# Mara's Secret

FELICIA ROGERS

δ
**Dingbat Publishing**
Humble, Texas

MARA'S SECRET

ISBN 978-1-940520-80-3

Published in the United States of America
Dingbat Publishing
Humble, Texas

Originally published by Solstice Publishing 2011–2012

# PROLOGUE

"Who *is* he?"

Ailin studied the unconscious man, the one who'd appeared out of nowhere. He sprawled in a crater the size of a railroad car, the remaining wet grass bent beneath him. Thick black hair lay rakishly across his forehead. Dried blood clotted upon his defined chin, as if he'd smashed his nose before landing in the field. His hands were clasped together before his naked breastbone in a prayerful pose. Ragged breeches made of some unusual material rested low on his hips.

Squinting against the bright August sun, Ailin pondered Dand's question. Normally the black gryphons, themselves included, would never have approached a human, but the unconscious fellow's arrival... well, that was different. The thunderstorm had caught their group out on patrol and they'd sheltered beneath the cleft of an overhanging rock. Rain had poured in sheets so thick a body couldn't see his hand before his face, then a misty haze had swarmed across the forest floor. The clouds had parted as if God Himself had ordered it and a shaft of light had shot through the darkness. Like a meteor, the young man fell from the sky and landed, creating the crater and incredibly, not dying.

Ailin stroked his chin. "I'm not sure." A glance down showed black fur too near his face. For a bizarre moment shock swept through Ailin, then he grimaced. He'd been a gray for so long; it still surprised him to see that hateful dark shade on his own hand.

Beside him, Dand fidgeted. "He doesn't look like one of us, but I felt the pull as we approached."

The pull of one gryphon for another. "As did I." Ailin hunched over the figure and touched his hand to the man's forehead, avoiding the dried blood. Heat pooled beneath the clear skin. With his eyes closed and mouth relaxed, the stranger looked very young.

"Should we take him with us?"

Ailin settled back on his haunches. The stranger looked harmless enough, but what if he was a gray? In order to save a village, Ailin had bargained away his own rights as a gray, but that didn't mean he was willing to turn someone else over to the black gryphons. He shook his head. "No."

"But if we leave him and he is one of us..."

The whiny voice trailed off, but Ailin knew what Dand meant. If they left the stranger behind and he turned out to be a black gryphon, then he could be taken by the grays. Thinking fast, he glanced around—forest, trees, more forest—then someone nearby started whistling a sprightly tune. He jumped. "We should leave."

The two blacks slid into the trees as a young human woman, carrying a basket full of flowers and a pail full of berries, skipped into the open. She stopped before the unconscious man. Her jaw dropped and she covered her mouth and stepped back. "Pa!"

Ailin started forward. No, it was too late, and he kept the last line of trees between his folded wings and the little clearing.

The stranger struggled and pushed himself up on one elbow. Voice thick, he asked, "Where am I?"

The young woman, skirts bunched in her hands, ran back into the trees and returned moments later, minus her berries and dragging an elderly gentleman behind her. Her animated face matched her fluttering hands. "There he is, Pa. I about stepped on him, I did." She leaned over and her lips twitched upward. "He sure is a beaut! We should get 'em home and have Ma put the kettle on. We'll be having stew tonight."

The stranger rolled to his side and blinked, eyes glassy, then he groaned and fell back into the grass. The older man didn't argue with his daughter, but hoisted the stranger over his shoulder and staggered back the way they'd come.

Ailin followed them for a hundred feet, carefully keeping his wings hidden amongst the trees. Today he'd been saved from making a decision; he just hoped letting the stranger go hadn't been a mistake.

# 1

Awareness swam slowly to the top of Dougal's thoughts. Voices… voices he didn't know.

"Can I keep 'im, Ma?"

Weird voices. Or at least, weird people.

"Maude, don't be silly. You don't have any idea where he's been."

A new voice, a male one, cleared his throat and interrupted. "T'aint it obvious where he's been? Look at all those scars. He's been in the war and from the looks of him, he must've taken a good beating."

War. That didn't sound good. Dougal risked slitting his eyes open. The old man who'd carried him sat at a plain wooden table, scratching his head and staring at Dougal. "I wish he was wearing more of his uniform. If he was wearing more blue, I'd put him back out in the field."

"Pshaw. You'll do no such thing," said Ma. The woman speaking bustled around out of Dougal's sight. A pan clanked down on a stove; at least there was one sound he recognized.

Pa shook his head. "Maybe he's a deserter. I'm surprised the feller ain't been shot. You heard about them two boys who were on their way home. Poor fellers were let out of the army, done injured and discharged. They got plenty close and the neighbors thought they'd deserted, so they shot 'em." He paused. "Maybe he didn't leave his company, maybe he was in a battle and they thought he was dead, and they left 'im behind. Could be that's why they didn't shoot 'im."

"Should we turn him in?" Another male voice, but younger.

Pa scratched his head. "Naw, Junior. Your ma's right. We should let the poor soul rest. Since we don't know where he came from or why he was about these parts, we should give him a chance to explain himself."

The voices continued, but they didn't seem to pose any immediate danger and exhaustion won. Dougal drifted back into a deep sleep.

Later, when he again awoke, his chest felt tight and heat tortured him. Pain throbbed in his forehead. A glance showed that someone had draped heavy covers over him. He grabbed the quilts' edge, flung them aside, swung his legs up and around, and settled his feet to the floor. The smooth-worn planks felt like a freezer's interior and he shuddered.

Sunlight filtered into the empty room through scrubbed-clean windows. The family from before—Ma, Pa, Junior, and covetous Maude—weren't around. The cabin was simple—thick logs planed smooth and grouted with mud, notched together at the ends. Dried pelts hung from the rafters. Metal cooking utensils hung from nails beside a stone fireplace. In the middle of the room stood a plain wooden table and six chairs. The construction details were different, but overall, the cabin reminded him forcefully of the primitive home where he'd grown up.

No people, weird or otherwise, darkened the interior. Good; he could think. Dougal grabbed his pounding head. Bits and pieces of the earlier conversation drifted back to him. They thought he was a soldier in a war with blue and gray, a soldier who had abandoned his unit or been left for dead. Did that mean he was in the United States during the Civil War?

No, that would be some bizarre form of time travel and that couldn't be right. How could that even be possible? His pulse pounded, matching his head, and he swallowed his fear.

"Get ahold of yourself, Dougal." His voice sounded thin and raspy, not reassuring at all. "Maybe you're in one of those reenactment battles or something." Right. "Sure, that's what it is." Oh, yeah, right.

Another shiver rippled through him, and he looked around for a pair of shoes, socks, anything to cover his poor cold feet. No clothing, but the shiver segued into a tingle that raced along his spine, as if someone had touched him with an electrical current. Dougal lifted his head.

She stood silhouetted in the open doorway, twisting her white, almost translucent gown between her slender fingers. Long black hair hung unfettered to her waist. Her eyes were the color of blue steel, her beauty like that of a statue in a world-famous museum. He couldn't look away, didn't want to, didn't want to ever look away from her again. The tingle up his spine deepened until he felt he'd shake apart.

As he stared, her breath burst in and out and her color melted away, leaving her ashen. He lifted his hand toward her, wanting to comfort her fear, but his throat had dried and all that came out was a croak.

Nope, that wasn't going to help.

She glared at his hand, her eyes widening. A moan escaped her. She turned on her heel and vanished.

A ghost. He'd been visited by a ghost, while trapped in a Civil War reenactment. Dougal collapsed back onto the bed and yanked the quilts back over him. Something—okay, *nothing* was right, but he couldn't put his finger on it...

Even outside, in the clear pine-scented air, Mara's chest heaved as she struggled to breathe. The stranger had *looked* at her. He'd even lifted his hand, as if he wanted to *touch* her! Just the thought made her tremble. She didn't like strangers. Strangers did bad things to people. Strangers tricked you into doing things you didn't want to do, like holding your tongue.

Still rattled, Mara settled on the tree swing, her favorite spot for thinking, and laid her head against the rope. She looked across the pond and eyed the cabin where the stranger lurked. Yesterday morning, when Pa and Maude had brought him home, the only clothes covering his body had been a pair of tattered breeches. The sight of his exposed chest had caused heat to flush her cheeks, and finally Ma had shooed her from the room. She'd climbed into the loft and peered over the edge, watching while Ma had treated the wounds carved upon the stranger's body and he'd groaned and moaned as if dying.

Pa said the stranger had received a beating and he was lucky to be alive. She didn't know if she agreed, but why else would the young man have been left in the field?

She glanced around the farmyard. The cow chewed her cud under a shade tree but otherwise Mara was alone. She bit her lip. Would it be safe to hum? Or maybe sing quietly to herself? Technically it wasn't talking if no one was listening, and the sweet sound of Sunday hymns took her mind off her troubles. Soon Ma would call her in for dinner and she'd have to blink, and play dumb, and help in her mute way.

Mara squeezed the swing's rope until frayed fibers cut into the tender flesh of her palms. If only she had stayed away from the creek.

When Dougal awoke again, the family sat around the table praying over a meal. He remained silent and peeked through his lashes. He needed more info so he could figure out what to do next. If he could only remember more—but there seemed to be a hole in his memory. Darkness, then light, then… something.

Middle-aged mother and father and three grown children raised their heads with a rousing "Amen!" Ma lifted a ladle and spooned steaming liquid into each raised bowl. The smell of rich broth tantalized him and his stomach growled. Loudly.

Maude swiveled around. She cocked a brow before pushing back her chair and ambling toward him. Blond hair pulled back in a severe bun highlighted her defined cheekbones and hazel eyes. Her small, round frame reached his side and she leaned over. A smile tugged at the corners of her rosy lips as her gaze followed the length of the bed.

No, not the bed. His body.

Great. The strange one. Not the silent, pretty one, staring at the table and shredding a roll with nervous fingers. Not even Ma, with her safe, wrinkled face and stern, measuring eyes. No, of course not. He had to attract attention from Maude.

"I think he's awake, Pa." The grin reached her eyes and Dougal gulped.

Pa didn't even glance up. "Good. Get him some food."

She patted his hand. "Are you hungry?"

Dougal nodded, and the girl shuffled back to the table and retrieved her bowl. When she returned, she dragged over her chair, settled her curved body with a wriggle, and began to spoon broth into his mouth.

It tasted as good as it smelled, all savory warmth and goodness. He twitched his lips upward in a practiced smile. A flush stole over Maude's face, and she blinked shyly and looked away. He hadn't had a chance to study his appearance since his arrival, but thankfully his good looks appeared intact. At least he still had the ability to make a young woman blush.

She fed him another warm spoonful. Maybe he'd get a chance to enjoy the meal, after all. At the thought, he smiled again—a real smile this time, surprisingly, not one of his practiced concoctions designed to get a reaction from a girl. Strange, how good a simple smile could feel.

Maude leaped from her chair. The bowl flew through the air, spreading his meal across the floorboards, and clattered to a halt upside down. Dougal sighed. It had been good while it lasted. He'd have to turn down his wattage.

"Maude, what are you thinkin', child!" Ma's voice sounded irritated.

Maude ran to the table, clutched her parents around their shoulders, and screamed with delight. "Ma! He smiled at me! Can you believe it? He is one mighty fine specimen. Should we send for the preacher?"

What twilight zone had he been dumped into? With two fingers, Dougal pinched himself. This had to be a nightmare, right? If not, he might soon be standing in front of a clapboard church with shotguns cocked on either side while he waited for his fate to be sealed!

The other girl, the quiet one, reminded him of the girl from his dream. Was she real? She'd held her peace, but at Maude's declaration, her steel blue eyes widened as if horrified.

Pa's spoon paused halfway up. "Now, Maude, you stop with such silly talk. You're upsetting Mara."

*Mara...*

As if Dougal had spoken the name aloud, the quiet girl glanced in his direction. His breath caught. It *was* her, the one who'd fled so fast she'd seemed to vanish, like a ghost. She was real and even more beautiful than he'd remembered.

The black hair that had hung freely was now braided and draped atop her shoulder. Her translucent gown had been changed for a yellow one, which highlighted her tanned skin.

Again he couldn't stop staring at her. He gave her the same smile, the one that sent Maude leaping for joy, but Mara trembled, shaking so violently her chair bounced. What was wrong? His looks had never caused that kind of response. Unless...

Ma cocked a brow. "Mara, what in heaven's name is wrong with you?"

Mara didn't reply. She shoved back from the table and bolted for the door, sending her chair reeling backward and crashing against the floor.

As if nothing had happened, Maude resumed her seat, plopped her elbow on the table, cradled her chin in her hand, and whined in a nasally wistful tone. "I ain't never gonna get married. Every time someone looks at me, you say no. It ain't fair."

"Now, Maude, we've done been over this. You are spoken for. You can't just go off and try for another beau. It ain't fittin'." Pa eyeshot a glance in Dougal's direction.

Maude's fingers plucked at a loose string on her dress. She looked up and her heated gaze fell on Dougal. *Great, just great.* He shifted on the bed. She smiled. "But he's so purdy."

Pa rolled his eyes. "It don't matter. If he's a deserter, they might want him back once he's well."

Oh, yeah, he needed to get out of this madhouse. He had no intention of marrying Maude or anyone else. Nor did he have any intention of being taken by an army he'd never joined in the first place. How he'd gotten there and why—those were his current concerns. Little else deserved his attention. Well, maybe Mara...

Ma frowned and patted Maude's hand. "We ain't arguing about that. What we're sayin'—"

"What do you mean?" interrupted Pa.

"Mean by what?" asked Ma.

"By what you just said?"

"I don't understand your question."

"Are you tryin' to say you find this here feller attractive?"

Ma leaned over the table and stared into Pa's eyes. "You don't need to worry, dear. I haven't seen an attractive man in the last twenty-five years."

Dougal restrained his laughter as the old man attempted to use his fingers to count. Perhaps he was trying to decide whether he should be offended or not.

# 2

Barry O'Brien stood in the doorway of his two-story colonial home, the old Wheeler place. August heat had brought drought to Wheeler's Landing and the grass was an ugly shade of brown. Perhaps Elijah, his head slave, needed to see that the lawn was watered. An issue to address upon his return, no doubt. At times, being the master of so much was an extremely trying occupation.

The day was Monday, the day he drove into town to manage his business affairs. The carriage waited in front of the house, the matched bay horses pawing and stamping.

"Elijah?" O'Brien called as he checked his gold pocket watch. He had a standing appointment with the bank manager, Thomason, every Monday morning.

"Yes, massa," came Elijah's reply from the far side of the carriage.

"Ah, there you are. I'm ready to go."

"Should we wait on the mistress, sir?"

"No. She won't be traveling with me today." An hour ago his wife had suffered a case of the vapors. He couldn't have been happier. Ivy could be quite demanding and he would accomplish so much more without her presence.

"Verra well, sir. Verra well."

O'Brien climbed inside the carriage and Elijah closed the door. He settled against the bench and braced himself as the driver snapped the reins and the carriage jerked into motion.

Elijah was his most favored slave and oversaw the entire household, both when O'Brien was in the country and when he traveled to town. Why, Elijah was almost like family. O'Brien had allowed Elijah to have a wife. He'd provided him decent clothing. And anyone could see how well the slave ate. Why, he had once even sat at the house's dining room table! The idea of a war to free the colored was naught but a way for the North to control the South.

But O'Brien wasn't overly concerned about the war. As long as he prepared for either side to win, he would survive.

When they were almost to town, O'Brien tapped on the ceiling with his cane. "Driver, take me to the hotel first."

Minutes later, the carriage eased to a stop. Elijah jumped down from the rear rumble seat and opened the door. "Here y' are, massa."

"Take my trunk upstairs and inform Mr. Johnson I will be utilizing my rooms for the entire week."

O'Brien didn't wait for an answer as he stepped from the carriage and walked toward the bank with a spring in his step. It was strange. He loved the old Wheeler home in the country. The huge, two-story white house had more rooms than he and Ivy would ever need. The ballroom, formal dining room, the running water... oh, yes, the home fit him perfectly. It demonstrated his prestige and importance. Yet inside, it was a miserable place, no matter how magnificent the furnishings. Drab, lonely, quiet, with no excitement. As much as he loved the house, O'Brien would rather be in town with the true action.

In front of the bank, two guards reclined on a wooden bench, their feet crossed at the ankles. A piece of straw dangled casually from one guard's mouth. A tip of the hat was the only acknowledgement O'Brien received as he passed.

"Oh! Mr. O'Brien, we weren't expecting you." Thomason, the bank manager, rose from behind the counter as O'Brien opened the front door and entered.

He frowned. "And why ever not? I come every Monday. And today is Monday, correct?"

The teller, standing behind Thomason, gaped at both of them.

"Uh, yes, of course. It's just we heard Mrs. O'Brien was under the weather and we assumed—"

"You need not worry. Mrs. O'Brien is under constant care. Why, her slave can do a much better job of caring for her than I. I'm only underfoot, you see. Besides, Ivy would worry herself sick if she thought the town's business suffered because of her illness."

"Of c-course." Thomason straightened his crooked tie. "I guess you would like to see the accounts."

"Yes, I would. I will retire to your office and you may bring them."

"Yes, of course."

For a moment, O'Brien paused and stared at Thomason. The man didn't seem quite himself. But it wasn't worth his time, so he shrugged and headed to the back office, the one with the glorious view of the lake. Every Monday he viewed *his* bank's accounts. Today would be no different.

But when he swung the door open, a pair of booted feet were propped on the bank manager's desk, a pair of long legs stretching beyond them. With the chair tilted back, the intruder's face was hidden by shadows.

O'Brien opened his mouth to yell for the guards. But the chair moved and light hit the stranger's visage. He froze and swallowed. "You!"

Dougal lost track of the days he lay in bed recuperating. With time, his physical strength returned, and with it came increased knowledge and understanding of the situation.

Every night before the family prepared for bed, Pa would read aloud, sometimes from the newspaper, and that was how Dougal heard about the recent siege of Vicksburg, Mississippi. He knew the siege had started sometime in May of 1863 and with the news reporting lagging a little behind the time's events, the current date was likely in late summer. Because of the family's accents, he assumed he was somewhere in the deep South.

What he didn't learn from the paper reading, he learned from private conversations between Ma and Pa as they snuggled in the bed across from his at night. In whispers, they often talked about him.

That night they talked again, discreet murmurs drifting across the cabin. Dougal yawned and blinked his heavy lids. He should ignore the conversation and go to sleep. Tomorrow he was going to figure a way out of this mess. But then he heard...

"You know, Ma, I believe finding that boy was a blessin'."

"What are you talking about?"

"I don't mean like the last time we found a young 'un. That was a different kind of blessing. What I mean is, we could sure use some help with the harvest. After all those irrigatin' ditches Junior dug, we're goin' to have a big take this year. Might even be able to repay the bank. Maybe if we let Maude marry this here feller, then he'll stay on and help."

"No. Maude is marryin' Beauford. His family and ours have been friends for too long to go back on our word now."

"But what if Maude is right? What if Beauford done up and died in the war? What then? We might lose half the crop without more help."

"You got Junior," said Ma.

Shifting sounds came from the other side of the room. Dougal strained to hear.

"Junior is just one man. A boy, really. Besides, if those soldiers come back through, he'll have to hide in the cave. His act won't be enough to save him forever. And what'll we do then?"

"Wouldn't the stranger have to hide, too?"

"I don't know. Maybe."

Dougal heard the contact of flesh on flesh, as if someone had been slapped.

"You aren't tryin' to say you'd let Maude marry a feller then let him be carted back to the war?"

"Now why'd you go and slap me?" Pa sighed. "You needn't worry, I would protect him. But not as much as my own kin."

"But him being married to Maude might cause you to have kin."

After a brief pause, Pa added, "Maybe he could marry Mar—"

Ma interrupted, her voice stern. "Flint Hess, you better hush. There'll be no marryin'. This feller has nowhere to go. Maybe even no family. We'll offer to let him stay on if he'll work. And that's it. You just keep them other thoughts out of your head."

Dougal stretched out on the bed with a smile and closed his eyes.

Mara was suffocating. The August heat made the attic room feel like the inside of a fireplace. Somehow Maude rested peacefully, a snore cracking the air every so often, which made her own suffering even worse. Mara rolled out of bed and slid her feet to the floor, enjoying the cool feel of the slats. Carefully avoiding the creaking boards—she knew them all by heart—she shuffled gingerly toward the window.

The white dressing gown clung to her frame and made a faint ripping sort of sound as she tugged it from her sweat-swathed skin. Easing back the curtain, she waited for a breeze to float through the open window. Even the slightest breath of wind would be a relief. But the night air was still.

Mara rested her head against the glass pane and enjoyed its coolness until her body heat warmed it. Then, as she peered down into the yard, moonlight struck the swing. If she visited her favorite spot, maybe the effort would tire her and the motion would create a cooling breeze.

Tiptoeing, she headed toward the stairs. Maude stirred but her eyes remained closed. The snores resumed within a moment. Good. Mara wasn't in the mood to stare blankly at her older sister, pretending to be stupid while Maude rattled on about whatever. She wanted to be alone.

With each step down the stairs, the worry of discovery gnawed at her. Mara placed her feet in the right spots to avoid loose boards. By the time she reached the first floor, sweat beaded her brow and trickled down her cheek, gathering at her collarbone.

Moonlight bathed the front room and she breathed easier as she crept toward the front door. To get outside, she would need to pass her parents and the visitor without waking them.

She had little fear Ma and Pa would wake. They were up with the sun and didn't rest until the sun set. Exhaustion was their common state and not much would wake them once they were asleep. But the newcomer was a different story. He'd slept off and on for days. With so much rest, anything might wake him.

On tiptoes, she reached his bedside and stopped.

The stranger lay on the bed with the homemade quilt wadded around his hips. Sweat twinkled on his exposed chest, highlighting the white bandage wrapped around his ribs. Black wavy hair lay across his forehead. Stubble poked through his bronzed chin. Mara sighed. Maude was right. No finer specimen had ever been seen in those parts.

Arms bulged, chest sculpted, hair like silk. Mara couldn't resist the urge to touch him. She reached forward. But a blue arc, like strange lightning, leapt from his body and struck her. Mara gasped and danced back, yanking her trembling hand to her heart.

Her pulse pounded and the sudden, desperate need to escape overwhelmed her. With one last look at the stranger, she ran on silent bare feet to the door. Opening it quietly, she slipped out into the starlit night.

It had taken Dougal forever to fall asleep. The overheard conversation beat like a drum between his ears. But now he was awake again.

Try as he might, Dougal couldn't understand what he was doing there, or how he'd arrived. One minute he'd been in the white tower; the next he was in the past. He'd been ready to listen to the wailing of trapped gryphons for eternity. Granted, he wouldn't miss that part. There'd been darkness, then light, then… he still couldn't remember.

Could he still change into his alternate form? He wasn't sure. There'd be no way to check until he could get away from the family's constant supervision.

Dougal rolled over in the bed and punched his pillow. The family had asked him no questions, which seemed ever stranger the more he considered it. Didn't they want to know who they harbored? Whatever their reasons, their lack of curiosity couldn't last forever. They were giving him time to heal, but after that the questions were sure to begin. Sure, Pa and Ma whispered words about him staying on in exchange for working on the farm, but Dougal found the idea hard to believe. They would want more, he was certain of it; and when they did, what would he do? What would he say?

A wave of rippling light shifted and played between the ceiling's open rafters, dancing off the cured hams. There had to be water nearby. Watching the phenomenon made him sleepy, and he'd used it for several nights instead of counting sheep. His eyelids drifted downward. Then he heard it—movement. Stealthy footsteps, like a thief in the proverbial night.

Lying perfectly still, Dougal waited. Even with his eyes closed, he could tell when she stopped and stared at him. He imagined her in his mind's eye, black hair unfettered, steel blue eyes in a face of innocence. Staring at her in his imagination was almost as satisfying as staring at her in real life.

But then a feeling like an electric jolt shot through his body, lifting the hairs on his arms and tickling the nape of his neck. A sense of massive power engulfed him, as if he'd been ambushed by one of the Ancient Ones, and the fresh scent of ozone invaded the cottage. It all caught him off guard and he needed every fiber of his being not to jump to his feet. Then a burst of hot, humid air passed across his tingling chest. He narrowed his eyes and peeked through his slit lashes.

She'd run outside, maybe because of the heat. The cabin *was* stifling. Still shaken, Dougal stroked his stubbled chin. That could only have been some residue of whatever power, whatever spell or freak accident or act of God had dumped him in a backwater, war-torn nation. It didn't mean anything. He could safely forget it.

On the other hand, what would Mara do if he showed up by her side unannounced? The thought caused an even stronger quiver to race through his body.

But what about her earlier stark terror when he'd looked at her? What was it about him that scared her so? The other family members didn't seem overly concerned by him. Maybe a mirror was needed, after all. *Oh, no.* His eyes widened in horror. What if during the time travel his good looks had been marred and Maude was too blind to see it?

Dougal kicked off the quilts and jumped from the bed. While resting and healing, he'd paid little attention to what he wore. But now, when he glanced down, his attire became a major concern. Bare feet; bandaged chest. A pair of long johns, several sizes too large, sagged on his hips. He rolled his eyes. How was he to attract a woman wearing that?

With his first step, the long johns sank to his knees. He grabbed a handful of material and yanked it up to his waist. Holding them with one hand, careful not to snare the covers with his shuffling feet, Dougal peered around for a mirror. The room couldn't be more than twenty feet by twenty feet and it didn't take long to conclude there was no mirror.

With his free hand, Dougal stroked his hair—it still felt thick and healthy—then yanked out a few strands. But the moonlight wasn't bright enough to show its color.

*This is ridiculous!* Good looks and charm were the two things he'd always depended on; that and his suave way with words. He possessed few other positive attributes. What would he do if his good looks disappeared?

A loud snore startled Dougal from his self-absorption. At least Ma and Pa Kettle, as he'd begun thinking of them—she'd said Pa's real name earlier, but Dougal hadn't caught it—were heavy sleepers. He sighed and glanced out a window. There it was, the small pond he'd seen reflecting off the hams and rafters. Light danced from its crystal surface, as if a thousand stars winked off and on.

Grasping the long johns tightly, he headed outside, easing the door closed behind him. Moonlight lit the yard surprisingly well, and nothing hindered his long strides. At the water's edge, he dropped to one knee, then both. Peering into the pond, he searched for his reflection.

Frustration mounted. It was hopeless! Every time he leaned forward to check his appearance, his body blocked the moonlight so he couldn't see! How was he to determine if his looks remained intact if he couldn't see himself?

Dougal slapped the water and leaned back on his haunches. Drops of tepid water trickled down his hand. Still holding up the long johns, he rose and shook out his legs. Maybe he'd be able to stare at himself in the morning; he'd just have to wait. But before he could take a step back to the cabin, a singing voice carried across the water. He turned, peering through the night.

On the other side of the pond, Mara swung on a tree swing. The rope made a squeaky noise as it rocked back and forth, her bare feet brushing the hard-packed dirt in passing. Her voice, clear and pure, moved up then down the scale. It felt like tiny drums beat in his chest and he closed his eyes, listening to the singing angel. Without thinking, he moved toward the music. Then the noise stopped. All of it—the rubbing, the squeaking, the singing.

Dougal opened his eyes. Mara watched him. To say he had never experienced anything like it would be an understatement. It felt as if the depths of his soul were pierced by hot knives. His breath came in short, rasping gasps. Sweat covered his closed palms and his heart raced. He clenched his fists to keep from rushing to her and enveloping her in his arms. Even Maddie's call hadn't been this strong. Who *was* she?

Eyes wide, Mara continued to stare back. He smiled, a real smile, not one of the calculating ones he'd flashed around Coal Creek High. But it seemed to have the wrong effect on Mara.

She jumped from the swing and ran.

Still not thinking straight, he reached out as she raced past. Air struck his exposed flesh. He sighed and dropped his arms to his sides. Cold; yeah, he felt cold. He looked down and groaned. It seemed he had lost something important. His long johns.

# 3

"Captain Herrick," O'Brien whispered between gritted teeth. "What are you doing here?"

The captain rose and sauntered around the desk, his blue uniform trousers wrinkled, his blue jacket worn, his riding boots scuffed. Battered spurs clinked as he walked. His Union cavalry uniform looked as if he'd worn it for weeks without a break.

O'Brien swallowed and looked away. Herrick was an enigma. He showed up at the strangest times and in the most unusual places. O'Brien would have told him to go elsewhere—*and bathe, if you please!*—but he was beholden to Captain Herrick. Half of everything he owned—and he owned a lot—he owed to the captain. Herrick had given him funds, which he'd used to build the spur railroad line into the valley, the depot, and even to renovate the hotel. And yet Herrick had asked for nothing. Of late, O'Brien sensed that last was in the process of changing.

O'Brien switched places with the captain and settled into the office chair behind the manager's desk. Herrick retired to the visitor's smaller chair. The wood creaked beneath his weight and O'Brien feared it would collapse at any moment.

Captain Herrick steepled his fingers. "Mr. O'Brien, we are friends, are we not?"

O'Brien's fingers automatically shifted to his collar, easing the fabric away from his constricted throat. "Yes, of course."

"I've done many things for you, yes?"

Had he ever. "Yes." O'Brien cringed.

"Good. Now we have that established, I have something to ask of you."

*Here it goes.* O'Brien's pulse increased. Time to repay his debt. Would he have accepted the captain's help in the beginning if he'd known one day payment would be required?

After taking several deep breaths, O'Brien realized there was nothing to fear. He might not be a young man, but in his day he had been able to handle himself. There was nothing Herrick could ask of him that he couldn't fulfill.

Too restless to sit, he rose and stalked to the window, turning his back to Herrick. Outside sprawled the town of Wheeler's Landing. Along the street, he could see the hotel, the general store, and the tavern, all bearing the name of O'Brien. Of course, all the signs had been replaced within the last twenty years. Before, everything in sight had read Wheeler's *this* and Wheeler's *that.* Personally, he thought the O'Brien name lent the place an air of class. *Wheeler, indeed.*

His faith in himself was restored. If he could control and manage his vast wealth, he could easily take care of any small request Herrick might make. Turning back around, O'Brien squared his shoulders. "What can I do for you?"

The captain studied his tanned hands, their overly long nails in need of a good trim. Even his beard looked shaggy and unkempt. O'Brien wasn't used to such company. Perhaps he should tell the captain to return when he was more presentable. *Yes, a bath.*

But before he could make the suggestion, the captain placed one dirt-encrusted fingernail in his mouth and scraped it across his pointed teeth. O'Brien cringed at the horrendous sound. *No, maybe not.*

"Not to rush you, Captain, but the bank manager will be along any moment. And I believe you wish to maintain the secrecy of our relationship as much as I. If you please." O'Brien held out his palm, hoping Herrick would take the hint and proceed.

"I wish for you to enter the abandoned silo northwest of town and tell me its contents."

O'Brien's eyes widened. Sweat beaded his brow. A Confederate unit was encamped around the silo; everyone knew that, knew that they were using the abandoned farm. He'd been the one to give them permission. Yanking out his handkerchief, he wiped his forehead. "You must be joking. There is no way I can—"

"There is. And you will."

"But—"

"O'Brien—I may call you O'Brien, yes? Of course I may. The fact is, you owe me. You would be nowhere without me. And I'm afraid it is time for the Pied Piper to collect his dues."

"Pied Piper?"

"You do know the story, yes?" The captain's voice grew gruff.

O'Brien bit the inside of his cheek to keep his lips from trembling. Showing weakness would be a disaster.

Herrick's little smile grew. "Ah, the Pied Piper of Hamelin. The piper agreed to rid the town of all the *rats* but in return for payment. When the piper completed his part, the townsfolk refused to pay. He promised revenge, and revenge he got. He played his pipe and lured all the children out of the town. Then he led them into the water—and they drowned."

The evil glint in Herrick's eyes caused O'Brien to shiver.

A piece of food lingered in Herrick's nail; he flicked it toward O'Brien and it landed on the desk in front of him.

"I think you will find I'm not nearly as patient as the Pied Piper."

O'Brien was afraid to inquire about who was being threatened, the children of Wheeler's Landing or his own son; instead he asked, "When should I start?"

# 4

The room Mara shared with Maude seemed smaller than usual. It only took five steps to reach one side from the other and Mara would know since she had spent the last several hours pacing back and forth across the already-worn floor.

Fear overwhelmed her. Had the stranger heard her singing? If he had, then... her fear gave way to anger. What right did he have to follow her in the middle of the night and intrude upon her personal time? On the other hand, did it matter why he'd followed her? If he'd *heard* her... the fear returned.

A chair sat across from the bed and Mara plopped into it, exhausted. The homemade structure groaned at her abuse, but Mara paid it no mind. Instead of pacing, she bit her lip. Who *was* the stranger? What kind of man ventured out in the dead of night for no apparent reason?

Ma and Pa assumed he'd been a soldier. Perhaps he was a deserter or one wounded and left for dead, as they thought. Or perhaps he was something entirely different. The thought sent a shiver rippling up her spine.

Looking at the bed where Maude still gently snored, Mara remembered what Maude had called him, 'a gift from the sky.' Maude seemed to think the stranger fell down from heaven, obviously because of his heavenly appearance. Junior, her brother, thought the stranger was a blessing as well, an angel. He said the stranger probably flew in on a pair of wings. Mara certainly hoped not.

She didn't know where the stranger hailed from, but one thing she knew: he should be glad Maude found him. Otherwise he wouldn't be alive. If she had discovered him, alone and helpless in the woods, she would have used a large rock to smash in his handsome face. She would never again risk being lured in by a stranger. The price was too high.

Dougal tossed his shirt over a nearby fence post and stretched. The too-hot sun felt good on his back, even as the work threatened to knock him back into bed. It had been, what, a century since he'd repaired a fence... if he went by his age... but if he was right about the Civil War, then that hadn't happened yet... and trying to sort that out would hurt worse than the work.

He leaned his chin on the wooden shovel handle and sagged theatrically. How much easier this would have been with a set of post-hole diggers. Or a backhoe. Caveman times, that's where he was.

Beside him, Pa crouched in the turned earth, working to loosen a tangled wire. The old man's face had seemed drawn and worn when he'd handed Dougal an armload of old clothing in the barn. Dougal had taken them reluctantly. "What should I call you? I can't exactly call you Pa." *Because I'm older than you... no, I'm not... yeah, I am.*

Pa had guffawed loudly. "I guess you might be right. Folks would think it mighty strange if I had a grown son just up and appear. Mayhap you better call me Uncle." He'd leaned closer, and the tired lines in his face couldn't be missed. "Listen, boy, I don't know where you hail from and right now I don't care. Fact is, for me, you're a blessing from the Almighty. We have a huge crop this year and with most of the strong young men either dead, lame, or off at war, there's no one to hire. So for now you'll take the role of my simple-minded nephew."

Simple-minded. Yeah. Uncle it was.

Dougal straightened and shoved the shovel in the ground, extending the trench further down the fence row. Somewhere nearby water sloshed as it hit the sides of a metal container. The faint scent of honeysuckle assaulted his nostrils. Then the sound of a skirt flapping in the breeze caught his attention. *Oh, yeah. Break time.* Dougal placed his best, most sultry smile on his lips as he lifted his gaze. But her response wasn't what he expected. The bucket dropped. The water spilled. Mara ran.

Envy of the ground plagued him as the water pooled and spread. So close to satisfaction, yet so far away. Dougal sighed and stared longingly at Mara's fleeing form.

Mara hunkered behind the barn. Fire burned in her lungs as she struggled to regain control and calm her rapid breathing.

As she'd hauled the water, she'd mentally prepared herself to meet the stranger, or at least she'd thought so. But then his dark stare had turned on her. A smile that reached all the way to his eyes had graced his perfectly formed lips. His exposed skin had glowed under the afternoon sun. Then her hands shook, her grip on the bucket slackened, her resolve disappeared, and she'd run away.

Carefully, she peered around the barn's corner. Pa glared in her general direction but the stranger studied the ground. The water formed a sad, tiny stream at his feet.

The stranger—Dougal, he called himself—picked up the shovel and rammed it into the little stream. His back muscles rippled; his tan skin gleamed. But beside him, Pa crooked his finger at her. Well, she *had* played the fool. Hands clasped tightly before her, Mara approached.

Before she arrived, Pa shouted, "Mara Hess! What in tarnation has gotten into you? We've been working all day in this hot weather and you spilled our water all over the ground."

Mara dropped her chin and bit her lip. Why couldn't she just explain that it was Dougal's fault for looking at her?

Instead of speaking, Dougal picked up the water bucket and the dipper. For some reason, that simple action made her heartbeat accelerate.

"Now, nephew—"

"Uncle, I don't mind helping. Maybe the bucket was too heavy for her. Direct me to the well and I'll fetch more water."

Pa shrugged and pointed the way.

Dougal pulled his shirt over his head and shrugged it into position before heading down the path. He'd only taken a few steps when he called over his shoulder, "Aren't you coming?"

Without a second thought, she joined him, and then passed him on the narrow path. *The bucket was too heavy. Humph.* As if she hadn't been fetching water for Pa and Junior for the last ten years of her life. A flush crept up her neck. She hoped it was anger, but just in case it wasn't, she walked on with her head down. Had he noticed she didn't speak? If he had, then he didn't mention it but just kept chattering away as if expecting a reply.

"I'm sorry I startled you earlier. I guess I don't know my own power."

Mara was glad he was behind her and couldn't see the smile tugging at her lips. It was evident he thought highly of himself, and he didn't need to know that she agreed.

"Perhaps it's my frightful looks which keep sending you away. I haven't shaved, bathed, or combed my hair in days. If I was to see myself in a mirror, I might run away as well!"

Her smile was winning. Imagine one such as *him* worrying over his appearance. The "beard" he was worried about, really just some stubble, made him look quite distinguished, although she preferred him clean-shaven, like when he'd been found.

And his hair! As black as midnight, and wavy, it touched the nape of his neck and curled under. The strands were smooth as silk and looked like a glimmering spiderweb.

And the bath he was wrong about. He'd received a very thorough sponge bath from Ma before she'd bound up his wounds. The thought of which sent a rush of heat to her cheeks.

Finally they reached the well. Mara erased her smile, pasted on a frown, then turned and reached out for the bucket, but he refused.

"Let me do it."

The well wasn't their only water source, but it was the best and where they drew their drinking water. It was fed by an underground spring, and the water was crystal clear and always cold. Dougal rotated the hand crank and lowered the bucket into the black depths, his dark eyes never wavering from her face. The heat was intense, as if he actually touched her, and she couldn't blame it all on the afternoon sun. Mara avoided his direct stare by glancing at the ground and kicking the dust this way and that with her booted foot.

"I don't believe we've been formally introduced." Holding the crank in place with one hand, he thrust out the other one. "My name is Dougal Lachlan."

Mara reached out politely, but before they touched an arc of energy shot between them. Yanking her hand back, she hugged herself. It hadn't exactly hurt, but... it was strange, and she didn't like strange, or strangers.

As she eyed the span of his shoulders, she reminded herself of that.

Dougal's eyes widened but he just said, "Your name is Mara, right?"

She nodded.

"I take it you don't talk much."

Mara blinked several times like she didn't understand.

"That's not a problem. In fact, this could be the best of both worlds. Not only a beautiful woman, but one who doesn't argue or complain."

She frowned and clenched her jaw. The audacity of the man! Unfortunately he didn't seem to notice her disapproval as he busily poured the water from one bucket to the other. Never before had Mara been so tempted to break her vow of silence. Someone needed to put him in his place.

Wherever that might be.

Dougal finished, drank two dippers full without stopping for air, and lifted the bucket. Mara swallowed just watching him. She could only carry it half-full, but he filled it to the top and lifted it with no effort, although it did make his shoulders and arm muscles flex; she could see it through Junior's old shirt.

Water splashed over the rim as they returned to the field. She could hear it sloshing behind her, hear his steady footsteps along the path. Ignoring him was impossible. For some reason she was too aware of his presence, even though he didn't walk very close, and it kept her breathing hurried and her face flushed. That was strange, too, and she didn't like strange.

From behind her, Dougal called, "It's kind of your parents to let me stay on."

Kindness likely had very little to do with it. Not that her parents weren't good people, but as far as Dougal Lachlan was concerned, they needed him. It was plain and simple.

"There are very few people left who take in strangers and help them. Where I come from, it's every man for himself. Everyone has so much, but only a special few share what they have."

She walked on, listening despite herself. What selfish people!

"And inviting a stranger into your home is an absolute no-no. Half the time the person steals from you; the other half he kills you in your sleep. If you see someone in need, you're much better off handing them a five-dollar bill and leaving them where they are."

Mara couldn't help it. She stopped in the middle of the path, turned, and glared at him. Where did he hail from? Where was that terrible place? And what in heaven's name was a five-dollar bill? It sounded like a huge sum of money!

But without looking up from the path, Dougal barreled into her. Water splashed and poured down her dress, seeping through to her skin. Mara gasped.

"Oh, lass, I'm sorry. You startled me. I didn't expect you to stop." Dougal set the bucket down. He pulled his grimy shirt over his head and offered it to her.

Should she take it? First of all, it was nasty. Second, if she took it, she would be acknowledging she understood his gestures. Third, she might experience the spark again. And that was strange.

Teeth clenched, Mara fretted. There was the vow to consider. If he startled her the way she'd startled him, he might surprise words from her, and she couldn't risk that. Which left her with only one course of action.

With a twirl of her wet skirt, she turned and skipped toward the house, swinging her arms wildly.

# 5

O'Brien stood on his hotel's porch and studied the mountains that towered behind his town. Little military activity and no battles had occurred in the sleepy valley. A small Confederate unit camped outside of town; that was all. The river bottom was thick with trees and foliage, which provided excellent cover for the Rebels and kept the Yankees at bay. *Most of the Yankees, at least.*

The valley seemed so peaceful, it was difficult to imagine war descending upon it. But a wise businessman prepared for all possibilities, and so he had. Whichever side won, his empire would prosper.

Hands clasped behind his back, he paced and waited for word. O'Brien had hired two local drunks to scout out the abandoned silo that had attracted Herrick's attention. He'd considered hiring more respectable persons, but decided against it when he realized that if the drunks were caught by the little Rebel unit, they'd be easier to discredit.

If all went well, his obligation to the captain would be fulfilled by evening and then he would no longer be under Herrick's thumb.

Wispy gray clouds cast a sickly pallor over the sky, hinting at rain that hadn't arrived all summer. A long, lonely whistle blew in the distance and O'Brien checked his gold pocket watch. The train was right on time.

Facing the street, he leaned on the railing. A block away, a shadow moved. He narrowed his eyes; no, there were really two shadows, staggering at an angle in his direction. Apparently his hirelings had taken the funds he'd provided and blown them on strong drink at the tavern before doing their job. O'Brien restrained his anger and waited for them to arrive.

"Mr. O'Brien?"

"Hush, you fool. Mr. O'Brien don't want no one to know we know him."

"Oh, yeah. I dun forgot. Umm, how *do* we know him?"

"We did a job for him, you big dummy. Just come on. I know everything."

"Well, that's good, 'cause I think I dun drunk too much at that there O'Brien tavern. Mr. O'Brien sure was generous, giv'n us a line of credit. Now we can drink until we can't drink no more and it don't cost us one red cent."

"You're right about that. But if we don't find him and give him his information, then you can forget your drinking for a good long time, 'cause you'll be in the O'Brien jail."

"How did everything in this town get named O'Brien?"

"Best I heard it, Mr. O'Brien made a deal with the devil to marry Ivy Wheeler. When her parents died, she inherited everything, all of Wheeler's Landing and half of Coal Creek. Then O'Brien went and renamed everything for hisself."

"Humph. Wonder how you go about sellin' your soul to the devil? I might have to consider it. Seems like it might be a lucrative prospect."

"Oh, you need to shut up. You ain't doin' no such thing. Let's get over there and tell Mr. O'Brien what we found out before he comes searchin' for us."

"You're just jealous about my plans."

"You fool, you don't need to sell the devil your soul, because he already has it."

O'Brien leaned back against the wall of his office. The voices of his hirelings had traveled along the entire street. They'd better have some mighty good information for him or he might not be in town long enough to pass it along to Captain Herrick.

# 6

Dougal shrugged back into his filthy shirt, retrieved the bucket of water, and headed out to find Pa and Junior as Mara skipped away. He couldn't help but wonder about her. She was a lovely lass, if a bit strange. The best he could tell, she never spoke. Sometimes she appeared to understand what people were saying, while at other times he wasn't so sure.

Back at the well, he'd witnessed that spark. The lass must have seen it, too, because she'd withdrawn fast. He couldn't remember anything like that happening before, not in his entire life among druids and gryphons and even the mother of all monsters.

Up ahead, Pa and Junior were buried by tall stalks of corn. Irrigation channels lined the field and fed water into the rows. At four o'clock, everyone dropped what they were doing and hauled water from the pond and the creek, filling the channels in every field. The surrounding forest was tinder-box dry, Pa and Junior said the other farms in the area were withering, but the Hess family's crops thrived.

These people, this family, was normal. Very normal, if a little strange at times. Ma, Pa, and three kids; they eked out a living, an existence, an honest profession. So why was he there? If he'd counted the years right, the black gryphons hadn't yet been trapped in the white tower. In fact, if he was correct, he hadn't even been born yet.

How had he gotten out of the tower? How had he traveled

back in time? Blackness, then light, then... he couldn't remember. Why was he there? Was he there to stop something from happening or to start something? What was his purpose?

As Dougal had observed during his convalescence, supper was a big event. The family cleaned up and gathered around the table. Ma, Maude, and Mara piled the surface with food, handing out plates, cutlery, and glasses of warm milk. The smell of fresh-baked bread, home-churned butter, roasted ham, boiled potatoes, carrots, and cabbage had Dougal salivating.

The women had cooked outside, but the main room was still stifling. The windows and doors stood open. The breeze, or lack of one, made the room uncomfortable but with the feast before them, no one complained.

Dougal was flanked by Mara and Maude; it was the best seat in the house. Directly across from him sat Ma. Junior and Pa presided at the head and foot of the table. Strange, how *right* it felt, almost as strange as how satisfying he found his exhausting day's work.

Before Dougal could reach for the potatoes, Pa held out his hand and Ma grasped it. With a jolt, Dougal remembered: the family always prayed. Hands reached out around the table, and he joined in, feeling even stranger; he hadn't prayed for what, a hundred years?

Maude squeezed his hand. No doubt she feared he would let go; but on his opposite side, Mara clasped hers demurely in her lap and refused to look at him. The urge to snatch her hand and intertwine their fingers assailed him. Would sparks fly? Or perhaps their touch would produce fireworks! He smiled at the thought, then shot a glance sideways to see if she felt the same. Disappointment filled him. She still stared straight ahead, ignoring him. He thought about narrowing his gaze and peering over her shoulder to see what she saw, but held back.

Pa cleared his throat and looked to Ma. Ma nodded and Pa proceeded to offer up a brief prayer. After the last word was spoken, Ma huffed. "Flint Hess!"

"Now, LouAnn, don't—"

"How many times have I asked you to pray longer?"

"Well, the good Lord—"

"Don't you give me that sorry line about Him not timin' you!

You've got blessing's comin' from every which way and you don't have the decency to take more than ten seconds to be thankful for it."

"But, LouAnn, the food'll get cold if—"

"Flint, how in tarnation can anything get cold in this heat? Now, you pray again and this time do it right."

"But, LouAnn—" Flint stopped.

Dougal agreed with that strategy. Ma's glare was too fierce for further argument.

He cleared his throat and fought to hold in his laughter as Flint tried to turn his ten-second prayer into something with more substance. Mara's pink lips twitched.

When Pa appeared to have said enough, he added the word "Amen" and looked at Ma as if for approval. Instead of responding, she picked up the basket of bread and passed it around the table.

The meal was consumed in silence, for which Dougal was happy. He was so exhausted from the heat and the day's work that he only felt like eating.

Junior finished first and scooted his chair back from the table. "Ma, that was some fine eatin'."

"Sure was," Pa said.

Dougal, feeling the need to join in, added, "Very fine indeed."

A rosy hue covered Ma's cheeks and a satisfied smile lifted her lips. The girls rose together and began clearing the table.

"Dougal, come sit with me on the porch." Pa grabbed his pipe and led the way.

Dougal trailed behind, surprised when Junior didn't follow. The teenager, big, blond, and lumbering, seemed to never be more than a few steps behind his father. But Junior grabbed a bucket and went to the well for clean-up water, leaving Pa and Dougal alone.

Pa settled in his rocker. "Sit, boy. We need to talk."

Dougal couldn't help it; he was worried. Finally Pa would want to know everything about him. Where he'd came from, why he'd been lying unconscious in the field, how he'd been injured. He settled on the wooden bench next to the rocker. A cool breeze blew and teased his flushed cheeks. Across the pond, the swing swayed beneath the maple tree.

"As I said earlier, I don't know where you hail from," Pa said around his pipe stem, digging out a match, "and I don't need to know. Seems like you're willing to stay on and work a while, and for that I'm mighty grateful."

Tension climbed Dougal's spine. Why did he sense a *but* coming? Was he receiving the big heave-ho speech?

Pa leaned back in his chair, the smoke from his pipe curling upward and creating a gray cloud.

Dougal waited, spine still tingling.

"I know you're a young virile man. I remember those days myself—oh, how I loved women." Pa sighed.

The tension and tingles gave way to shock. Dougal wished he could erase the images flashing through his mind.

Pa looked at him. "But you have to stay away from Maude."

Dougal choked.

One quick nod was Pa's only response. "I know. Maude is a rare specimen. Round and full-figured and all. Special girl, she is. I realize this might be a shock to your system, but Maude, well, she's engaged. Her fiancé, Beauford, went off to the war but he's coming back for her and I can't have you interfering."

"I understand." Dougal cleared his throat. His voice sounded strangled.

"Well, of course you do. The thing is, Maude don't understand. The poor girl has her heart set on you, now that Beauford's out of her sight. Ma tried to tell her to leave you be but the lass is obsessed with you." Pa cocked an eyebrow.

No way would he comment.

Another nod. "Ma and I have been talkin' and I got her to realize that the best way to get Maude to forget about you is to tell her you're Mara's betrothed. She knows we found you in the woods unconscious and all, but if I tell her we was expectin' you, she won't question it."

*Mara...*

"Now, I know Mara's a tad simple. Touched in the head, some say. She ain't spoke one word in the last ten years. A'course, that's not a bad quality for a woman, if you ask me!" Pa slapped his thigh and stared at Dougal, no doubt to gauge his reaction.

But no words could force themselves past the fullness in his throat. *Mara...*

Pa's grunt sounded disappointed. "You don't have to actually marry Mara, just pay her some attention. Do some courtin' and a little bit of wooin'. Once Maude sees your interest lies elsewhere, she'll leave this foolish notion behind her." He took a long draw of his pipe. "What do you think?"

Dougal didn't know what to say. He was being offered the opportunity to woo Mara? Her father thought Mara was simple-minded, but Dougal didn't believe it, not for a moment.

He massaged between his brows. There was an attraction between the two of them; it was almost electric, like that between Chase and Maddie. A memory—Maddie touching Chase and then *poof*, Chase changing forms—caused Dougal's stomach to clench.

If he remained near Mara too long or touched her, would he change to his gryphon form against his will? In front of *everybody*? Love did weird things to a gray gryphon. Was he one of them now? Sacrificing himself had changed something inside him, but had it changed enough?

Was he still a destroyer or was he now a protector?

Motionless as a marble statue, Maeldun's only movement while the table had been set had been the occasional flick of his eyelids. But once the meal had begun, he'd clenched his claws tightly around the limb supporting him and finally scooted from side to side to get a better view. He had sighed with envy as the stranger stared at Mara. The look of attraction the stranger sent Mara's way had made the black blood boil in his veins. Even through the open windows, the undercurrent between the human and Mara could be felt. Who *was* that stranger?

But finally, watching the spectacle of love made him sick. He stretched his wings and took flight, soaring to the next post. Again he landed outside the big house and settled on a branch to peer inside. *She* would be by at any moment... and *there*. With his eyes fixed on her, Maeldun quivered as Ivy passed.

In all the years he'd watched her, her beauty had not diminished. Silken golden tresses interspersed with stray strands of gray flowed gracefully down her slender back. With his snout lifted, he breathed deeply and was rewarded with the faintest scent of petunias. If only things were different. But alas, to achieve his goals, he couldn't let personal desires get in the way—not yet, anyway.

One more deep breath and he took to the skies.

The men under his charge were no doubt waiting for him. He needed to return and see if anything new had developed.

Soaring on an updraft, Maeldun surveyed the land. The

mountain trails would only be passable for a few more months. Then the snows would come and help to protect their stronghold. The railroad's pass would remain open longer, but even now plans were being finalized. The time chosen to attack would be when the townspeople had little or no means of obtaining assistance.

While closing in on his men's position, Maeldun spotted a small furry thing stuck in a thicket. Flapping his large wings, he swooped down for a closer look. He bared his fangs and used a clawed hand to free the helpless, quivering creature. As it scurried away, it glanced back over its shoulder, as if searching for danger. Laughter filled him as he pounced on the tiny animal. His claws dug into the ground; he lifted it by the scruff of its neck and peered into its tiny black eyes. They resembled those of the stranger who gazed longingly at Mara. Anger consumed him. He squeezed. When he was finished, he shook his hand, freeing it of the blood, gore, and fur. The creature's remains landed with a plop in two pieces at his feet. The *rat* would pay.

# 7

All during clean-up, Mara had gazed out the window and wished for a dip in the stream. Just thinking about the water, cooling with night's fall, sliding over her sweaty skin and washing her clean… she shuddered and hid it by fetching more dirty dishes from the table.

Once they'd finished, she snuck upstairs and gathered her things. As she slid out the door onto the porch, her father's voice stopped her.

"Now, I know Mara's a tad simple. Touched in the head, some say. She ain't spoke one word in the last ten years. Course, that's not a bad quality for a woman, if you ask me!"

Then Pa asked Dougal to woo her. Her pulse thumped wildly in her chest, and heat infused her cheeks as images of a shirtless Dougal raced through her mind. The way his muscles rippled as he'd lifted the shovel and thrust it into the ground. How the sweat had beaded and run down his spine toward his tapered waist.

Catching her breath became increasingly difficult, until Pa added, "You don't have to actually marry Mara, just pay her some attention, do some courtin' and a little bit of wooin'. Once Maude sees your interest lies elsewhere, she'll leave the foolish notion of you two behind."

Everything stopped, especially her heart. In other words, Dougal could pass along words of love and make meaningful gestures, but they didn't have to mean anything. Her shoulders slumped and a single tear slipped from her eye. She should leave the two of them to their plotting, go to the stream as she'd planned and enjoy a nice cool dip in the flowing waters, but she couldn't go, not yet. She needed to know Dougal's answer.

Remaining in the shadows and waiting was almost unbearable. Her throat burned with restrained tears. The thump of her pulse echoed in her ears.

"I would be honored to woo your daughter."

The next tear froze in its track.

The sound of a back being slapped echoed across the porch. "Well done. I'm obliged to you."

"No, Uncle, I'm obliged to you. I was lost, but you found me and took me in." There was a pause. "Please, I know you say you need me to help work the farm. But I say you could have turned me over as a deserter; you don't know that I'm not one. I'm more than glad to help in any way I can to repay your kindness."

"Good."

The discussion continued, but her sudden anger drowned out their words. She stalked to the opposite end of the porch and stepped off. Shoulders rigid, she headed for the creek. There, hung between two trees, was a rope. Rocks covered the creek banks. On Fridays they washed their laundry and hung it out to dry.

Mara settled on the smooth boulder Ma preferred for scrubbing shirts. Sometimes—not when they were doing laundry, of course—but sometimes when she was alone and her work was done, she would sit in this spot and sing. The place held a magical feeling that drew words from her despite her best intentions. But each time the sound came through, she knew she put her family in danger. Why had she been such a nosy child? Why had her curiosity driven her to places she wasn't supposed to go? Because of her inquisitive nature and the event it caused, she had not spoken to another human being in over ten years.

Mara prayed that singing quietly to herself didn't break the vow. Sometimes she wanted to shout to the world. For surely *he* had left by now; he had to be long gone. But still Mara was afraid to risk everything to find out. So far nothing had happened when she sang. Surely singing again wouldn't cause any harm.

"Whoa, that was some bird!" Pa exclaimed. "I might oughta tell Junior to check on the scarecrow. If something like that gets in our corn, there won't be nary a thing left for us to eat!"

A weird feeling invaded Dougal's gut. His pulse quickened, and he leaned over the porch railing and peered into the sky. That was no bird! And he'd seen Mara sneak by some time ago. "Why don't I take a look around?" He fought to keep his voice calm, to not alert Pa to the danger.

The shadow's path had made a beeline in the direction Mara had taken.

"Maybe that'd be for the best." Pa started scouring out his pipe. "I guess I'll wait here until you get back."

Dougal stepped off the porch and kicked his legs out as he strode toward the trees. Once hidden from Pa, he ran. His feet hit the ground in a blur, and he considered trying to transform. He hadn't tried since he'd arrived and he could reach her much faster if he flew. But… something he didn't understand held him back. His breath came in short quick gasps, the blood rushing between his ears. Why did it feel as if time was running out?

Bursting through the trees, Dougal lifted his head to the night sky. Brassy orange and yellow painted the sunset sky. The shadow had disappeared. Had it merely been a large crow flying toward the corn, as Pa had suggested, or was it something more?

He lowered his chin. Beside the chattering creek, Mara lay awkwardly across a large boulder and stared blankly up at the brilliant sky.

It seemed like… no, there it was, the gentle rise and fall of her chest. Was that a red stain on her white gown, or a reflection of the evening sky?

A stick snapped beneath his feet. Mara bolted upright, her hand flying to cover her heart. Before he could say anything, her eyes widened, and she jumped from the boulder and scurried underneath a nearby willow with huge overhanging limbs. Her arms wrapped around the tree trunk's girth, and she moaned as her head twisted from side to side.

She never once looked at him, though.

That seemed weird. Dougal searched the skies while walking backward toward the willow. Nothing grabbed his attention. The brilliant sky still looked clear, but appearances could be deceptive.

He ducked beneath the branches into Mara's sanctuary and moved slowly toward her. Skittish as she seemed at that moment, the last thing he wanted was for her to bolt. But she peered up through the branches toward the sky, as if mesmerized by the colors.

"Mara," he whispered as he approached. "Mara, it's me. Dougal. I'm here to help you."

A noise echoed around him and he stopped. What was that? He snapped his head around. There it was again. It sounded like mocking laughter. Maybe the crow was cawing? If that actually had been a crow, of course.

Shaking it off, Dougal refocused on Mara. "Mara, look at me. I'm going to take you home."

Laughter; there it was again. This time, even Mara peered around. It had to be the wind, right? Or maybe a murder of crows?

"Please come to me. Let me help you."

"Mara, Mara, please come to me. Let me help you," came a mocking voice. "Now what have we got here?"

Dougal stiffened. Not the wind. Not a crow.

With the house behind him, O'Brien watched the slow river and listened for the slightest sound. He wiped his damp forehead with a white linen handkerchief, causing the dock to sway beneath him. But the heat and humidity were relentless and again sweat gathered on his face and neck. A faint morning mist hovered over the water, giving the landing an eerie appearance.

Months ago, when the Rebel officer had approached him about using an abandoned farm with an empty grain silo and a half-collapsed barn, O'Brien had thought nothing of it. He was patriotic, or patriotic enough. Besides, it didn't take a genius to understand Jefferson Davis... or at least *someone*... might reward him mightily if the South won, and if it didn't, well, he could just tell the victors he had had no choice in the matter.

But now Captain Herrick demanded he investigate that same piece of property. The farm in question was south and a little west of his own, almost directly south of the Hess place. Checking the silo's contents should have proved an easy task. He was a Southerner. The Rebel commander was a Southerner. He should only need to ask.

But still… putting his own face on the project rankled. Herrick knew something, or at least suspected it, and trusting Herrick was a fool's errand. No, the job called for agents, preferably agents that couldn't be traced back to O'Brien.

The spies he'd hired in town had proved completely worthless. Perhaps giving them a line of credit at the tavern hadn't been the best choice for the two most notorious town drunks, but there was little else which would get them to work. And now they languished in the jail that bore his name and he was unable to gather any information they might have gleaned. Not that it would have been trustworthy after it had been obtained while they were soused.

Removing his pocket watch from his vest pocket for the tenth time in less than twenty minutes, O'Brien sighed. What was taking the new spies so long? They had deserted from the Confederate army and swore they had no intention of returning, which made them the perfect candidates. All they had to do was sneak through the Confederate lines, open a door—

The water rippled. O'Brien peered around the cypress tree, but still… no boat. Enough! He would go to the barn, saddle his horse, and ride into town; he had business to see to. Elijah could wait for the fools. Why should he stand there all day? Besides, if Ivy spotted him hanging around, she would become suspicious. Sweat greased his palms and he wiped them against his trousers.

Yes, he'd leave. Decision made, he clumped across the dock and climbed the lawn toward the barn. But before he took two steps on dry land, a big shadow fell over him. He jolted to a stop. Blocking his path stood a horse, with a man sitting on high. The early morning sun rested behind the intruder's back and O'Brien lifted his hand to shield his eyes.

"Who goes there?" He hated the quiver in his voice.

"Mr. O'Brien, *Barry,* I have yet to hear from you."

"Captain Herrick?" What was he doing there, on the old Wheeler property—on *his* property?

"Aye, it is I."

O'Brien shuffled his feet. "Captain, I-I was j-just about to receive word."

"Truly?"

"Oh, yes. This very instant my spies are on their way to give a full report on the silo and the supplies within. I will have your information by the end of the day."

"And what of the other informants you hired?"

O'Brien gulped and ran his finger between his collar and his throat. How did Herrick know about the other informants? He'd told no one. Must have been when those fools yelled out his business along Main Street.

The horse muttered and pawed at the ground. Captain Herrick shifted in the saddle, his hips following the horse's movement. An odor of sulfur wafted toward O'Brien, which he refrained from commenting on. For some reason that odor happened quite frequently in the captain's presence.

O'Brien thought fast. "Captain, I'm sorry to say the intelligence gathered by my first informants was not as reliable as I had originally hoped. That is why I hired new spies to bring me better information."

"And you are certain these new spies are doing as they were told?"

"Oh, yes, Captain Herrick. Most certainly. They came highly recommended. There is no doubt in my mind they are on their way here as we speak."

Two raggedly dressed men stepped from the bushes. Gray uniform jackets hung open on their skinny frames. Between them they carried a small dingy. Wicked grins split their faces.

Dougal stepped out of the trees, hoping to lead the men away from Mara.

"I'm upset, Jude. Are you upset?"

"I sure am." Jude, the taller of the two, scratched his head. "But why are we upset?"

"Well, Jude, this young lady here was about to take a dip in the stream and I haven't seen a pretty lady in a while. First a stupid bird scares her, and now this no-account shows up, thinking to haul her away. *That* upsets me."

"Yeah, me, too, Jake." Jude nodded his head with increasing speed.

"So what do you think we should do about it?"

Bouncing from one foot to the other, Jude said, "I don't know. I don't know. Wonder if they have any food on them? Do you think they have some food?"

A slap landed on the back of Jude's head. "Of course they have food. Just look at them; well fed, they are. No doubt because of all their slaves."

Muscles tense, Dougal planted his feet firmly and shook out his arms. These two wouldn't give up without a fight. Blood raced between his ears as he steeled himself for the altercation. When a hand squeezed his shoulder, he startled, jumping a few inches off the ground. The two soldiers laughed and heat flooded his cheeks.

He glanced over his shoulder. Mara stood there, too close, and his thoughts started to frazzle. But then her fingers strayed to her mouth.

Dougal whispered, "Are you wanting to offer them food?"

She nodded.

"Mara, I don't think that's a good idea."

She stepped in front of him, her head bowed as if in prayer.

"You think it's your Christian duty?"

Another nod.

"Yeah, that's right, little girl," Jake said. "Your Christian duty."

Mara rounded on them, eyes blazing.

The two deserters backed up a step. She turned back to Dougal. Her expression begged for understanding.

Dougal's shoulders relaxed. "As you wish. But only if you do exactly as I say."

Mara nodded but this time with a smile twitching at her lips.

Dougal turned to the two deserters. "You will walk in front of me and the girl down this path. Stray from the path and I will break your necks. Do I make myself clear?"

A sarcastic "Humph" came from Jake.

With almost supernatural speed, Dougal shoved Jake against a tree, wrapped one hand around his neck, and lifted. Jake's feet dangled, his eyes bulging.

Dougal ground his teeth. "Do you understand?"

While Jake tried to claw Dougal's hand from his throat, Jude rushed in. Dougal lashed out with his other hand. The flat of his palm crashed against Jude's chest. Reeling back, Jude banged into a boulder. Blood gushed from his nose.

Dougal turned back to Jake, whose face was turning a nasty purple color. If he held on for much longer, the boy in gray would never bother another person. Was that what he wanted? To be as he was before?

Nausea climbed the back of his throat. Dougal let go. Jake

collapsed in a heap, clutching his throat and gasping for air, as Dougal stepped back, protecting Mara.

When Jake spoke, his voice sounded like a croaking frog. “Who are you?”

Dougal glanced at him again. Jake backed away, grabbing a dazed Jude by the jacket. “Let’s get out of here!”

Jude held his bleeding nose and stumbled away in Jake’s wake, abandoning the boat they’d carried. A few times they glanced back over their shoulders before disappearing into the trees.

Dougal sighed with relief. Mara was safe. He felt good, until he saw Mara.

She’d stepped back, away from him, back toward the boulder where he’d originally found her. As he watched, her dainty hands settled on either side of her narrow hips. A scowl marred her beautiful face. Gone was her fear, replaced by anger.

“I see you’re mad.”

She narrowed her steel blue eyes until he felt like a wilting flower in a hothouse. Raising hands in a defensive gesture, he said, “I know you thought we should feed them.”

Mara nodded, her tense posture slowly relaxing.

“I know you think they were just starving soldiers.” She nodded again. “But the truth is, they were dangerous, and in more ways than one. If they were truly Confederate deserters, they might have robbed your family. And if they were working for the Union, they could have brought the whole army down on the farm. You would all have been in danger.”

Mara’s face fell.

Dougal stepped closer. He was normally confident and self-assured, but for some reason he was afraid to touch her—and not because of the electricity between them; he enjoyed that. Something else stole his confidence. Fear. He stroked the tip of his finger along her well-defined chin, forcing her face upward. “Besides the risk to your family, they threatened to harm you.” The words glided from his lips smoothly and ended in a harsh whisper. “And I will *never, ever* allow anyone to hurt you.”

Her rosy lips parted and Dougal tensed in anticipation. When she didn’t speak, he shifted his gaze to her mouth. She bit her lip. Dougal struggled to read her expression.

Originally, Maddie and Chase had shared a link because Draoi made it so. Dougal had known things about Maddie because of Serena’s magic. But Mara was an enigma. He knew nothing but wanted to know everything. Pa's invitation for wooing could be the answer to his dilemma. It gave him an excuse to pursue everything there was to know about the lovely young lass.

The electricity that had shot through him the last time they'd touched became a strong, steady pulse. He sensed a humming, like a beehive. It was comforting, enticing. Just one finger and a small touch. What would happen if he touched her more? If his whole hand cradled her face? If the silken black locks that cascaded down her back poured through his fingers like a waterfall?

Without thought to the consequences, he leaned in, until their breath mingled. The vein in her neck throbbed as her heartbeat increased. A smile of satisfaction tugged at his mouth. Even though he had yet to see himself in a mirror, his good looks were obviously intact.

Mara pushed herself up on tiptoes. Dougal couldn't have been more pleased. His head lowering, his tongue darting out to moisten his dry lips, he envisioned kissing Mara. It would be like a July Fourth fireworks display, exploding from within his body. It would be like orbiting the moon. It would feel like a rush of sensations and pleasures beyond words.

His pulse increased in anticipation. Only one second more...

# 8

Mara glared at Junior as she used a wet cloth to clean the blood off Dougal's temple.

"Don't look at me like that," Junior said, crossing his arms over his barrel-shaped chest.

In her rigid anger, Mara forgot that not only was she supposed to be mute, but simple-minded as well.

"I came across you two, and I reacted," Junior said peevishly. "Dougal was about to kiss you. He has no business doin' so."

Pa ran a hand through what was left of his graying hair. "Junior Hess! Do you know what you've dun? You've dun knocked out your sister's beau."

"Beau?" Junior shot glances between Mara and Dougal.

"That's right. Dougal asked permission to court Mara."

Mara kept her head down. Dougal openly stared at her, and she couldn't help but peek up through her lashes. The black depths of his eyes took on a bronze glow, unreal and gorgeous.

"But... but what would he do that fer? She can't even speak!"

Pa smiled. "You act like that's a bad thing."

Mara stiffened and Dougal clasped her hand and squeezed.

"But Pa, he was goin' to kiss her!"

Pa heaved a sigh. "Well, I agree it is pretty quick. I'll talk to the lad about slowing down a bit. But you have to promise to stop punching my help and your future brother-in-law!"

"Yes, Pa," said Junior, narrowing his eyes and dropping his chin to his chest.

"Now, did you fix the scarecrow?"

"No. There weren't no need. That big bird never even went to the garden. No, it headed straight for the creek, hovered there for a while, it did. Then it took off toward the old Wheeler place."

Mara froze. If they asked if she'd seen anything, she'd act dimwitted.

Pa drew his brows together. He opened his mouth to speak, but before he could, Maude skidded into the room. Her rounded form gave her extra momentum, propelling her forward. She smacked into Junior and bounced.

She widened her eyes. "Junior! Why are you standing in my way? Ma said you hit Dougal. I need to tend to him." She rested her hands on her ample hips. "And why were you hittin' Dougal, anyway? He ain't dun nothing wrong."

Junior peered into Maude's eyes. Pointing his finger at Dougal, he said, "I hit that feller 'cause he was tryin' to kiss Mara."

"*What?*" Maude rested her fluttering hand over her heart.

"Yeah, I could have saved my hand some pain had I known Dougal asked to court her."

"Asked to—"

"Court. Can you believe it? Don't know why any man would want a woman that can't speak. But Pa keeps callin' it a blessin'." Junior shook his head.

Maude stared at Mara and Dougal.

Mara felt sorry for her sister, but there was nothing she could do but remain silent.

Maude faced Pa. "Pa, how could you? You knew I fancied him. You knew!"

"Now Maude, you're taken. What would Beauford think if he came back and found you hankerin' after another man? Why, then he wouldn't marry you and we would never get our land attached with the Wheeler place."

Maude appeared ready to argue, but quickly clamped her mouth shut and dropped her arms to her sides. She walked in front of Dougal and bumped Mara out of the way. Leaning over, she allowed Dougal an eyeful of her well-endowed bosom. "You are goin' to regret your choice."

Mara resisted the urge to push Maude away. Fortunately,

Maude moved before Mara needed to take action.

Dougal winked at her, as if he wasn't at all concerned by Maude's threat.

Mara tried to take solace in his confidence and resumed cleaning his wound. As the rag touched his broken cheek, her exposed skin connected with his and caused an electric pulse to race through her body. Where did that strange feeling keep coming from? Maybe it was some kind of magic—like voodoo.

She peered at Dougal to see if he noted the reaction. His pupils dilated; his tanned skin turned pale. With a hand across his stomach, he stood and lurched out of the room, leaving Mara behind, confused. What on earth...?

# 9

Captain Herrick turned his horse away, leaving O'Brien standing near the dock. O'Brien was as nervous as a cat on a hot tin roof. Good. He needed to know his life rested in Herrick's hands.

A smile tugged at his lips. Since coming to Wheeler's Landing, he'd seen no action, even though his Union troops were encamped no major distance from the Confederate unit near the silo. His primary function was to hold the area against dissidents to the Union's cause. That was where he could do the most damage, or the most good.

After returning to town, he gave over his horse to the stableman and searched out his men. They rested in the tavern, enjoying the drinks offered. The townspeople were oblivious to their true identity. A change of clothes was all it took to keep his spies hidden.

Herrick left them and went to his own room at the hotel. Rummaging through his things brought about a familiar urge. Checking on his future bride several times throughout the day exhausted him, but he needed to satisfy that drive. If only there was a way to *hear* her, *feel* her. Their time apart was maddening.

He opened the window and peered out at the street. Below him staggered two stragglers. They wore ragged blue-gray pants and torn white shirts. Perhaps the rips were an attempt to shed their identity before entering the Southern town; however, Union trousers were nearly the same shade as those worn by

Confederate soldiers.

At the first building on the street, they increased their pace. They reached the middle of the street and shouted, "Help! Help! There's a madman out there. He tried to kill us."

The sheriff stepped off the boardwalk. A cigar dangled from his mouth. He flicked it to the ground directly in front of the yelling pair and approached them with a confident swagger. He lifted a booted foot and ground the still glowing cigar with his toe.

The two men gulped, their eyes widening. They must have just realized their mistake. Herrick leaned against the window jamb and waited.

"Well, well, what do we have here? Look, boys," the sheriff called to a group of watchers standing outside the tavern door. "It looks like we've got ourselves a couple of Union soldiers."

"Sure does," said one bystander.

"And what do we do with Union soldiers?" asked the sheriff.

Herrick couldn't hear all the suggestions. One he did hear was "Hang 'em."

The two soldiers looked at one another and then turned and ran. Tripping and falling over one another, they made it to the depot before they were caught. The sheriff laughed heartily as the two were bound and escorted to the town jail. They screamed that they didn't belong to no "stinkin' Union," but it did no good.

Herrick shook his head. There would be no information today. Those two idiots were almost certainly the men O'Brien had hired.

He paced his hotel room. To return and tell the leader he still knew nothing... well, he'd rather not.

Good help was so hard to find these days. He could easily have gathered the information required. How hard would it be to learn the silo's contents? Why, it would be nothing at all, but for some unknown reason Colonel Hastings wanted the information to come from Barry O'Brien.

Only one chair fit in the hotel room beside the bed, and Herrick fell into it. Perhaps if he begged, Hastings would allow him to do his own scouting. They could still use Barry O'Brien, just for some other purpose. It would be easy. The man was an utter fool. An elaborate plan wasn't required. Why, if anyone wanted to take O'Brien down, all they needed to do was study his business practices.

Pain clenched Herrick's stomach and he doubled over. A masochistic grin spread across his face as he reveled in the pain. The change hadn't hurt this much since his first time. Could his dark leader be doing something without his knowledge? He bent over and clasped his arms around his middle.

Dougal tumbled from the farmhouse porch. Not now! No, he couldn't change now! Where could he hide? A copse of trees loomed ahead, bordering the largest cornfield. He glanced over his shoulder; no one followed.

He staggered toward the trees. Changing; he had to be changing; but it felt different. Always in the past he'd controlled the change, but this time the change controlled him, and the helplessness was scary.

The large maple tree with Mara's swing provided shelter as the change occurred. Dougal stretched from his normal six-foot height to over seven feet. His fingers lengthened and claws sharpened. A fine fur covered his body. He stretched his wings beneath the maple's branches.

Air rushed between his teeth and he closed his eyes. The change. It felt good. Normal.

Sweat beaded his brow. What would he see when he opened his eyes? Matted black fur or pristine gray? He was such a wimp. He could deal; he always had before.

Light blinded his sensitive eyes as he looked at his new body. His fur was gray. *Gray.* He touched his face, but it wasn't enough. He need to see himself. Nobody was in sight. One peek in the pond wouldn't hurt.

He leaned over the clear glassy surface, careful not to block the light. There he was in all his gray glory. Brows were neatly trimmed, as if he'd gone to a salon. Eyelashes curled upward. And the snout was shorter, unlike that of a black. So the sacrifice had worked. Hadn't he felt it, the difference? No longer did he carry the mark of a black gryphon. Now he held the seal of a protector. It was what he'd always dreamed. Since childhood he'd wanted nothing more, and now here he was—

Behind him, a twig snapped. His pulsed jumped in his neck. He'd been followed. He flew to the top of a tree and settled on a branch. The leaves barely hid him. Was he bigger now?

Like it hadn't been hard enough to hide before.

*Mara.* Of course she would be the one to follow him. The silly girl. She was scared of her own shadow, yet she came after him. If she saw him, her steel blue eyes would widen and lock in place. Her lip would quiver like a small animal caught in a trap. His gut clenched. He needed to get out of there.

She kept walking until he could no longer see her. This was his chance. He leapt and took flight.

The sun descended behind the mountains, creating a halo of light. Treetops brushed the tips of his wings, sending pulses of static along his nerves. He inhaled deeply. How he'd missed the feeling of freedom. The air shifting through his fur, the beauty of the scenery. Perfect. Everything was perfect.

*Mara.*

Maybe everything wasn't perfect. He'd traveled through time and now he'd changed into a gray gryphon. And then there was Mara. Why did she get to him so much? Her eyes. Her touch. The electric energy they shared. There was something there he was missing. He needed a place to rest and think. But where?

At the risk of being seen, Dougal soared higher. Bare patches dotted the mountainside in random patterns. He narrowed his eyes. Another positive to being a gryphon was increased eyesight. He'd always loved that particular ability. He could spot a tick on a dog's back from a hundred yards away. If only tick-finding was a useful thing.

The first place he located was little more than a rabbit hole. He couldn't exactly hide there unless grays could shrink. Now there was an ability he could get used to, if it existed.

Another opening, not far from the first one, seemed to go all the way through the mountain. That would be a great way for the Union army to secretly move their weapons or supplies. He needed to remember the location and report it back to Pa. If he'd paid more attention in history class, he might know if that had happened.

*Note to self: if I ever make it back to the present, pay more attention to history.*

The trees thickened. Too bad he didn't know where he was in the great South. He might have visited the area before. He doubted it, though. The place wasn't a touristy spot—unless you liked bird watching.

Ah, there was another opening. It was larger than the first

one and more sealed off than the second one.

He landed on the lip. The rock was damp. Water trickled somewhere inside, striking an even rhythm. One beat, two beats, three beats. It sounded like a heart.

He ran his hands over the thick gray fur of his forearm. He actually felt cold. Wait, that wasn't cold; it was foreboding. Yup, definitely a worry. A rush of protective instincts welled inside him.

His gut seized and his chest hurt. He couldn't breathe. He ran from the cave and took to the air. So much for resting and figuring things out. Was this how Chase had felt when he'd protected Maddie? An overwhelming sense of dread and fear? How had he coped? Responsibility for others stank.

The sky darkened. He narrowed his eyes. What was he looking for? It was probably something stupid. One of the Hess family members might have stubbed a toe or—

*There*, just ahead—Mara, tense with fear, was sliding off the edge of a cliff! Her arms flew over her head as she plunged. A yell stuck in his throat as he formed the shape of a bullet and dove underneath her. She landed in his outstretched arms and almost bounced out. Quickly he pulled her to his chest. The normal electricity that arced between them would be exhilarating. He waited.

But she beat his chest with her fists. Um, something wasn't right. Shouldn't she be grateful?

Gruffly he said, "If you want to live, you need to be still."

Maybe she didn't believe him. She continued to beat and claw, even embedding her teeth into his shoulder. He grunted, but a smile tinged his lips. If he loosened his grip just a little, she might straighten up.

Then she kicked her legs and he almost lost his grip for real.

Playtime was over. "I'm telling you to be still."

He needed to find a place to set her down. Perhaps he could explain that he was trying to help her. Or something that would be more fun—touching her. Would the electricity in the new form be more powerful? He hadn't felt it yet. Maybe being a gray made it defective. That would be just his luck.

A black dot appeared on the horizon. It moved closer fast, increasing in size. Long feathery wings flapped. But it wasn't a bird. Could it be another gryphon? Who did he know that could be alive? Gregory. The foul-mouthed, disgusting creature could easily be alive. If Dougal had calculated the years correctly, Cian had yet to imprison any of the gryphons. That meant Dougal could find himself in the midst of a war between the two gryphon factions. Not good, definitely not good.

The flying creature closed on their position.

“Crap!” It *was* a black gryphon!

What should he do? Confront or run? It really depended on why he was there. If he’d been sent to change the future by altering the past, then to hurt a gryphon, say Gregory, would perhaps harm Maddie and Chase. But if he’d been sent there to protect someone, then harming the gryphon might be exactly what he needed to do.

His head hurt. He hated being confused.

He tightened his hold. Mara stiffened in his arms. Great. She must have noticed he wasn’t the only beast around. Way to keep her calm.

She tightened her grip on his arm. Tiny bursts of pleasure radiated along his limbs, until he felt weak. So the electricity wasn’t defective. This was a great time to find out. He needed to land. Now.

Dougal touched down in a clearing and jogged to a stop. Mara lifted her head from his chest. Her blue eyes were wide. Probably with fear. Falling off a cliff couldn’t have been a great experience and following it with two beasts, well, not too good either. He’d love to reassure her, but how? Right now he couldn’t even reassure himself.

With as much gentleness as he could muster, he placed Mara on the ground and kept his hands on her shoulders until she was steady. “Don’t move.”

Mara gasped. That didn’t sound good, either. He turned. The blow struck his side, shooting shafts of pain along his spine and sending him to his knees. He needed to get up and protect Mara.

The black drew in, like he meant to strike again. Dougal extended his claws and scraped them down the black’s face. Instead of a howl of pain, the black gryphon roared with laughter. That wasn’t the reaction such a blow normally received. But this didn’t seem like a normal gryphon, and a strange knot of fear tangled in Dougal’s chest.

“I see you’ve taken a special interest in my *friend.*” The gryphon sneered, drool dripping from his sharp fangs.

Was he talking about Mara? Dougal didn’t like that.

Mara's trembling set his pulse racing. He needed to gain control of his emotions. Dougal ignored the pain in his side. "Who are you? And what do you want with the young lass?"

The gryphon reared back his head and laughed louder. When he lowered his head, his eyes had widened to the size of saucers and his lips were drawn back over his fangs. The black gryphon was maniacal. Nope, not good.

"It matters not who I am. The girl is *mine*."

Dougal raised his hands defensively. "No worries. I didn't want her anyway. She's nothing but a bunch of trouble. You see this blood." He pointed to his shoulder. "She bit me. So you can have her. I'll just find me another." Mara's swift intake of breath added to the effect of his words. Did she know he was lying? He just needed to keep up the act long enough to find an escape. Sometimes it stank, not having a friend, or at least an ally or sidekick for his adventures.

The stranger drew his bushy brows together. Should he tell him to get a trim? Probably wouldn't go over too well. And look at that long snout! Had he really looked like that? So ugly.

"Do you think I was born yesterday?"

Dougal shrugged. "No?"

The dark gryphon spat. "I know you want her. The stench of a fresh change is all over you." He paused. "I haven't seen one of your kind in a long time."

"I feel insulted. I thought I was one of a kind." He smirked; it felt like old times.

"Oh, a smart Alec, I see. I believe you will find me more amicable when I'm not in a foul mood." He leaned over and pawed the ground. Air whooshed from his nostrils.

Yup, not good. "Moody, are you?"

Breath left him as the black gryphon struck him in the chest and flung him to the ground. Mara scurried backward, right in time to keep from cushioning his blow. The black crossed his arms over his chest. Perhaps aggravating the beast hadn't been his best idea.

"Reckless. You're obviously new, so your power is limited. Do you just want to die?" The stranger rubbed his palms together. "Because I can help you with that."

Dougal snorted a half laugh. It hurt like the devil.

"Let's make a deal. You leave the girl with me and I won't kill you."

His breathing was labored as his body repaired several broken ribs. It wasn't the most comfortable feeling, but it was better than the alternative. And then there was the other problem to add to his growing list—no power. How could he protect Mara? Brute force didn't seem to be working, and the black was obviously not affected by witty comebacks. Waiting on the cavalry would take too long, like a century too long. He needed another plan. "Why d-do you want the girl?"

"Why do you?"

The gryphon shifted. Did he just cock a hip? No way. This day just kept getting weirder.

Dougal shrugged. "She smells good."

The black snickered. "An honest answer. Perhaps you should join me. I can teach you how to really live."

Join the hideous beast? The black's fangs dripped with sulfurous venom, his claws were gnarled and twisted; a visage once beautiful was now grotesque from transgression. Had *he* looked that way? Bile rose in his throat. He would never go back to that life; even if it brought his demise, he would remain on the side of good. Now was the time to prove his intent.

Dougal rotated, hugged Mara, and flew straight up. It wouldn't take long for the black gryphon to follow them and catch up. Recovery had always taken a lot out of him and now that he was like a newly changed creature, it was going to be worse.

Trees loomed below them. Mountains lined both sides of the valley. They needed a place to hide. Something about this place seemed familiar... Coal Creek! He was in Coal Creek! But where was the town? In his day, Coal Creek had been a thriving little city. He shook his head. It was a hundred and fifty years too early, but maybe he could still use his knowledge of the area to his advantage. The lair! If it was already there, then that would be the perfect place to hide.

The distinct rock face came into view and he scanned the base of the mountain. The opening!

Dougal took a circuitous route before entering. Now all he could do was pray they hadn't been seen.

Dougal parted the hanging vines and peered into the dark, gloomy depths of the mountain lair. Tenebrous tunnels should lie ahead. Webs hung from the ceiling and clung to the walls, but he was lucky—the tunnels were there. He stopped in an antechamber and lowered his cargo. Mara staggered backward into the wall, hugging herself.

It was really a shame that he hadn't had time to explain. Then maybe she could cut out the timid act and be a little more grateful. Of course there wasn't a lot to be grateful for just yet. They were hiding in a dark cave after being pursued by a crazed, obsessed black gryphon.

"Gray, show yourself!"

Dougal moved closer to Mara. His voice was husky. "You stay here. I'll come back for you."

"*Yes...*"

Her dark blue eyes glowed. He blinked. Had she spoken? No, it had been more like a feeling that raced over him. A feeling that he wouldn't mind getting lost in. It was like lying on a bed of flowers and staring at the afternoon sky, or—

"Gray gryphon! The girl is *mine*!"

That was *it*! He'd been thrown into a tower of wailing gryphons, sent back in time, taken in by a family of bumpkins, and now this jerk had the audacity to threaten him while he was in the midst of enjoying a woman! Dougal twirled on his heel and rushed to the cave's entrance. The rocks groaned, the mountain shuddered, and the trees sighed as he pushed through the hanging vines like lava being expelled from a volcano. He flew a hundred feet from the entrance and landed in a clearing, and struggled to catch his breath as he faced his enemy. Dougal hoped the gryphon was ready, because he wanted this over with!

The black landed, the ground shuddering beneath his feet. "Where is she?"

"Who are you?" Before he ripped the gryphon's head off, he needed to make sure it wasn't Gregory.

The black's tone deepened, playfulness gone. "I could ask you the same thing. But I care not who you are. Once you're extinguished, the girl will be mine once more."

Presumptuous fellow. Why couldn't he fight an incompetent gryphon for a change? "And why do you assume I'll be the one to die?"

"Because I want you to. And I always get what I want."

Dougal drew his brows together. This gryphon sounded familiar. Now he really needed to know. "Gregory?"

White fangs gleamed in the waning light. An odor of sulfur

floated from his mouth. “Gregory? I know not of this Gregory you speak.”

“Ailin Colin?” Dougal tried Gregory’s gryphon name. It was possible with the time travel that he hadn’t changed it yet.

“Are you serious? Now I know you value not your life. Imagine insulting me thusly.” The black pecked a curled nail upon his forehead. A new light entered his eyes. “Do you know where Ailin resides? Perhaps renewing our friendship would be *beneficial.*”

The grin that covered the black’s snout when he said “beneficial” had Dougal cringing. No doubt Gregory, or Ailin, was not on the best of terms with this black.

“Well? You’ve had plenty of time to consider my offer. What is your answer?”

“Offer?” What was the black talking about?

“Are you as dimwitted as the humans? I would think it was obvious. You give me the girl and I will consider letting you live. If you decline...” he shrugged his black shoulders, “...you will die. I believe I’m being more than generous.”

Unperturbed, Dougal asked again, “Who *are* you?”

“Determined to know, are you? Very well. I am Maeldun, second in command to Cahal.”

Cahal! He’d been right. He’d come back to when Cahal and the others had yet to be imprisoned. The urge was there again. *Father.* What harm would it do to seek him out? Maybe just for a moment... Flashbacks of their first and last encounter flashed through his mind. A lot of harm.

Maeldun meant *devotee of the dark warrior.* The name almost made him laugh. “Your name is not very creative.”

Maeldun scowled. “And what is your name?”

Dougal thought for a moment. He was no longer Doran, *the exiled one.* Now he was something completely different. Shouldn’t his name reflect the new person he’d become? “I am Nuada Lear.”

Maeldun’s head reared back with laughter. “Newly-made gray! And you say I’m uncreative.”

His stomach tightened. He tucked his wings to his back and raced forward. Claws and fangs bared, he ripped and tore at Maeldun. The movements of his arms were so fast he appeared as a blur. When he finished, blood oozed from gaps in Maeldun’s flesh. Breathing in short rasping gasps, he grasped Maeldun, and with one final stroke he drew a talon across

Maeldun's neck. The black collapsed to the ground. Blood drained from his body, causing him to jerk and convulse. Blood lust burned within Dougal as he stumbled away.

Thirst clawed at his throat. Water. He needed water. Briars snagged his skin until he reached a slow-moving stream. He dropped to one knee, took a handful of water, and poured it over his head and down his back. He almost felt normal again.

Red dripped from his hands and he trembled. He'd done it again. He'd gone back to what he'd previously been so soon. How did this behavior fit with his new life? His name meant newly-made, but now he felt like he always had. Self-loathing overcame him.

He stood shakily to his feet. His heart hammered in his chest. Had protecting Mara been his purpose? Was that why he'd been thrust back in time? Now would he return to his own time? Would he go back to the tower as a prisoner? Or would he be free?

He sighed, his body changing back to his human form without giving him a choice. His reflection stared back at him. Scratches and scars melted away, but his clothing was in tatters. He bit his lip. How would he retrieve Mara now? She expected a gryphon or at least someone fully clothed.

Before he decided what to do, he should probably check on Maeldun. It only took a moment to return to the clearing. The black gryphon still lay unmoving on the ground. Dougal drew closer until he leaned over the prone form. Blood seeped from the black gryphon's wounds and covered the ground. He put his finger under the black's long snout. It was so different from his own now. Definitely much uglier. He would have tried for gray status much earlier if he'd realized.

He waited a moment. Nothing. Maeldun was dead.

He moved away from the body and sat on a log. What was he going to do about Mara? He could return to the farm and direct the Hess family to her location so they could find her. Mara should be safe until then.

Dougal stood and walked backward from the clearing. He reached a dirt road on the other side of the trees and ran. His boot slid in the dusty road and he tripped, slamming down hard. Pebbles embedded in his hand. He didn't have time for this. Maybe he could fly a little closer and then change. He closed his eyes and scrunched his nose, but nothing happened. No pain, no change, nothing. Great. He was a gray all right;

they couldn't change unless they needed to save someone, and there was the love thing, which he didn't know how it worked. Guess it was back to hoofing it.

As he reached the edge of the Hess yard, he heard worried voices.

"Flint, where could she be?"

"Mara!" yelled Junior.

The popping of a slap echoed through the valley. "You dummy. Do you think she'll yell back?"

"Well—"

"The girl ain't spoken since the last time she disappeared when she were but seven years old."

"Well, I know, but she's still got a tongue, so maybe she has the ability to talk but she ain't had nothin' to say. Unlike some people I know who think they have to do all the talkin'."

"What? Why, you are the stupidest boy I've ever known," replied Maude.

Junior mumbled, "Probably the only boy you're likely to know."

Maude turned with a scathing retort upon her lips. Before she spoke, Ma yelled, "Dougal! We've been lookin' for you. Have you seen Mara?"

He ran his hand through his hair. Now he needed to think of a way to direct them to Mara without revealing how he knew where she was. It would have been better if he'd knocked Mara out and brought her back on his own. Why hadn't he thought of that before he ran all the way here?

# 10

Maeldun detested the act of pretending, yet he had dropped to the ground, writhed and moaned, and eventually laid perfectly still. The gray gryphon had shuffled away. In an unexpected stroke of luck, he'd morphed into his human form. But black hair and a tanned back were all Maeldun could make out. That wasn't enough.

*Face me, Nuada.*

The gray-in-human-form had complied and he'd almost cheered, until he'd noticed the gray's route. He'd quickly closed his eyes as Nuada had paused and stood directly above him. Maeldun had held perfectly still, held his breath, until he finally heard the grass crunching beneath the retreating gryphon's feet.

Now Maeldun sat up and dusted himself off. The small pool of his blood had already absorbed into the ground. He should have allowed more to flow. He'd cut his ruse too close.

The gray had grossly overestimated his power. Maeldun's first assessment had been correct: Nuada Lear was a new creature. The strike across Maeldun's neck had barely penetrated enough to pierce his skin and allow his dark blood to flow. In fact, he had leaned into the slice to get the cut deeper. He sighed; the things he had to do for Cahal.

Maeldun perked his ears and listened for movement. Nuada's shuffling feet grew muffled by the thickening trees and finally fell silent. At least he was alone. Now he had other things to concentrate on—*Mara.*

One glance told him Mara wasn't close. So the gray wasn't completely inadequate. He'd hidden the girl *then* returned to fight. Smart.

Frustration mounting, Maeldun flared his wings. Sunlight filtered through the thin membrane. Nuada had failed to cut off his head, but he had sliced his patagium. The wound was minor, but would make flight near impossible. Not to mention that it hurt. He should have been more careful. Walking annoyed him. It reminded him of human frailty. Granted, that was one thing he did enjoy thinking about.

He changed into his human form and headed toward camp. It would take longer to heal in this form, but at least if he was spotted he wouldn't be shot because of his beastly appearance.

He sniffed. Pine trees, the scent of fresh water, but still no Mara. Nuada and Mara had been together moments before the gray had reappeared in the clearing. So she had to be close by, but where?

He could look for the girl and abandon his idea of updating Cahal. What would he report, anyways? "There's a new man in town"?

But the leader had a vicious nature. He didn't appreciate failure, and at the moment Maeldun *was* a failure. He had no information on the silo, and he had lost Mara—again. He sighed. They'd waited ten years on the lass; what was a little longer?

He approached the camp. A soldier gave him the once-over. "Captain, what happened to you?"

Mara huddled against the cave wall. Pain radiated through her ribs. The gray creature had squeezed hard—too hard. Maybe she should be grateful that she hadn't fallen. But something kept her from happiness. Probably the fact that he'd left her in a cave without even telling her where she was or where he was going. That could have something to do with her ungratefulness.

She should have fought harder to get away. Maybe falling off a cliff wouldn't have been so bad.

If she hadn't gone in search of Dougal, none of this would have happened. And of course she wouldn't have gone after him if he hadn't run out of the house as if her touch had burned him. And she wouldn't have touched him if not for Junior. Why had he gone and struck Dougal for trying to kiss her?

Heat rushed to her cheeks. She would have enjoyed that kiss; she was sure of it. But now she'd never know. Dougal had run off. She'd tried to go after him, but he'd just up and disappeared.

Twigs had snapped and been pushed off the trail. She'd followed them like clues to a treasure. When the trail had ended at the cliff's edge, she'd turned in a wide circle and walked backward a few steps, and that was when the ground had given way. Next thing she'd known, warm furry arms had wrapped around her and she was sailing through the air. If she'd been a talker, she'd have had a story to tell.

Rumbling rolled from her throat as hunger gnawed at her empty stomach. Chill bumps dotted her tender flesh. Did the cooling air mean the sun was descending? If she didn't escape while there was light, then she would be stuck—alone—in the dark. She didn't like the dark. Too many noises in the dark. Too many creatures in the dark. Too many strange, unexplainable *things*.

Her legs trembled as she used the wall to scramble to her feet. It was damp with no grooves or indentations that might lead her out. That fool beast might have thought to trap her, but he was wrong. She wouldn't give up. She'd been through worse. This was a minor setback, no more.

She scooted her feet along the narrow path, sometimes bumping her toes but mostly meeting no resistance. Finally, red and orange shafts of light peered through what looked like a hanging wall of greenery. Vines! Hanging vines. She pushed them aside slowly and stepped through.

Boulders formed a square on all sides. This wasn't the entrance the gray had used. This one was more hemmed in—more secluded. What now? She could go back into the cave and try to find another exit but the dark—the dark wasn't appealing. She'd rather try her chances where she was.

Light streamed from above and struck a crevice, showing just enough room for her to turn sideways and slide through. As she did, uneven rocks snagged her dress and scraped her exposed skin. She released her clenched stomach as she exited to the other side, outside the boulders.

Broken tree limbs were scattered through flattened grass. Blood dotted the exposed ground.

She ran her hand around a knothole. The trunk was completely shattered. Not even Union cannons could have inflicted that kind of damage. The world was definitely dealing with something much more nefarious, and powerful. Much more dangerous.

Thoughts of hunger dissipated. The beasts had been there. They'd fought. If she wanted to survive, she needed to get home before they returned.

Dougal cringed as Junior eyed him. Curiosity wasn't good right now.

"What happened to you? You look like you was mauled by a bear."

Yup, he should have found a way to change.

Pa pushed Junior aside. "Please tell me Mara wasn't with you when you were attacked."

The world suddenly fell out of focus. Queasy; his stomach felt queasy. What was happening? Something wasn't right. "She was by the river." Why did his words sound so garbled?

"Bless you, son."

Was that Ma?

He reached out his hand and staggered toward what he hoped was the river. Whatever was happening to him wasn't good. He needed to hurry before he blacked out completely. Mara would never forgive him if she wound up stuck in that dark cave. Of course she didn't know he'd put her there, but that wasn't much consolation right then.

Pa wrapped an arm around his shoulder. "I don't know what got you, but you might oughta go back to the house and lie down. We'll find Mara."

"No." Dougal groaned. Without him they would never find her.

Blackness swirled behind his eyes. He stumbled. The ground didn't look very forgiving as it came up to meet his face.

Mara drew her mouth into a thin line as she skirted trees and obstacles on her way back to the farm.

Brambles caught her dress, ripping and tearing the thin fabric. Her legs ached and her lungs burned with exhaustion.

She needed to rest. A rotted log made the perfect seat. She removed her shoes and massaged her sore feet.

One of these days, her life would be normal. She would have her own family. Her own home. Her own children. She wanted a whole gaggle of them. But right now she needed to get out of this mess and that meant knowing where she was.

Everything looked the same. Trees, grass, downed limbs, pine needles, wildflowers. Maybe everything was similar because she was walking in circles. But she did feel a draw in this direction, so surely she was going the right way.

The sun set to her right, which meant west. But where was home?

She rubbed her aching temples. It was official. She was lost. And no one but a beast knew where she was.

# 11

Herrick had cleaned up and now stood at attention before his superior, Colonel Hastings. Unlike some other leaders in the Union army, Hastings was stern but fair. His five-foot-five rotund frame, beady eyes, and bowed legs suggested he was incapable of leading a military unit, but looks were deceiving. Because Hastings' appearance denied him respect, he was apt to place people under him whose looks and bearing made him appear more competent, which was the reason Herrick had been chosen as his emissary. Herrick didn't mind. His position in the Union army served him well.

Spies and scouts had been hired to discover needed information but had failed on more than one occasion. Time was running out. The Union army was on the move and Hastings was determined his unit would lead the pack. However, without the necessary supplies and weapons his unit wouldn't survive.

"Herrick, do you have anything new to report?"

"I'm afraid to say O'Brien has yet to be successful."

Hastings paced, stomping. He flipped over a corner table, sending a flurry of papers through the air. "This is unacceptable!"

Herrick didn't flinch. He'd seen worse tantrums. "Yes, sir. I've told him that."

Rounding on Herrick, Hastings asked, "Does he still wish to help us?"

Herrick clasped his hands behind his back and looked forward. "I think so." The fool kept hiring incompetents to perform the task, but at least he was hiring someone.

Hastings sighed and plopped into a chair. It cracked and groaned from his weight. "This is impossible. The information is critical. Do you understand? Critical! I need to know what is in that grain silo. Our supplies are running out. And the generals in the Union army don't have enough sense to keep us from going so far out ahead of the battle lines that we can't reach our own supply lines! If the Rebels knew of our predicament, we'd be sitting ducks."

"Yes, sir." What else could he say?

Hastings ran his hand over his balding head. It was a sign of frustration. Compared to Herrick's other leader, though, his behavior was mild.

Hastings tapped his finger to his chin. "This is what I want you to do."

Herrick listened. A couple of times he cocked a brow but remained silent.

"What do you think?"

Herrick scratched a spot between his brows. "Well, sir, it is an interesting plan, to be sure."

"Interesting, you say. I believe it's brilliant. The question is, do you think it will work?"

Hastings expected a reply. Like a child, he needed encouragement. And Herrick didn't care either way. He needed to know the contents of the silo, both for Hastings and for his other leader. If one wanted to pin the treachery on O'Brien, then he was content to assist, as long as it didn't anger the other. "Yes."

"Good. Get started right away. And I don't want to see you until it has been completed. Do you understand?"

"Yes, sir." Herrick saluted and exited the tent. It was going to be a long afternoon.

# 12

*Honeysuckle...*

Dougal's eyelids were so heavy he couldn't open them. And the voices. They sounded so far away. But he smelled honeysuckle.

Had he passed out again? If he did that every time he battled, he'd be in trouble.

Rough bark scratched his back. He was cold. So cold.

He blinked. He was beneath a shade tree and the Hess family was nearby, scouring the sides of the riverbank. So he'd gotten them this far. That was hardly enough. The cave was a considerable distance away.

Wind caressed the hair on his arms. There was that smell again.

He walked out from beneath the tree. "*Mara...*"

She swiveled and ran toward him, landing in his open arms. He planted a chaste kiss on her forehead, and she didn't pull away, but rather buried her head against his chest. It felt good—right.

Dougal pulled back and smoothed her hair from her forehead. "Are you all right?"

She nodded.

"Good." He wished he had a better word, but he was just so grateful she was safe that he couldn't think.

She caressed his stubbled cheek. Her hand came away with a drop of blood. She arched her brow.

He grinned. "You should see the other guy."

An intense scowl settled over her face.

Dougal raised his hands, palms up. "Sorry, it was a bad joke. I'm just happy to see you."

A single tear slipped from the corner of her eye and trailed down her dirt-stained cheek. He gently wiped it away with his knuckle. "Don't cry. You're safe."

He stared at her midnight black hair. If only she could speak, he would ask her how she'd gotten to the clearing. Or if she remembered what had happened. Or if she knew he was involved in what happened.

Leaves rustled behind them. Mara's parents were coming.

He placed his hands on her upper arms and gazed into her eyes. "Mara, I need to tell them I found you."

She removed herself from his hold, smoothed down her dress, and placed her hands demurely together before her, then nodded.

She knew they'd be upset so she was trying to present a positive front. It was as he'd suspected. The dimwittedness was an act.

He drew in a deep breath. "I found her!"

Pa, Ma, Maude, and Junior fell over each other as they crashed through the foliage, and in a single mass of bodies they enveloped Mara.

"Oh, my baby. I'm never letting you out of my sight again."

"LouAnn, please. Don't smother the girl."

Ma dropped her arms and Pa stepped in and took her place, repeating Ma's words verbatim.

Maude moved back, rolled her eyes, and placed her hands on her hips. "She's fakin'."

Pa and Ma froze.

Maude's suspicion was a complication he hadn't foreseen. How could a mute girl explain her disappearance?

She stalked forward and stood before Mara. "Admit it. I'm tired of you bein' an attention hog."

Mara lowered her chin to her chest. He should defend her but bit his tongue. He couldn't risk revealing his involvement in her disappearance. It would be a Pandora's Box that he couldn't close.

Maude wagged her finger. "I'm tired of your silent treatment. I'm tired of you playin' the victim. Always gettin' the man." Envy laced her voice. Yup, she was jealous and he'd made matters worse. Why hadn't he just brought Mara directly to the Hess farm instead of hiding her?

Pa and Ma turned red. Were they embarrassed or angry? He'd go with angry. He was getting there himself.

Junior grabbed Maude's arm. "Come with me."

She attempted to shake him loose. "Remove your hands from me."

Junior bent his head and whispered something.

Dougal could have tuned in to the conversation but he didn't want to. He stepped under the overhang of the weeping willow before sinking to his knees. An outsider might have thought he was praying, and part of him did give thanks, but the real reason he knelt was because he could stand no longer. Being a new creature was more exhausting than he'd thought possible.

# 13

O'Brien started toward home. The two spies had failed to return and he was steamed. He was an idiot. Why had he told Herrick he could provide answers? Repercussions. There would be repercussions. But would they be against him or another in his family?

He ran his hand over his head. Strands of hair tangled around his fingers. Soon he'd be bald. Worry. It was the stress that came from burning the candle at both ends. It would be the death of him.

He crested the hill. His home spread before him, and for a moment his heart sang. But then a wisp of fabric passed the upper right-most window, and his pride vanished. Ivy waited upstairs, looking out. Since their son Beauford had joined the Rebel army, she had waited for his return.

He'd tried to hide his son away, but Beauford wouldn't hear of it. He'd said he didn't like the idea that they might lose everything if they lost their slaves.

O'Brien didn't care one way or the other. After his fool driver ran off a few days ago, Elijah and Ellie were all they had left and whether the South or the North won, he would still keep his property. He could rebuild his slave population later, or hire workers to replace them. Right now he just needed to keep both sides, North and South, happy.

But since Beauford's departure, Ivy was a mere shadow of the girl he'd married. At one time, she had been full of life. Then her family had perished unexpectedly and their son had left for war. Now he was all she had left and lately she didn't want much to do with him.

The feeling was mutual. She wouldn't understand his goals. She'd never understood his desire to lead. She'd been content to be pretty, which was why he'd married her. That and her property rights. But now with her youth and beauty diminishing, he wondered if he'd made the right choice. Maybe if he'd looked longer he could have found someone with a stronger constitution. He could have found someone who would have stood with him in his goal to win, no matter what.

He headed toward the stables. He had been away from town for too long. Perhaps if he returned, he could find others willing to search the silo. Captain Herrick's patience would only last so long. He'd thought of going himself, but he couldn't risk being caught working for the North. It could jeopardize his relationship with his Southern neighbors and he couldn't have that. No matter who won the conflict, he planned to come out on top.

Elijah hitched the horses to the carriage and O'Brien climbed inside. His head drooped as they bounced along the rutted road. He hadn't been sleeping well since Herrick began forcing the issue of the silo. The captain just didn't understand how hard it was to find good help with all the boys off to war.

The carriage stopped at the hotel and he dismissed Elijah. People milled about but ignored him as he climbed the rickety stairs and let himself into his regular room. A lingering odor of smoke smacked him. A side window was open. Had someone opened the window to allow air inside? Others used the room in his absence if the hotel was full. So maybe a guest left the smoke behind and the window open.

He crossed the room, grasped the wooden frame, and lowered it before engaging the lock. A whoosh of air struck his back and he swiveled. Captain Herrick stretched upon the bed, his booted feet crossed at the ankles.

O'Brien swallowed. Hadn't the bed been vacant just seconds earlier?

"What took you so long?"

O'Brien shook his head and pursed his lips. "I don't know what you're talking about." Or how he got in the room.

"I knew yesterday your spies weren't returning with the information. You should have contacted me so other arrangements could be made."

O'Brien straightened his collar and put on his best air of confidence. "That's interesting. You seem to know way more than I about my hirelings."

Captain Herrick cocked a brow. "Did your men find you?"

The answer was written all over his face, but he said it anyway. "No."

Captain Herrick worried at a loose string on the coverlet. "I know where they are."

"You do?" That couldn't be good.

"Yes. They reside in the town's jail."

"The jail?" He couldn't breathe. This couldn't be happening. Both sets of informants—in the jail! If they told the sheriff that he'd hired them, then the town might discover his double status. He'd be hanging by evening.

"It seems they straggled into town appearing to be dressed in Union garb and rambling like crazy men, and they were immediately arrested."

"No." The word was dragged from his throat.

"Yes."

He moved his hands through the air. "What am I going to do? If they tell the sheriff I hired them to search the—"

"They won't tell."

He narrowed his eyes and scrutinized Herrick. "What makes you so sure?"

"They're much too concerned with what happened to them in the woods to even remember your involvement."

"I don't understand."

"It seems they decided to leave the river before they reached your place. Who knows why? Perhaps they thought they could sell the information to the highest bidder. Anyway, they ran into a young man and woman and proceeded to attack the young lady. They were hungry, you see. You really should feed your people before you send them on a job."

O'Brien frowned and clenched his fists to his sides. Herrick would do well to remember *he* was the one who needed the favor.

Herrick continued, "As I was saying, they attacked the woman but the man who was with her took care of them."

"What do you mean?" How did Herrick make everything so dark and ominous just by adjusting his tone? He really was a creepy fellow.

"They claim he held them up against a tree with one hand and threatened to break their necks."

He dropped his hands to his sides. "Great." He paced. "And the first thing those idiots do is run into town, in what looks like Union garb, and tell the sheriff."

"Precisely."

He fell into a rickety chair. "This is a disaster."

Captain Herrick shifted to the edge of the bed. "Yes, it is. But it can be rectified. You will go to the jail and talk to them. Get all the information they have."

"Are you crazy? If I ask questions, the sheriff will realize I know them! I can't be caught fraternizing with possible Union soldiers!"

The captain tapped his finger to his forehead. "Hmm, this is true. But I don't see that you have a choice. We had a deal and if you don't fulfill your end of the bargain, then I suffer." He smiled without humor. "And if I suffer, then you suffer."

O'Brien gulped. With a shaky hand, he grabbed his silver-tipped cane and shuffled toward the closed door. Herrick had left him little choice. He marched from the room and to his destiny.

# 14

*The sounds. Day and night, wailing and moaning. It was as if a thousand people were on the verge of dying, all at the same time.*

*If he survived the noise, then there was the smell. With every exhalation, sulfur flowed. Inhale the smoke, exhale the sulfur. Over and over, in and out.*

*If he could tune out the sounds and the smell, then there was the heat. Heat so intense he thought he walked on the surface of the sun.*

*But worst of all was the darkness. Dark so thick that even when he touched his nose he couldn't see his hand. The absolute absence of light was worse than any punishment he could have imagined.*

*Every day was the same. There was no rest, no peace. Wailing and gnashing of teeth, the smell of burning flesh, and the darkness were his constant companions. It was no less than he deserved. He was no better than those who'd entered this place before him. He had sought to kill and destroy the same as them, even if it was on a smaller, less grand scale.*

*He could go completely insane in a place like this. When you thought of it in terms of eternity? A few hundred years on earth as a tormentor would be nothing compared to the punishment suffered; the ultimate torture, the absence of everything except misery.*

*The only hope he had was in sitting still.*

Be still, and know...

*Where had he heard that? He wasn't sure, but it seemed to work. Amidst the chaos, he closed his eyes and embraced the stillness. It wasn't much but it was the only hope he had. Maybe it was just a fantasy, but it seemed to relieve the pain—a little.*

*If only he could change the past. But people didn't get second chances and traveling to the past was foolish.*

*His eyelids burned. He needed to open them for just a moment, but he dreaded the pain that would follow. Best to just get it over with.*

*He opened his eyes. He squinted. He must be seeing things.*

*He rubbed his eye sockets. It was still there. A tiny pinprick of light.*

*He stood from his folded position upon the cold stone floor. His muscles ached from lack of use. How long had he been there? How long had he been in that position?*

*As he stumbled toward the ray of light, hope filled him. Amazing how light and hope held a connection.*

*He touched the light, and the pinprick grew into a gaping hole. It grew larger and larger, creating a sort of vortex. It tugged at his hand and arm. He should hold on to something, but what?*

*He stopped trying to fight and relaxed, allowing himself to be taken. The light grew brighter, surrounding him, until it was almost blinding.*

*He stretched out his hands and staggered forward. Without sight, he felt lost. More lost than he had in the darkness.*

*A voice. A familiar voice. Speaking a strange name that, strangely, spoke to him.*

*"Nuada Lear..."*

*He followed the sound. It was a relief to hear something other than wailing.*

*Joyful singing and then, again, "Nuada Lear..."*

*The voice was insistent; he should answer. "I'm here."*

*"Come to me."*

*"Yes." He took one timid step at a time. The blindness hindered his progress and it seemed as if he would never reach his destination.*

*The voice grew stronger, and closer. "Stop. Look at me."*

*Fear gripped him. He blinked. Madness—he was going mad. He should beg to shut his eyes—that would help.*

*But the hand on his shoulder was gentle and brought a sense of peace. Then like magic, he could see, even in the light's brilliance.*

*"My son, welcome."*

*Cian. What was he doing here?*

*Cian pulled him into a fierce embrace. "We've been expecting you."*

*"But—" How could Cian have expected him? He hadn't seen him in over a hundred years and he'd had no plans to come to such a horrific place. The light helped, but it wasn't where he thought he'd be.*

*Cian's upraised hand halted his words. "Please, Nuada. Do you like your new name? From Doran, 'the exile', to Nuada, 'a newly made creation'."*

*What was he talking about?*

*"Allow me to explain why you are here."*

*The room was made of mirrors or glass. White and sterile. Yeah, he could use some explanation about now.*

*"Your sacrifice has not gone unnoticed. Those in charge have decided you will be removed from the tower and brought here to live."*

*"Here?" In this white, sterile room? At least it was quieter and smelled better, but he was still confused.*

*"It is the true white tower. But—"*

*"But?" Wasn't there always a but?*

*"Nuada, while you have been given this gift, I do have another offer."*

*"Well, lay it on me. You said we didn't have much time."*

*Cian sighed. "Always the impatient one."*

*"Not much has changed, I'm afraid."*

*"That is where you are wrong, but there is no time for discussions of that past."*

*Was there another past? Cian had grown even weirder. Had to be the whiteness of the room.*

*"Perhaps you don't remember, but the gray gryphons have always been the protectors of the weak, the innocent. Since my time on earth, the grays have diminished, yet the dangers have remained."*

*Dougal frowned. "You said I have a place here, but you have something else to offer me. What?" He was ready to get on with it. Dark room, white room, just tell him where he was going.*

*"There is a black named Maeldun. At one time he was the captain of Cahal's army and he has placed his sights on a certain girl. This girl must remain safe. He must not be allowed to*

*harm her."*

*Dougal crossed his arms over his chest. Sounded like he was being sent on a quest.* Wonder if there's a reward? *"So what do you want me to do?"*

*"I need you to travel back in time and protect Ma—"*

Mara's chest hurt.

Ma and Pa were patting her down and all she wanted to do was find Dougal. Where had he gotten off to? He'd been with her, then her parents had pulled her out from under the tree. If only she could scream his name, or even whisper it—but she couldn't. Too much was at stake.

Pa stopped first. "Well I'm glad to see you're unscathed. I guess we better get home." He turned in a circle. "Where did Dougal go? One of these days I'll get to stop searching after my children because they'll stop running off, but I guess today ain't that day. Come on, let's find the poor feller. He must have come from the city and not know about the bears roaming the woods. I guess I should have told him."

Ma, Pa, Junior, and Maude went in separate directions. Mara bit her lip. There were lots of places to hide in the thick wood. But most likely he was still where she'd left him. She hoped.

She pushed willow branches aside. Her breath caught. Dougal lay curled into a ball, his head lying against the trunk.

She took a step toward him and stopped. Why did she want to go to him so badly? Just yesterday she hadn't wanted to be around him at all, and now she wanted to race to his side and see his chest rise and fall with each breath. It seemed odd, but what could be considered odd when she didn't speak for fear of flying creatures attacking her? Maybe it was part of the strangeness that Dougal brought with him. His strangeness, his voodoo.

*Help.* She couldn't call for help, but she needed to alert everyone to Dougal's presence. The paleness of his face didn't bode well. He might be hurt.

Mara stepped from beneath the tree. Junior was the closest. She ran to him and grabbed his forearm. He lowered his chin and looked at her like he was really paying attention.

She motioned for him to follow and he parted the sagging branches. "Well, what do you know? That bear tuckered him out and he had to take a nap." Over his shoulder he hoisted Dougal like a sack of potatoes

So Pa hadn't been kidding. She massaged her neck. What a crazy day! Two flying beasts attacked her and Dougal fought off a bear! Pa was right. The woods were dangerous.

Junior sauntered past Ma and Pa. Everyone followed him to the cabin, as if everything was normal, *usual*—but life would never be normal again.

Junior deposited Dougal on the bed in the living room then leaned against the wall, breathing heavily.

Dried blood covered Dougal's forearms and hands. Before Mara could react, Ma scooted her aside. She wiped him clean, then removed his ruined clothing and dressed him in a new pair of long johns.

Her lips twitched. *Wonder if this pair will fall down around his ankles like the last pair?* Dougal had a real problem with clothes.

Sunlight filtered into the room. The night had passed and they hadn't slept a wink.

"Guess we better get started on the chores." Pa's statement pulled groans from Junior and Maude. "Mara, you best stay inside and keep an eye on Dougal. Let us know if he wakes up."

A tear slipped down her cheek.

Pa smiled and wiped it away with his knuckle. "Now, there'll be none of that. We'll see you in a bit. And if you need anything just call."

She wouldn't be doing that, but it was the normal thing to say.

Ma pushed Junior and Maude out the door. Mara leaned back and closed her eyes. Now that they weren't hovering and whispering, she could finally relax. It wasn't easy, acting stupid all the time.

Dougal rolled over. She wet a cloth and dabbed his fevered brow. The rag grew hot and she rewet it.

He'd not awakened since Junior had placed him in bed. Why had he been out? Had he been searching for her when the bear attacked? It was all her fault. Everything was always her fault. Just like that day in the woods; if she hadn't...

Heat surrounded her fingers and she forced back a cry. He squeezed her wrist. Breath rushed past her lips as she looked at him.

His black eyes glowed bronze. He stared forward, but was

he seeing her? She didn't think so.

His grip tightened. She squealed, but instead of dropping her hand, he lifted his head from the pillow and kissed the tender spot where the blood raced through her veins. As he pressed harder, her blood pumped faster and faster. What was he doing to her? How was he doing it?

He released her hand and palmed her cheek, caressing her tender skin over her cheekbones. She closed her eyes and sighed. Everywhere he touched, tiny electric pulses radiated across her skin. Involuntary sounds of pleasure left her parted lips. Now she was really scared. The feelings he brought to the surface were new, different. She wasn't sure if she liked the control he seemed to have over her body.

*Mara...*

Had he said her name aloud or did she just feel it in her soul?

*Mara...*

She bit her tongue. Telling him how she felt would not be a good thing, would it? Maybe she should tell him. But if she spoke, the creature might come back. Twice in a lifetime was enough.

The shocks stopped. The feeling of flesh against flesh disappeared. She felt empty—lost. She opened her eyes.

Dougal lay against the pillow, his ebony eyes staring at her from behind his thick lashes. "What's wrong?"

Heat rushed to her cheeks. His hands were neatly tucked to his sides. There was no way he could have touched her. Had she been daydreaming?

She moistened her dry lips then parted them to speak, but quickly clapped her mouth shut. What was she doing? She couldn't talk. Dougal was making her lose her sense of reality, the reality where she did what the beast said or she lost her family.

He blinked. "What am I? A weakling? Every time I turn around I'm laid up in this bed." He lifted the sheets and sighed. "And is there nothing else for me to wear besides Junior's cast-off underwear?"

She covered her mouth and her giggle. He *would* try to make her laugh.

"Don't think I'm ungrateful. It's not that." He raked his hand through his black wavy hair and her heart skipped a beat. "I just miss my old clothes. You wouldn't believe the style

I had."

He flung the covers back, sat up, dropped his legs over the side of the bed, and settled his bare feet on the wooden floor. When he stood, the long johns slipped, and he grabbed the waist quickly and tugged them back up. "I'm going to the... umm... outhouse."

The tan glow of his skin, the muscles flexing in his arms, his tapered waist. She really should stop looking at him, but she couldn't. She just couldn't.

She failed to notice when he stopped moving until he turned. His grin was rakish. He'd caught her staring. Her embarrassment turned to mortification and this time heat crept from her toes to her hairline. His gaze followed its ascent. He laughed faintly as he backed out the door. Yup, he knew she'd been ogling him. He was very conceited and he didn't seem to care.

It felt as if hummingbird wings beat a rhythm within her chest. First the static shocks and now this. She should find Ma and Pa and wave her hands around until they came running. Being alone with him now or in the future didn't seem wise.

# 15

Dougal leaned against a tree and closed his eyes. He felt like he'd been run over by a Mack truck, but all his wounds had healed. He hoped the family forgot about the supposed bear attack. Explaining that one away might take some time and explaining his wounds healing might take even longer. Being a flying creature with strange supernatural abilities... should be easier.

He sighed. That crazy dream had awakened him. It had seemed so real. He'd been surrounded by light and then he'd felt a cool cloth on his forehead. Suddenly Mara's silken wrist was in his hands. Electric charges had rolled along his arms. He hadn't wanted to wake. He could have stayed in the dream forever, his hands cradling her face, his heart racing, but something had pulled him out. *The dream.* He needed to analyze it.

He ran his hand over his hair. In the dream, he'd been ordered to protect Mara... maybe. He might have been ordered to protect Ma or Maude. Why couldn't Cian have finished the sentence before he'd woken up!

And once he figured out *who* he was supposed to protect, then he had to figure out what he was protecting them *from.* Cian hadn't explained very well. It figured that Cian would send him to his doom and not tell him why. They meet again after a hundred years and that was all he got—a cryptic message and then shoved back in time. Was he being punished for not sticking around in the past? Cian should have understood the reason he'd had to leave.

Steam rolled from the cabin's open windows. He didn't look forward to returning inside. But what of Mara? She waited there. Perhaps for him to return and resume their private moment. He wanted that, he did, but he needed to think.

The sun crested over the mountains. Ma and Maude exited the barn carrying huge metal pails filled with fresh cow's milk. Junior wasn't far behind. His shirt, pinched and held at the corners, formed a bowl in which he carried fresh eggs. Pa stood before the meat house holding a slab of pork. At least food wouldn't be on his list of concerns.

The rough bark scratched his cheek. Outhouse smells filled his nostrils. He could have picked a better location to think, but at least it was private.

He bit his lip. If only he could have slept just a moment longer... but it had to be Mara; she was the only person who made sense. Especially after Maeldun had come after her. Black gryphons didn't choose just anyone to hunt, and he should know.

Since he'd killed Maeldun in that encounter, it should be over. *If* that was the reason he'd been sent back in time. So now he should just return home. It was a theory, at least.

He stared longingly at the house. Maybe there was more for him to do. He kind of hoped so. He didn't really want to leave. He'd never belonged to a real family. And then there was *Mara*.

He took a step forward. Mara exited the cabin, wearing a homemade light blue dress that swirled against the ground as she walked. The simple bodice was form-fitting and tapered at her small waist. White lace trimmed the collar and sleeves. The blue fabric matched the hue of her eyes, and mimicked the color of the sky.

It had to be Mara. He'd changed—for her. When she'd needed saving, he'd changed. No incantation had been needed, as he'd needed in his real time line. It had just happened... *Mara...*

He relaxed his grip. Cold air struck his legs.

Junior's long john's fell to his feet. He rolled his eyes and bent quickly.

He needed new clothes. Wearing Junior's castoffs wasn't going to work. As long as he was staying around, he had a woman to woo.

The next morning everyone gathered for breakfast. Dougal kept his gaze downward, only occasionally looking up. Ma and Pa set their worried eyes upon Mara. She lowered her head and stared at the table. Maybe it was because she was shy, maybe it was because she was reliving all the things she'd seen the day before, and maybe it was because he sat at the table with only the lower half of his body covered. No one had offered him a shirt. Probably because he continued to ruin Junior's clothing, and he might not have any more to spare.

Dougal grabbed a biscuit. Maude yanked the biscuit away and took a bite. She winked. So she wasn't giving up without a fight. Great. A continued complication he could have done without. Too bad he couldn't temper his charm, but it was just natural.

He grabbed another biscuit and shoved the entire thing in his mouth. Let Maude try to get that one.

Maude muttered under her breath and Mara widened her eyes. He should have tuned in, but he didn't care what Maude thought. He was hungry and he wasn't interested. She would just have to ignore his animal magnetism and wait for her own man to show up.

Chewing echoed between his ears. Surely someone would speak soon.

Pa slathered butter on a biscuit. "I was thinkin' maybe it's time you get some new duds, Dougal."

"A trip to town!" Maude clapped and bounced in her chair.

He'd known town was a big deal, but this seemed kind of over the top.

"But we'll have to wait until we finish the rest of the chores."

A collective groan went around the table, except for Mara. She still wasn't expressing an opinion.

Pa quickly added, "We can't have Dougal runnin' around in Junior's skivvies all the time, and the boy is so danger prone we can't risk any more of Junior's clothing."

Dougal fiddled with the waistband of the borrowed long johns. Might as well just say what he was thinking. It was going to come out. "I don't have any money."

Pa stroked his chin thoughtfully. "I gathered as much. Seein' as you've barely been clothed since we found you."

Would his embarrassment never end?

"But don't worry; we'll purchase the material and Ma will make you a few things. Besides, we should have enough from this year's crop to pay back the store and you're helpin' with that, so it only seems fittin' that you benefit."

Maude crossed her fingers. "Are we all goin'?"

"I reckon so. Don't seem right to leave anyone behind."

Ma dipped her brows. "What about Junior? If someone sees him and reports he didn't go to war, they might come and take him away."

"That's a good question. I don't think it'll be a problem if he's discreet. Do you think you can be discreet, son?"

Junior nodded like a bobble-head doll. Dougal didn't like it. Junior was a towering giant and a bit of a lunk-head. He could bring the whole Confederate army down on them. And Dougal needed to remain hidden until he went back to his own timeline. Maybe he should help...

"I'll stay with him. Ma can pick out fabric for my clothing."

Pa twisted his lips to the side as if considering the proposal. "Dougal's got a good idea. You two could look out for each other." He slapped his thigh. "It's settled. After lunch we'll hitch up the mules and drive into town." Pa scooted back his chair. "Daylight's a wastin'. Let's get these dishes cleaned and finish the mornin' chores."

The family went to their respective places and completed their daily chores. Junior handed him a cloth bundle. "Try not to ruin them."

Dougal gave him a mock salute.

Junior shook his head and left.

Dressed, Dougal went outside. Maude and Ma pulled weeds from the small herb garden. Junior and Pa hoed corn. Mara carried a pail to the well. Pa hadn't given him any marching orders.

A grin tilted his lips. Looked like he could do what he wanted. *Mara.*

He drew alongside her and she hugged the pail to her chest. He was a little envious, but it didn't matter; her arms would be around him soon enough. If he was allowed to stick around that long.

"Rough couple of nights, huh?"

Mara continued to look straight ahead. He'd expected that. She was good at her farce.

He shoved his hands in his pockets. "I was thinking, when we visit town maybe we could have a picnic or something."

She stopped and faced him, cocking a brow. So she admitted understanding. About time.

"I mean, I don't know what Wheeler's Landing looks like or how far away it is, but I'm assuming it'll take us awhile to get there, do our shopping, and get home, which means we'll need food. So why not pack a basket and take it with us? As the ducks waddle by and the squirrels scurry up trees and the birds chirp a love song to one another, maybe we can lay back on a blanket and talk about our future."

Mara's arms relaxed. The empty metal bucket fell, slamming into his toe. Pain shot up his leg, and he hopped on one foot and bit back a yelp. How was he supposed to impress Mara when he looked like a jumping fool?

At least she covered her mouth and her laughter.

He clenched his jaw to hold back his own laughter. This could work to his advantage. "Are you laughing at me?"

She shook her head, her hand clasped even tighter across her grinning lips.

He'd elicited another response! "You're laughing at me! I'll get you for that."

Her eyes widened as she clasped her skirt, and she took off at a run. So she wanted to play cat and mouse—his favorite game.

He limped after her. The wind lifted his hair and tickled his neck. It was the most fun he'd had in a long time. A really long time.

Mara stopped in the middle of the path. He smacked into her, throwing his arms around her as they tumbled to the ground. She was beneath him, her chest heaving and touching his, sending electric pulses throughout his tender body. If he leaned forward an inch, their lips would touch. Would it be like fireworks? And if it was, what would he do when he had to leave her?

He rolled off and onto his side, rising on his elbow. "Are you okay? I didn't mean to hit you." It was the best he could do.

Mara nodded.

He should have expected that. Just because she'd laughed

didn't mean she was going to speak.

He flopped onto his back, and painfully hit his head. Stars. He saw nothing but stars. "Ow. You're a dangerous girl to be around."

Mara rose and pointed a finger at herself. It seemed like she was saying *"Me?"*

Dougal responded as if she'd spoken. Maybe if he misunderstood, she'd open her mouth and correct him. "Yes, you. Every time I'm near you, I either ruin my clothes or get hurt."

She frowned.

Oops. That was almost an admission that he was one of the gryphons from earlier. Almost. "I guess I should retrieve the water bucket."

He jumped up and ran back along the path, retrieving the bucket. He went on to the well and filled the bucket with water before starting back toward the house. He passed Mara but didn't speak. Ignoring her worked… because she followed.

He'd start another conversation. She'd be forced to speak sometime. "I don't know what to do today. Pa didn't ask my help with anything and I'm so tired I don't know if there is much I can do. So why don't I just help you with the water? Does that work?"

She nodded. Mara had to be tired as well. If any of them had suffered an ordeal, it had been her. If only they could talk about it. That would have helped them both, but he couldn't reveal his secret and she wasn't about to loosen her tongue and reveal hers.

A smile tugged at his lips. There were other ways to make her loosen her tongue and he looked forward to trying them out.

# 16

O'Brien once heard, "The only way to ensure something is done right is to do it yourself," and whoever said that was a genius.

Out the side door and onto his veranda, and the afternoon sunlight smacked him with its heat. He swung the cane and struck his leg. It hurt, so he moved it further away but continued to swing it. Peering across the lawn, he narrowed his eyes. The stables. Horses were beautiful and useful animals, but also disgusting. He hated working with the filthy creatures, but Elijah was repairing a fence. So he would be forced to undertake the chore himself. When the war was over, he was going to make sure he purchased more slaves. One just for the stables. No, several.

Inside the dark building he found a riding horse, saddled it, and climbed astride with the aid of the mounting block. A tug of the reins aimed the horse in the right direction, and O'Brien dug in his heels.

The horse's rough trot and the rutted dirt road jostled his less than stellar frame. In years past, he'd put on a few pounds and nothing proved this more than trying to get comfortable on the four-legged beast. His behind ached from the abuse.

He slowed the horse as the silo came into view. Confederate patrols were on an hourly rotation, but he didn't know when the hour began, which just meant he needed to hurry.

He dismounted, tied the horse to a handy branch, and cautiously approached the silo. No one appeared. So far, so good.

A simple wooden beam barred the silo's door, with not a padlock or hasp in sight. The whole thing was too easy. He should have done this ages ago, instead of wasting his time and money on useless hirelings.

He pushed upward on the beam, but nothing happened. Over and over he pushed, but the beam was wedged tight. He needed a plank or something for leverage, some way to shove it out of the cradling supports.

O'Brien found a tree limb, half buried in mud next to a creek that flowed nearby. With much finagling, he leveraged it under the beam and pried. It snapped. Wood splintering echoed through the tiny valley, sending birds into scattered flight. He cringed. Anyone within hearing distance would be alerted. He would need an excuse, or maybe he'd be lucky and make it into the silo first...

"What are you doin'?"

No, not lucky. He turned on his heel and licked his lips. An excuse; he needed an excuse.

"I asked you what you're doin'?" A young officer had rounded the silo and stood in plain view, but too far away for O'Brien to grab him.

His cane leaned against the doorframe. If he moved quickly, perhaps he could reach the cane, swing it hard, and smack it upside the officer's head. But what if he was caught in such an act? It would mean hanging. No, a bluff. He'd been told he was good with words he didn't mean. Now was the time to test that theory.

He straightened. "I'm the mayor of Wheeler's Landing and it is my duty to protect my people and their interests. It has come to my attention that this silo contains weapons that could be used against the town. So you can see that I'm honor-bound to investigate." Huh. Not bad, if he did say so himself. The speech felt effective, but the posturing would have been more professional with his cane. He'd remember that for the future.

The Confederate soldier drew his brows together and scratched the spot between his eyes. "Of course there are weapons in there. We done told everybody to keep out. We're the Confederate Army and we're here to protect your *little* town. I don't see any reason why you need to be snooping around. No reason at all." He folded his arms over his chest.

So the young man wasn't fooled. O'Brien scowled and

forced himself not to swallow. He needed another reason for breaking into the silo, and quick.

But before he could speak, the officer dropped his arms. “Listen, if you really want to know what’s in this here silo, so you can go back and relieve your town’s fears, then just ask the general. I’m sure he’ll let you in. Why, we’ve had people coming and going all week long. That’s why I wasn’t at my post. I had to escort a group back to their boat. Why people don’t know how to walk on our marshy ground is beyond me. You put some lily-livered government feller in here and they can’t figure out how to put one foot in front of the other.”

O’Brien sighed with relief. The man had given him the solution. “I would be delighted to meet up with your superior officer. Where might I find him?”

“Just over that ridge. There’s a huge flat field, used to be a farm, I think. All our tents are pitched there while we wait for orders.”

O’Brien hefted his silver-tipped cane, nodded a cool salute to the officer, and headed for his horse. Hoisting himself into the saddle wasn’t as easy without the mounting block and he felt the young officer’s scrutiny. If only the dratted beast would stand still!

He hopped along with the side-stepping horse, struggling to slide his foot into the stirrup. The boy guffawed and O’Brien shot him a glare, making him cover his mouth and turn his face away. Boys shouldn’t antagonize their elders or they might find themselves in a heap of trouble someday. He would be on the winning side of the war and that came with influence.

Once astride, he headed for the Confederate camp, ignoring the snickers behind him.

# 17

After lunch Mara clambered into the back of the flatbed wagon with Junior, Maude, and Dougal. Quilts covered the rough surface, but they did little to protect one's bottom from the pain caused by constant bumps and thumps as the wooden wheels hit the ruts in the dirt road.

Overhanging trees provided shade and protected them from the sun. She closed her eyes and breathed in the scent of wildflowers. On her right, Dougal was crushed up against her. Ignoring him was becoming harder and harder. The incident with the pail still brought a smile to her lips. He'd been so cute hopping around on one foot. And the picnic idea had been brilliant. Fortunately Ma had thought of it on her own, or it wouldn't be happening.

So thinking, Mara twirled a strand of hair around her finger.

Without warning, Dougal slid his hands around her waist, lifted her without effort, and plopped her bottom onto his lap. A moment later, the wagon dropped into and then heaved out of another rut. Dougal's lap cushioned the blow. She gasped, but her tingling flesh distracted her.

The bump past, Dougal resettled her beside him. But this time, his arm snaked around her middle and pulled her tightly to his side. Those Dougal-caused tingles and shocks which normally rocked through her body became a cornucopia of much nicer sensations. Pleasure engulfed her until she almost rolled her eyes back in her head. She had never felt so protected, so good. Nothing could ruin this moment.

On the other side of the flatbed, Maude crossed her arms over her ample bosom and her lips fell. "Pa said you could woo her, not take liberties."

She took it back. Maude could ruin everything.

Dougal grinned broadly, his eyes crinkling at the corners, but a harder light shone behind the mischief. And then Maude's lips twitched, starting at one corner of her mouth and sliding over to the other. Relentlessly her lips curved upward and stretched wider as Maude's face transformed into a mask of happiness. But although her mouth spread as far as it would go, displaying an eerie, almost sinister grin, her eyes bulged, as if gripped with fear.

Mara shook her head, turned away, and peered over the side railing. Had Dougal *made* Maude do that? His charm was electric, but causing someone to smile when she clearly didn't want to seemed beyond human capabilities. It seemed *strange.*

One look and the man could cause a lady to go weak at the knees. She'd experienced that fully, but making Maude smile? That was impossible.

She couldn't help it. Mara glanced at her sister. Maude glared back and narrowed her eyes. Yeah, Maude would be angry later. She would purposefully do little things to make Mara's life miserable. She would start with insults.

*Timid Mara.*

*Simple-minded Mara.*

*Mara with the pond water in her head.*

After the insults, she would throw Mara's clothes out the attic window. Or use all the covers on the bed and refuse to share; normally the cover torture occurred during the cold winter months, leaving Mara silently shivering.

But despite the abuse, Mara felt sorry for Maude. Her sister wasn't a bad person; it was the jealousy that caused her to do those things.

Tears pricked at her eyes. She wished she could talk. If she could, then she would share with Maude that Dougal's attentions were fake. That he was taking their father's invitation to woo her so Maude wouldn't get any ideas. Then perhaps instead of Maude's wrath, she'd receive her sympathy.

Mara scooted away from Dougal and drew her knees to her chest. He tried to pull her back, but she wouldn't budge. His touch was nothing more than a way to keep Maude from becoming interested in him. It hurt. She had tried to ignore the conversation on the porch because of the feelings his nearness aroused, but the words kept coming back and haunting her. She should have slapped him or done something to put him off.

He scooted closer. She'd show him he couldn't intimidate her, no matter how handsome he was. She scooted further away. He followed. She scooted until she rested on the wagon's edge. Then of course they hit a rut. Balance wavering, she flailed her arms.

Dougal grabbed her and yanked her to his side. He whispered in her ear, his hot moist breath sending chills along her spine. "Why do you run from me?"

Did he really expect an answer?

"Do I offend you?" He was persistent; she had to give him that.

With one finger, he traced tiny circles around her wrist. The tingling intensified. Her pulse raced. Why was this happening to her? Was it him or would any man cause the same reaction?

"Do you dislike me so much that you want to fall off the wagon to get away from me?" His hot breath moved from her ear to her flushed cheek.

She swallowed. If only she could tell him that she'd overheard that awful conversation. Maybe if he looked into her eyes and studied her face, then he would understand. Or maybe it would intensify the feelings she had when in his presence.

The black depths of his eyes bored into hers. He grabbed her shoulders and held her steady. His head dipped until their lips were inches apart. Their breath mingled. The rush of wind carried his scent of coffee and bacon.

Dougal's lips grazed hers. She sat mesmerized, transfixed. She couldn't move. He leaned back, his black eyes flickering with bronze flecks. He moved his hand beneath her hair and pulled her head forward. Her heartbeat roared in her ears until she couldn't remember where she was or why she was there. Dougal was all that mattered. Nothing else existed.

They eased closer together and she closed her eyes, awaiting the kiss. Moments passed. Tense moments. Had he forgotten her already?

She fluttered her eyelids open. He no longer looked at her; instead he focused on something behind the white pines that lined the road. The expression on his face sent terror into her heart.

Sweetness lingered from their brief touch and tingles shot through Dougal's body. He couldn't seem to get enough of her taste; it was like a drug. And man, if he could bottle that one...

During the brief moment their lips touched, the world had faded away. His hand had slipped unconsciously behind her head, fingers sliding through her soft hair. In a strange way, he could feel their lips crushed together even though he'd only brushed over them. Nothing else existed. Nothing else mattered.

But at the same time, hairs rose on the back of his neck. Someone watched and not just Maude and Junior, who were doubtless aghast at his temerity. Who would have thought he'd attempt to kiss Mara in such a brazen way, with Ma and Pa sitting in the front of the wagon? But he couldn't help himself. Destiny had thrown them together. Who was he to turn his back on Fate?

But those telltale hairs rose again. Warned, he dragged his attention from Mara and studied his surroundings.

Tightly clustered trees lined the dirt road; leaves and overhanging branches clipped the wagon's sides as they passed. Not a threat themselves, but the trees could hide anything. As a gryphon, he could focus his vision and zero in on distant objects. When he did, his pulse jumped into his throat. Men with guns trailed alongside them, hidden only by the thick trees.

He forced himself to stay still. Probably Confederate soldiers on patrol. If attacked, he would defend the family regardless of the consequences, but he hoped it wouldn't come to that. Now wasn't the time to reveal his true identity.

Mara's forehead creased, drawing his glance back to her. What was she thinking? Was she upset that he'd stopped their connection? If so, he understood; he felt physical pain at the disconnect himself.

He pulled her closer. "Junior, we're being followed."

"Yup." Junior stared at the wagon's floorboards, as if embarrassed by Dougal's display.

"What?"

"If you stopped making goo-goo eyes at Mara long enough, you might've noticed the Rebels have been following us since we left the farm."

How had he failed to notice they were being tailed? Even if he'd come back in time for a reason besides Mara, he still couldn't let her be harmed. Yet he'd lost all sense of the dangers around them. He needed to step up his game.

Sidling away, Mara folded her hands in her lap. She looked like a small child. Her black hair swept back into a French braid, tiny wisps escaping and framing her face. His fingers ached to tuck those wisps back into place.

"Dougal? Are you listenin'?"

He shook his head. He really needed to snap out of it. "Yes."

"I said they've been followin' us since the farm. I don't think they mean no harm. They just want to protect us."

"What about your call to duty?" Had Junior forgotten he was a wanted man? How had he stayed free so long if patrols followed them whenever he left home? Pa's description of discretion didn't fit Dougal's image of Junior.

"Oh, that. Most of these boys think I'm not all here." He tapped his head. "If they get real close, I'll start moanin' and groanin' and actin' like I'm about to die. Generally, they get all scarit and take off back to the woods. That's one reason the farm ain't had too many visitors of late. They think I have the madness."

"I see." Dougal refused to grin, but the image in his mind was funny. Junior was probably excellent at playing crazy.

Junior leaned forward, the wagon bouncing him up and down, making his voice tremble. "Do you want to see?"

He didn't really, but Junior seemed so eager. "I guess so. But shouldn't you warn your parents?"

He waved his hand. "Naw. They know what to expect when we go to town."

"You've done this before?"

"A couple of times. Like when the recruiters come around and I don't make it to the cave in time. That's why Ma and Pa weren't worried about me going to town. A'course, you offering to help watch after me didn't hurt none." He paused. "Are you ready?"

If he said no, would it make a difference? Doubtful.

Junior stood and screamed, a raw, loud sound that rose and fell with the wagon's bouncing. Next, he jumped from the moving wagon and lumbered around like an ape, scraping his knuckles on the ground. Before the wagon got too far away, he jumped back inside. Crouching near the edge, he wailed and moaned, beating his chest.

No one in the wagon acted like anything unusual was happening. And that probably scared the soldiers more than his actual histrionics.

The men in gray pulled back as Junior finished his performance. A smile of satisfaction rested on his face. Fighting laughter, Dougal couldn't help but wonder if he would be required to behave the same way to keep interest away from himself. If so, he wouldn't do it. He'd rather break every soldier's neck than look crazy and weak.

Dougal had discussed the area with Pa and learned that the future town of Coal Creek was currently just a community of interconnecting farms. Wheeler's Landing, which in the future would be no more than a few ramshackle buildings and some old whitewashed houses, was currently the place to be. But it still wasn't what he expected.

A bank, a general store, a tavern, a hotel, a post office, and a train depot. No more. If he'd blinked, he'd have missed it, even at the wagon's tortoise-racing pace.

But still, the town was busier than he'd expected. A dozen people were rushing aboard an idling train, their valises and satchels showing bits of clothing poking out, as if they'd packed in a hurry. Dougal couldn't blame them. War was coming to their tiny town. The gray-clad soldiers strutting around with rifles slung over their shoulders proved that.

Not long after Junior's exhibition, Mara had closed her eyes and her breathing evened. He'd allowed her to move away, but only by a few inches. He couldn't have her flying off the back of the wagon again.

More people arrived, running into the depot, and now a mass of them—too many to count—pushed and shoved into the train's passenger cars. Family men raised their fists in anger. Women shielded their children but didn't back away.

Dougal leaned forward. "Where are they going?"

Maude picked at her teeth, then spat. What a lady.

"Why, they're leavin'. Don't you see all the gray coats about? Most of these people were farmers and their farms bit the dust, so to speak. Probably all headed out west or up north, any place that might be safer than here."

"I'm afraid they can't avoid the war." He'd read some history books; the South would burn. Could they really reach the North or the West in time?

"We know they can't run, but it don't matter. Everything is about perception. At least that's what Pa says." Maude pulled her shoulders back with an air of importance.

"He's right." In a way, at least. Dougal tried not to reflect on what people's perception of him must have been in the past. No matter the truth, he'd been perceived as a monster. That perception had affected what he'd become. He'd fulfilled exactly what they'd expected—at least until Maddie came along and changed everything... changed him.

Maude tilted her head. "You know, it's goin' to be mighty hard to woo a girl who don't know her head from a hole in the ground. Mara don't speak. Don't you think you'd be better off with someone else?" She leaned forward and batted her short lashes.

Dougal stared back. She wasn't unattractive, even if she was a bit on the hefty side. Her long blond hair curled down her back and her green eyes were as vibrant as the grass. But he felt no connection to her, no chemistry. Even if Pa had told him to woo Maude, he would have declined. Mara was the only girl for him.

Perhaps it showed on his face, in his eyes. Tears spilled down Maude's cheeks. She turned away and stared out at nothing. Dougal's innards squirmed. He was such a cad. He needed to dismiss her, yes, but he could have been nicer about it.

Without stopping to reconsider, he took her hand. Maude's head whipped around. He brushed a tear away with his knuckle, and her eyes widened.

Dougal softened his voice. "Maude, you are a very beautiful woman."

A flush crept up her neck and she parted her lips.

He placed his finger across them. "But you're spoken for."

She tried to pull away but he held tight. He was determined to get the words out. "Beauford has waited for you. And, well," he paused on a sigh, "I've waited for Mara." There; he had said it. That made it official... almost. Of course, he would have to convince Mara, but that shouldn't be hard. He oozed with natural charm.

"What?" Maude sounded breathless.

He scooted closer to her side, but their thighs made contact and he scooted away again. "I cannot explain it. Mara calls to me. She is the yin to my yang. The peanut butter to my jelly. The—"

She lifted her hand, palm out. “I don’t have a clue what you’re talkin’ about. But I understand—you have a thing for Mara.”

“Yes.” She *did* understand.

“And I’m guessin’ you want me to step back and let you do your wooin’.”

He nodded. “Do you think you can do that?”

She crossed her arms over her ample chest. “It ain’t fair.”

“Maude, I wouldn’t worry. I’m sure Beauford will be home any day now.”

“Humph. Beauford O’Brien will come home when he’s good and ready. He better just hope I haven’t found someone else by then.”

He didn’t plan to argue with her.

The wagon shuddered to a halt. Pa yelled, “All of you young ’uns get off now and let’s go to the general store for supplies.”

Dougal trudged obediently behind the others. It was going to be a long day.

Contrary to what he’d said to the young officer, O’Brien had no desire to visit with the Rebel general.

Instead, he rode his horse to town and stopped at the bank. In the office he settled behind his desk. Statements littered the surface. Figures waited to be tallied and entered into the books. Those figures were depressing. The crops in the surrounding area had diminished greatly since the war began. First the young men had gone off to war, leaving fewer behind to work the farms. Then the slaves had started disappearing in droves, leaving even fewer workers. And then even God almighty seemed to take a hand, by holding the rain at bay. The drought was terrible. Everything and everyone was against his success.

He ran his hand over his balding head. Where was his blasted pipe? Impatient, he riffled through the papers until he found it. He tapped some tobacco inside, struck a match, and lifted the pipe to his lips. Smoke filled the room as he took several draws, calming his frayed nerves. He couldn’t delay forever.

He glanced at the top paper. One farm seemed unaffected by the drought, producing corn and other crops at a record rate. How had they managed to keep up production when so many others had failed?

He took another draw and studied the figures. But only a reference number identified the form. He remembered seeing a name referencing this paper; where had it gotten to?

Before he could find the information, he inhaled the wrong way and a fit of coughing assaulted him. He pounded his chest with his fist then gulped tepid water, which made him sputter and cough some more. Perhaps air would help.

He opened the window and a burst of hot air rushed in. Sweat popped out over his body, and his heavy clothing stuck to his frame. He peeled away the coat and fanned himself. The tiny bit of air only served as a reminder of the heat.

Suddenly the room spun. Staggering, he leaned his head against the wooden window frame. It felt cool. Stars danced before his eyes and he struggled to remain upright, dropping his chin to his chest. If something happened to him, what would become of his legacy? He couldn't let the town falter.

He looked down into the street. His soldiers lined the avenue, rifles at the ready.

He'd sent for them after Union soldiers had moved into an encampment not that far away. But upon first seeing the ragtag young men, he'd been vastly disappointed. Half of them appeared barely out of diapers, their uniforms hanging from their malnourished bodies. He had felt insulted. No way could he allow such men to walk through the streets of *his* town. Why, it would be a disgrace!

He'd insured every one of them received new clothing, then he'd rewarded them with a night at the tavern, where they'd been fed, cleaned, and allowed to rest. Now, months later, the soldiers were fiercely devoted to him. They had no qualms about doing whatever he asked, regardless of what that might be. A good thing, too, because soon he might ask something of them which might test their limits of conscience and loyalty.

O'Brien narrowed his eyes. At the end of the street loomed a lone rider with a hat pulled low over his eyes. He wore the clothes of a civilian, but O'Brien wasn't fooled. Captain Herrick waved—at him.

Sweat pooled beneath his collar. He had yet to get the information Herrick sought. If he didn't get it soon, there would be severe repercussions. The captain was known for his cruelty. Like ripping out fingernails or washing a man's long johns while he was still in them. He'd heard the rumors. The Confederates were terrified of being captured by the captain.

Rumbling shook the window glass. He peered out again, ignoring his watcher. The Hess family entered town, their horses stirring up dust. A grin split his face. The task for Herrick might not be going quite as planned, but that didn't mean he couldn't work on his own personal gain when the opportunity presented itself. And the opportunity had just come knocking.

# 18

Mara worried with a loose string on her sleeve, playing the part of dummy until she thought she'd be sick. The casual touch Dougal and Maude had shared was almost more than she could bear. A few times she almost yelled, but she kept silent. Watching Dougal touch another woman, even Maude, had been pure torture.

The wagon lurched to a stop and Mara jumped out of the bed. She was the first one to reach the porch of the mercantile. She leaned against a post and waited for the rest of the family to join her. If she was lucky, she'd miss it if Dougal touched Maude—again.

An elderly gentleman sat on the storefront's bench. He smiled, revealing a row of missing teeth, and touched his hat to her. "Howdy, miss. Haven't seen you in a month of Sundays. Why don't you come and sit with me and tell me how you been?"

Mr. Armstrong was a regular fixture in town. No one had ever seen him move from his spot on the bench, although of course he had to do so. But every time the Hess family visited town, she would sit beside him and he would *pretend* to hear her speak. More than once, she'd had to stifle a giggle at some of the outlandish things he claimed she'd said.

She perched on the edge of the bench and placed her hands demurely on her lap.

He scratched his head and beamed. "Well, you don't say. Why, now, that *is* somethin'. A beau? Yeah, I see him. Mighty strong lookin' feller. You better be careful. Oh, you already know, do you?"

Her breath caught as she studied the old man and his rheumy eyes. How did he know about Dougal? How did he know she needed to be careful? Everyone said Mr. Armstrong had "the sight." Could that be true? Did he see the future? Or were her feelings written all over her face?

Breathless, she waited for him to continue.

"Now, Mara, dear, don't you fret. I can see the young feller has a thing for you. I don't think there's much that will keep him away from you, neither. But you see the man on the horse at the end of the street?"

She lifted her head to stare, but he stopped her. "Don't go gawkin', girl! Could be dangerous. Just kind of peek, like. Yup, that's the way. That man there on the horse at the end of the road, why, he's what you need to worry about. I know you think your sister is your only worry, but you're wrong. Your sister is goin' to marry and have her a mess of young 'uns like this county has never seen. But you, you're special. And I'm afeared the man on the horse knows it as much as I do. You need to stay away from that one. And you keep this new feller close by your side, do you hear me?"

Her blood rushed in her ears. Peering from beneath her lashes, she eyed the stranger on his massive horse. His looks were as dark as Dougal's. His bearing was erect like a soldier. His eyes were narrowed in a sinister fashion. And Mr. Armstrong warned her away from the stranger? Not really a problem. She wasn't friendly with strangers, at least not any more.

She patted the elderly gent's hand, reassuring him, and then Junior came over. "Mara, get in here. Ma's been searching everywhere fer you. One of these days, you're goin' to get lost and we ain't goin' to be able to find you."

Junior's words held an air of premonition as the heat from the stranger's gaze bored into her soul.

Cloth hunting proved to be a tiresome chore. By the time Ma decided on what she needed, Mara was ready to collapse from exhaustion. Her one consolation was that Dougal and Maude had maintained a safe distance between them. What could he have said to her that would keep them both silent and avoiding her? Maybe he'd decided to go against Pa's request to woo her instead. The thought hurt.

Mara trailed three steps behind the others as they grabbed baskets from the wagon and made their way to the pond. The wind floating over the water made it about the only place in town where a person could meet with a cool breeze during the summer months.

When they arrived, she stayed back and held her hands awkwardly before her as Ma and Maude arranged the food on a blanket.

But as she waited, the hairs on the back of her neck prickled. When she glanced up, Dougal focused his dark gaze on her. The sun reflected off the tiny flecks of bronze in his eyes. He watched her like a meal to be devoured. No, he hadn't told Maude he was available. That thought brought a certain amount of relief, but her attraction to him was maddening. If only he would hold her hand, or place the tips of his fingers against her cheek, just one more time.

A breeze blew. The cool wind lingered upon her lips like a caress and she remembered the feel of his breath mingling with hers. She closed her eyes and sighed. If only she could tell him how much she enjoyed his touch—just once—then maybe her silence wouldn't be such a big deal.

She peeked between her slit eyelids. Dougal still watched her, his lips twitching in amusement.

Heat infused her cheeks. She jumped to her feet and awkwardly strolled toward the water's edge.

Ma yelled, "Don't go too far, dear."

Mara made no acknowledgement, but obeyed. The water rolled onto the shore. Tiny white waves crested. A visitor to the town once had said it looked like a miniature beach. He had described the ocean, a limitless expanse of water as far as the eye could see. The townsfolk claimed he was addled and sent him on his way, but she'd believed him. Certainly there were wonders in this world she had never seen, nor would she ever see. But just because she couldn't see something didn't necessarily mean it wasn't true. No, the things she had problems with were the things she *had* seen.

A huge rock, naturally molded into the shape of a throne, perched close to the water's edge. Next to it someone had carved a stone heart on a pedestal. Couples came from miles around to get married at the Throne of Hearts. Rumor was if you married at the throne, then you were guaranteed a happy marriage. She'd imagined her own wedding there, but that fateful day at the creek had changed that dream.

She lowered herself onto the rock seat and stared across the water. Nothing seemed right; the world was topsy-turvy. Dougal acted as if he liked her, but agreed to fake-woo her. Mr. Armstrong had insinuated Dougal would protect her from the stranger, and that Dougal was safe. But why would a strange *human* be after her?

She leaned back and threw her arm over her face. If only she could share her worries with Dougal. But the last time she'd opened her mouth, not one but two flying creatures had materialized. She would *never* speak again.

"May I join you?" Dougal's deep timbered voice had her bolting upright. The sun shone behind him, putting his face in shadow and hiding his expression.

She clasped her hands and prayed he would leave.

"I'll take that as a yes."

So much for that prayer.

He settled next to her on the throne, not quite touching, resting his hands on his knees and staring straight ahead. "This is a beautiful place. Your pa said he and your mother married here. He explained that marrying here helps a couple endure."

She didn't respond. Let him wonder what she thought; maybe he'd go away.

He dug in his breeches pocket then brought out his closed fist. "I have something for you."

She narrowed her eyes. When had he had a chance to get her something?

He unfurled his fingers and revealed a perfectly oval, gleaming white egg.

She placed her hand over her open mouth.

"I know what you're thinking. Well, maybe I don't. I probably don't want to know." He grinned. "Anyway, I know flowers, chocolates, jewelry, and those kinds of things turn a girl's head, but I have no money. And besides, you seem like a lady who enjoys the simpler, more practical pleasures in life. So I brought you this."

She tilted her head. Would he continue this insanity? An egg, indeed!

"I can see from your expression you don't understand what

I went through to get this." He rubbed a spot between his brows. "Let me explain. This egg, this porcelain white egg of hardboiled perfection, was reflected in your brother's eyes. It was the last one and he wanted it bad. But of course I'm quicker and I grabbed it first. I even told him finders keepers, but I don't think it mattered too much to him. See this?"

She held back a snicker as he pointed to a small red mark on his tanned cheek.

"First, the big oaf tried to skewer me with his fork, and then he cuffed me! Over an egg! Anyway, I'm glad I expended the effort. The look on your face was worth it all. Here you go. You deserve it."

He thrust the hardboiled egg in front of her, and she had no choice but to take the offering. A smile tugged her lips up as she deftly cracked the shell, peeled it off, and placed the entire egg into her mouth.

As she ate, her cheeks bulged and the yolk broke deliciously on her tongue. Dougal fidgeted, appearing nervous and frustrated as if he waited for her response. Didn't he know better by now?—she was dimwitted.

The light-hearted moment passed. "Listen, Mara, I know you understand me. I also know you can speak."

She almost choked on the mouthful of egg and raised a hand to prevent unseemly spillage from the corners of her mouth.

"One night while you were swinging, I heard you. So don't deny it. Not that you ever would, since that would require you to open your mouth and make sounds. I don't know what has caused your silence. I don't know if you're afraid or angry. All I know is this." He paused, taking her chin in his hands, and staring intently into her eyes. "You *will* speak to me." Thumb underneath her chin, he rubbed back and forth in a rhythmic motion. He cleaned a speck of yolk from her lip and sucked his finger clean.

Mara gulped and tried to look away, but he held tight. His head dipped. She held her breath. This was it. A kiss. Her skin burned, her bones melted, and she sighed. But there was no kiss. His warm breath mingled with hers and right when she thought she would explode from waiting, he pulled away and placed a casual arm around her shoulders, hugging her roughly to his side.

"Now, that's what I'm talking about." His gentle laughter rumbled against her.

# 19

Maeldun's claws gripped the gnarled and twisted tree limb until it snapped in two and sent him plummeting to the ground. His wings expanded, but they were too big and their deployment too late. He slapped the hard earth. He thrust his clawed hands outward to keep from slamming vital parts. Sharp, stabbing pains shot up his legs and he pulled his lips back over his bared teeth in a snarl.

Rising from the ground, he made sure no one had noticed his fall. Securely hidden behind a row of trees, he zeroed in again on the couple. Their breath mingled as one, intertwining and wrapping around and around in a spiral of colors. Mara's was the color of pink roses. The stranger's was gray and wispy. Their scent wafted through the air. Bile rose in the back of his throat as he recognized the odor of love.

His injured hand ached to surround the stranger's throat. Something about the young man seemed vaguely familiar. Nose crinkling, he noticed a new scent of unwashed bodies, rotted teeth, and feces. Stragglers strutted along the bank of the pond.

He had no desire to be seen. He had enough troubles.

The injured leg didn't hamper his retreat as he left the safety of the trees and headed for a more open area.

He had a lot to think about. Such as who was this stranger with Mara and what was he going to do about him.

O'Brien studied his sore fingers. The nails were jagged from biting—a nasty habit he exercised in the worst of situations. If his present worries continued, he would have no fingernails left.

How long had he stared out the window, waiting for the Hess family to return from their meal? Seconds, minutes, hours? First they'd entered the general store and finally come out with so much cloth they must have been dressing everyone on this side of the Mississippi. Then they had disappeared by the water's edge and as of yet hadn't returned.

O'Brien paced. He wanted to talk with Flint Hess about *things.* Yes, they had many things to discuss. Like how did the Hess family have so much when everyone else mimicked the poverty of Job's turkey? Why were their crops thriving when everyone else's suffered from the drought?

And then there was his own son, Beauford, marrying Flint's daughter. It had been pure stupidity on his part to take the boy along to make the arrangement. His plans would have worked better if Beauford had picked the mute girl to wed. One wailing woman in the household was enough. But against his wishes, Beauford had accompanied him.

And then, after the brief time he'd spent with Maude, he'd claimed they fell in love. If O'Brien had been closer to his son, he would have told him love had nothing to do with it. But alas, he had given in. In the end, was it really so important? Beauford would marry one of the Hess girls and that was what really mattered.

Again he peered out the window. Still they frolicked by the water's edge. Perhaps he ought to pay them a little visit. Flint would think nothing of it. They were on good terms, after all. Otherwise Flint wouldn't have agreed so readily to Beauford's marriage proposal.

He grabbed his cane and reached for the back door handle, but it swung open before he touched it. Captain Herrick stood on the threshold. O'Brien froze. Breathing became harder. Had all the air been sucked from the room?

"What are you doing here?" Had the question come from him? He wasn't sure. Maybe he was dreaming.

"Is that any way to greet your partner?"

He pulled the captain inside and closed the door, praying no one had overheard the statement. "I don't have what you seek. I'm still working on it."

Herrick scowled. "My patience is waning."

He wasn't the only one with waning patience. O'Brien patted the air in a shushing gesture. "I understand. Just so you know, I went myself to investigate the silo, but I'm afraid my attempt proved unsuccessful, too. That silo is locked up tighter than a drum. An officer guarding the place offered to let me speak with the leader of the Rebel forces, but I didn't think we needed the extra attention."

Herrick paced. "No, we do not. But I'm here to inform you it no longer matters what the silo contains. We're coming anyway."

Sweat popped out on O'Brien's forehead. "Coming anyway?" Not yet; he wasn't ready. There were still things he needed to have in place. Beauford wasn't home. The Rebels hadn't vowed to protect his home place; nor had the Union, for that matter. The money in the bank hadn't been moved. Too many things hung in the balance. He needed more time!

Herrick sat behind the desk and propped his feet on the corner. A moment passed. He grimaced and pushed himself back up. "I need to discuss the details of the attack posthaste. My men will arrive in five days. You must be ready."

"Five days?" he whispered. His throat was constricting. He might pass out in front of the captain if he didn't get air soon.

"Yes. Your job is to ensure your people know to politely step aside. If they do as we ask, no one will be harmed. We'll take care of the Rebels and then we'll possess the silo."

The familiar faces of *his* soldiers flashed before his eyes. He'd housed them, clothed them, given them the confidence to protect his town... and now he was supposed to just let Herrick roll in and take care of them? Did he have a choice? The way Herrick said *possess* sent a shiver along O'Brien's spine. Why did he feel as if he had just made a deal with the devil and everyone he knew would suffer for it?

# 20

Maybe it was some kind of voodoo magic.

Hairs prickled along her arm. She hadn't seen him move, but now Dougal stared back, his mouth widening into a slow grin. His eyes twinkled. Mara could feel a tug pulling her toward him. She could add that to his list of voodoo powers. He wrapped her trembling fingers in warmth, and lifted her chin until his black and her blue eyes were locked. Tingles raced across her sensitive skin. Her heart leapt in her throat and her chest tightened as his black eyes glowed bronze. How did his eyes change color? Had to be the voodoo.

"Mara, do you know how beautiful you are? Do you know how your flesh sings to me?"

She should pull away, but it was impossible. His hand didn't hold her in place, but his gaze was magnetic.

"Mara, don't turn away. I want you to speak to me. I want you to tell me you feel it, too. Tell me you feel the tiny pulses of electricity that run across your skin. Tell me you yearn to kiss me as I yearn to kiss you. Tell me when you close your eyes at night I'm all you see." The words dripped from his lips like liquid honey.

He eased closer, erasing the gap between them. Did the others notice? Did they see that Dougal had bewitched her?

Hot moist breath struck her cheek as he planted a chaste kiss there. It felt as if he'd singed her with fire. Was this the "electric" feeling he kept talking about?

His supple lips left the teased skin of her cheek. He grabbed her hand and planted kisses along the length of her forearm, paying special attention to the vein that beat wildly at her wrist. She sucked in a breath and moistened her dry lips. Would he do it again? Unrecognizable feelings assailed her. She wanted the kiss. Needed it. Craved it. It was his voodoo witchcraft. He'd done something to her and she didn't even care.

She leaned forward. Heat spread through her body as she anticipated the simple union. Then something changed. Instead of leaning forward, Dougal again wrapped his arm across her shoulders and held her against his side.

Mara collapsed against him, working to calm her racing heart. She knew what he wanted. This voodoo trickery was his way of making her talk. He didn't realize he'd given her another reason *not* to speak—his safety. If the beast heard her, then he was one more person who would be in danger, because now she cared about him. Life wasn't fair.

But held so close to Dougal's side, Mara had trouble thinking clearly. One minute she was dying for him to kiss her and the next she was furious that he'd tried. If only she could allow herself to enjoy this moment, then perhaps she could be happy, even if just for that moment.

Dougal insisted she would speak. More likely, he thought she would beg. And maybe with time, if he kept tormenting her with the hint of kisses and affection, she would do just that.

She imagined tilting her head back and his lips coming down upon hers. It would be just a brief touch, like a whisper of wind, like the barest flutter of a hummingbird's wings. It would be mind-numbing, skull tingling. The ground would shake beneath them, and—

"You have to quit doing that."

She popped her eyes open and angled her head. He smiled and she cocked a brow. She wasn't ready to speak just yet, but she could give him an expression.

"Aye, I see you understand me. That's a start." He rested his chin atop her head. "Your sighs of contentment may initiate my undoing."

She stiffened. He'd *heard* her? Could he make people smile at will *and* read minds? That was a disturbing thought.

But he shook with laughter. Obviously he enjoyed her discomfort. Perhaps he used her for personal amusement. She bit her lip. How could she extract herself from his grasp? Being used wasn't something she wanted.

Twigs snapped. Dougal pushed off the rock and took a wide, protective stance in front of her. The line of his shoulders was rigid and she imagined his eyes growing darker, those bronze flecks peeking through.

She peered around Dougal's side. The intruder lifted his hand in greeting. She knew him; he had come to the farm unannounced, with his son. When the visit had concluded, Maude was betrothed. She hadn't trusted him then and she didn't trust him now. But she did know him. It was the mayor of Wheeler's Landing, Mr. Barry O'Brien.

Mara touched Dougal's back and leaned around his broad shoulder.

O'Brien's chest puffed out. "Hello. I'm looking for Mr. Hess. Do you happen to know where I may find him?"

"I might." Dougal crossed his arms.

"Oh." O'Brien scratched his forehead. "I see you hold concern with my inquiry."

Dougal didn't speak again. His back muscles flexed and unflexed. His arms snaked around behind him, wrapping her in a cocoon of protection. Fear rose in her throat, not for herself, but for O'Brien.

"Not a big talker, I see. Not a problem. Ask Mara there; she knows me. My farm borders the Hess farm. We're neighbors. Flint's daughter and my son Beauford are betrothed. When I saw Flint ride into town, I thought I would be neighborly and come say hello. Now, would you politely tell me where I can find him?"

Rarely did Mara regret her vow of silence, but today she did, from both the missed opportunity to share her feelings for Dougal and now, when she could have shared her thoughts on their "neighbor". Although every word O'Brien spoke rang true, she still didn't trust him. She closed her eyes and wished for Dougal to keep O'Brien as far from her family as possible.

But Dougal spouted off directions. Really, she couldn't blame him. The man presented himself as the epitome of an upright citizen. Tall and slender and dressed as if headed to a formal dinner, his black tailcoat hung open revealing a white shirt and a gray vest, perfectly creased gray trousers, tie uniquely straight, and a top hat which shone in the afternoon light. The hair that peeked out was covered in grease and looked almost as shiny as the hat. Yes, the man exuded style and prestige.

Again O'Brien puffed out his chest. The cane struck the dry earth and pushed him even more erect. All in all, he presented a picture worthy of the grandest artist. She knew, however, his surface was nothing more than that, a surface. Underneath the fancy clothing and the smelly pomade was what worried her most. *Wolf in sheep's clothing.*

O'Brien tipped his hat and walked off in search of Pa. She gave him a head start before ducking around Dougal, hitching her skirts, and running after O'Brien. Dougal could stay behind or follow; she didn't care. She just wanted to be near her family.

She passed O'Brien and skidded to a halt beside Pa. Her father gnawed a dried stalk and eyed their coming visitor.

O'Brien struggled to keep the revulsion from his voice as he spoke to Flint Hess. The man was attired in a pair of well-worn breeches, a white cotton shirt, and a tweed coat. The clothing was clean and pressed but frayed at the edges. O'Brien could have looked past all that if the man hadn't been chewing on a piece of straw. It reminded him of a cow chewing her cud. Why, that very piece of straw might have come from the feed trough! LouAnn waited nearby, with Maude hidden behind her. She coyly batted her thin lashes. Yes, he would have preferred his son marry the other one. Not her.

Sighing under his breath, O'Brien said, "Flint, would you care to come to the hotel? We could have a drink with our discussion." *Please say yes.* Then at least he would only have to look at one of them.

Flint's forehead furrowed and he spit out the straw. "Why do we need to go to the hotel? Is Beauford back?"

Those words gained Maude's attention and she hopped back and forth from one foot to the other. Well, at least his son would get a woman enthused about him.

"No, I'm afraid we've had no word." That settled the girl down. "The reason I asked you to the hotel was to—to—" How could he explain his desire to understand the family's financial and agricultural success?

"Mr. O'Brien, my family and I only come to town a handful of times a year. We're tryin' to enjoy our time. If what you need to discuss can wait, then I'd be much obliged."

"Y-yes, of course. It-it was noth—nothing. I-I just thought I would stop by and say hello. Perhaps before you leave town, you wouldn't mind coming in and sharing a drink with me."

"Don't drink." Flint withdrew another piece of straw from his pocket and slid it between his lips.

O'Brien massaged his chin. "You don't drink. That's fine. Then perhaps we should have a bite to eat?"

Flint looked at the ground behind him. A cover lay across the thick grass, littered with plates of half-eaten food. "I think I dun ate."

O'Brien blinked. Why would the man not speak to him alone? Stubborn and difficult farmer! "Mr. Hess, I know my boy has yet to return, but there are still many things we need to discuss before our children wed."

"Such as?"

"Well..." Now what? Looking down, he tried to think of a reasonable excuse. Pressure to blurt out the real reason assailed him. But one couldn't say *Because I want your property, you idiot!* No, that would never do. There had to be a better way to get this simpleton to sign his land over without all these complications.

"Listen, Mr. O'Brien. My wife there, LouAnn. Do you see her fidgetin'?"

"I do." Where was that going? Ivy fidgeted all the time.

"Well, you see, I don't get her into town much because of all the work we have on the farm and she looks forward to just gazin'. Why, she considered stopping over at the church just to stare at the new addition. I can see that look in her eye. Can you see it? Well, of course you can't see it. But I tell you I see a look in her eye and it is sayin' *Finish with your business, Flint, so I can go see my stuff.* That's what the look is sayin'. And you know what, I think I better listen to it."

He didn't know what to say, standing there amongst the family as they packed up their picnic remains and prepared to leave. He could threaten to break off the wedding proceedings if he didn't have a talk with Hess right away, but it wouldn't benefit him. Taking a deep breath, he tipped his hat in the family's direction—they ignored him—and said his goodbyes.

The tip of the cane stirred up dust as he strutted back to the office. A couple of old-timers rested outside on the storefront's bench, eyeing him curiously. One spat a wad of tobacco juice, barely missing his shoe. The disdain the community felt for him showed, and it hurt. Most believed he'd bought the town without any regard for the townspeople, and so he could follow personal pursuits. Perhaps they had a point.

The funds he had inherited by marrying Ivy had certainly taken a beating. He blamed it on the blasted war. How did anyone make money in such an economy? The idea of acquiring wealth through Confederate money was preposterous. Why, anyone with sense knew it would be completely worthless if the South lost.

He continued toward the tavern. Drunken men down on their luck littered the walkway. A hand snaked out and grabbed his cane, almost sending him toppling toward the ground. He righted himself and tried to yank his cane out of reach, but a hand reached from the building's shadows and held it tight.

The shadowy form said, "Care to buy a soldier a drink?"

O'Brien huffed. "A soldier? I see no solider. I see nothing but a drunk trying to make people take pity on him, which I don't take kindly to. Now, let go of my cane this instant or I will have you thrown into jail."

"I wouldn't do that." From behind the lounging drunk, a second voice spoke in a whisper, but it set his heart thudding.

Herrick. He leaned against the tavern's wall, a booted foot planted behind him, a hat slung low over his eyes. O'Brien wondered if there was more than one copy of the dratted man. Every time he turned around, Herrick waited ahead of him.

O'Brien pointed at the lounging drunk. "What is this man to you?" He'd never been so bold, but the circumstances of the day pushed him to it.

Herrick shrugged. "That isn't important. What I want to know is why you're here alone and Flint Hess isn't with you."

"How did you know I—"

"It's my business to know. Now, where is he?"

"He's not coming, but it doesn't matter. I can get the information without him." Had he said that aloud? Herrick didn't know that he had other designs besides learning the contents of the silo. Did he?

"I already told you, don't worry about the information. Just be ready. And stop playing games."

"Games?" O'Brien's heart pounded a dull, heavy rhythm. What did Herrick know?

Herrick sneered. But instead of approaching him, Herrick pushed off the wall and crossed into the road, striding like a hunting cat. The drunk yanked the cane from O'Brien's hand, threw it aside, and straightened. Face to face with O'Brien, the drunk seemed to shed years. He straightened. His eyes glowed. O'Brien inched backward. Then suddenly and strangely, the young man jumped at him, laughed, and ran off after Herrick.

O'Brien's pulse pounded harder, faster. What did Herrick want with Flint Hess? What did the captain know about his business with Hess? He'd mentioned the information to stall and distract Herrick. Flint's property was nowhere near the silo. The deal with Hess and the deal with Herrick were two completely different situations, and O'Brien intended to keep them that way.

The pair retreated down the street. A sinister laugh floated back, sending cold chills down his spine. He would need to be more careful with his dealings. He had no intention of sharing the Hess land with Herrick or anyone else.

# 21

Sated, happy, and loaded with cloth, the family headed home. The sun dipped behind the mountains, causing an eerie halo of light to ring the green peaks.

Dougal leaned against the side of the wagon. He'd not gotten Mara to speak, but he was close. He could feel it.

Tonight he hoped to have another dream about Cian. While he had been in that room flooded with light, Cian had told him things. But Cian had not said near enough, or maybe he couldn't remember everything. He thought he was there to protect Mara. If he completed his task, he'd be forced to leave, but he didn't want to. He was *happy*.

He studied Mara. She had contributed to his contentment, but it wasn't just the progress he'd made with her; it was also being part of a real family. He hadn't belonged to a family since his youth and even then he'd been shunned by many of the villagers; he had never experienced true acceptance—until now.

"Junior, I tell you, the girl was makin' googly eyes at you. You should tell Pa and then see if you can court her."

Junior waved Maude's statement away. "Naw. I'm not interested in no girls right now. Although it makes me wonder why she didn't pay attention to me when we was at school?" He bit his lip. "Do you really think she looked at me?"

"Yup. She was lookin' at you." Maude rolled her eyes. "And why wouldn't she be? You're the only man anywhere about these parts."

Junior drew his brows together and Dougal lowered his head, hiding his growing smile. Yep, he'd been accepted. They were ribbing each other in front of him—couldn't get more accepting than that.

Mara's shoulders shook, too. It ran through him like another jolt. It felt so good to feel her happiness.

Finally the wagon halted before the house, and he jumped down and helped Maude to the ground. Before Junior could reach for Mara, he grabbed her waist. He lowered her before him, but didn't release her immediately.

Curse nineteenth century clothing! If they were in modern times, Mara would be wearing skin-tight jeans, her hair would be pulled back in a ponytail where he could reach her neck, and she would have a T-shirt which rode up and allowed him access to the flesh beneath. But unfortunately, this wasn't modern times.

Instead, Mara's gray gown swooshed against her ankles. Three-quarter length sleeves ended in four inches of white lace. The thick material had to be torture in the hot August sun, yet she never appeared to sweat.

He dug his fingers into her sides. She didn't squirm, but cocked her brow. Even though she never spoke, she expressed herself very well.

"I guess we better get these things unloaded." Pa grabbed a box of supplies.

Guess that was a hint for help. He released his hold and Mara stepped back.

The family moved like a machine, each person playing their part. He waited to grab a box, but everything was taken by the time he reached the wagon bed. Dougal scowled. Maybe he was just fooling himself. He was like an extra. Here he'd thought he was finally part of a family, but not really. Maybe there wasn't a reason to stay, after all.

Ma, Maude, Pa, and Junior laughed as they strode up to the house. Mara followed behind silently. He was left leaning against the wagon. He rolled his eyes. What was he doing there? He could travel anywhere he pleased. He could meet Abraham Lincoln or Robert E. Lee. He could play riverboat casinos or travel to Louisiana and get a houseboat on the bayou.

But what about Mara—he needed her. Right?

He stared into the distance, feeling the tug at his wayward spirit. He'd always been a drifter, an explorer, and there was a whole world to explore.

In this timeline, he hadn't been born yet. When his life did begin, he would live in Ireland for many years. His first trip to the United States wouldn't occur until much later, as an escape.

If he used his historical knowledge, just think of all the things he could accomplish. Think of all the money he could make. But what of aging? Things seemed different now; nothing was like before. His body didn't seem to work the same. He was even losing some of his cockiness and charm. That was a tragedy to the entire human race if ever there was one.

Grays were protectors of humans, and only lived as long as a human. The blacks, however, were the fallen. They were beings who'd decided to give their lives over to selfish desires and pursuits.

At first, they had all been protectors, and then the rebellion had happened. Cahal had declared his superiority, proclaiming himself the leader of the gray clan in a direct violation of the understood law. So Cahal had been cast out. A third of the gray gryphons had followed, suffering the same fate; their punishment was to live apart from the grays and the humans.

Then all the grays that left to follow Cahal had changed. No longer were they gray, beautiful creatures; instead they darkened to black. For hundreds of years they'd roamed free, terrorizing villages. Then one arose from the gray clan, a warrior mighty in stature and pure in heart. He'd thought to speak with the leader of the black gryphons and perhaps convince him to change his ways.

What happened, though, had been an entirely different scenario. Which left him in his current situation.

Should he stay or should he go?

"Dougal?" Pa interrupted his thoughts. "Are you comin'? Ma has coffee ready. We's gotta finish the chores before the dark completely sets in."

Dougal nodded. A sense of foreboding surrounded him. The wind of change was in the air. The only question was whether he would stick around to find out what it meant.

# 22

O'Brien checked his gold pocket watch for the tenth time.

"Dear, please sit down."

"Ivy, I don't wish to sit down."

"Pacing doesn't do any good. We've discussed how you wear down the carpet when you do so. And you know how this distresses me. I'll have to call Ellie in with the brush to fluff it again."

He plopped into a nearby chair. "Ivy, please. I'm trying to think."

"I don't know what for. You've been in town all week and had plenty of time to think." His wife, Ivy, lounged on a paisley-covered chaise in the front parlor. It was almost dinnertime and she still wore her nightgown. A kerchief sat askew upon her head, and golden curls peeked around the edges. Worn slippers covered her dainty feet. She threw her arm over her eyes. "Just imagine, leaving me here all the time. I tell you, I'm not safe."

"Ivy, what could you possibly be worried about? Our only neighbors are the Hesses and what would they want? We don't have anything." Bitterness crept into his tone. The Hesses were probably better off than he was at the moment. Granted, he *owned* the town. But lately it didn't feel as if it was worth much, and he couldn't avoid the feeling that everything was falling apart around him.

She rose, snapping erect. Red flushed her face and her eyes dared him to speak. "I don't know what *it* wants. But I tell you it hangs on the side of the house and stares through the window. I saw it just the other day, all black and furry. Drool dripped from its fangs and I swear it was clicking its teeth in anticipation."

He straightened. "What?"

Ivy slapped her thigh. "The beast, Barry! How many times must I tell you? It's coming for me."

He waved away her fears, his sudden rush of worry fading away. Ivy was getting worse. "My dear, it is nothing more than your fevered imagination."

She scoffed and crossed her arms over her chest. "Humph. Last time you claimed it was nothing more than a trick of the light. So which is it? My imagination or the light? If Beauford was here, he would believe me."

It was all so tedious, and his patience was waning. Where was Ellie? She needed to entertain Ivy so he could have his meeting with the general, the commander of the Rebel forces near the silo. Probably after his attempted break-in, the solider had ratted him out. Then, when he hadn't shown, the general had decided to visit himself and had sent a note informing O'Brien of his impending visit. It was a disaster.

"Are you listening to me?" He'd missed something, and as a result her voice had sharpened.

With an effort, he focused on Ivy. "Of course. I know you think Beauford would believe you. He always did give in to your... well, oddities."

"You are too unkind." She swiped a tear from her cheek.

A grin spread across her face.

She stared into space. "When is Beauford coming home?" The sharpness faded from her voice and the red from her face. Now she just seemed lost and strangely alone, despite his presence. She asked the same question at least five times a day.

More and more, he wished he had the answer. "I don't know."

"Where is he? It shouldn't take this long to milk the cow." Ivy furrowed her brow.

O'Brien sighed. It was always the same. She was perfectly fine one minute, well aware that Beauford had gone to war; then the next she imagined him off on some meaningless errand or chore. Then she would go on to say he was taking too long. Next, the questions about when he would return would start.

He didn't have the patience to deal with it tonight. "Ivy, perhaps Ellie should put you to bed. You look a tad peaked."

"I do?" She patted her cheeks.

"Oh, yes. I think you need to lie down and rest." He almost felt guilty. Company calling, even in the guise of the general and his staff, coupled with acting as the lady of the house, might have brought her back to reality, but he couldn't risk it. The future was too unclear.

"Perhaps you're right. Maybe when I wake up, Beauford will be back." She stood, her legs wobbly.

He pulled the bell rope.

Ivy leaned against the wall. She stared at him. "But what if *he* comes back?"

"If you have a black beast outside your window, maybe you should just open the shutters and ask him what he wants."

Ivy nodded. "That's a good idea."

Ellie appeared and escorted Ivy from the room. Finally he could relax. A mint julep in one hand and cane in the other, he leaned back on the settee and prayed the forthcoming meeting would be brief and painless.

O'Brien jerked awake. Evening light filtered through the parted curtains. The pocket watch hanging from his side showed half past six. Where was the Rebel general?

Ellie should know something. He grasped the bell rope, but jumped as banging rattled the front door. He waited for Ellie to answer, but she must have been attending Ivy, because she never arrived.

He huffed, pushed himself up, and strutted to the door. Why must he do everything? He was the head of the household. One day people would wait on him hand and foot, which was why he'd made the deal with Herrick. He had to remember that.

He pulled the door open. The general stood there, head up and shoulders back. Behind him, twenty Rebel soldiers smiled broadly. This wasn't good.

"Hello, Mr. O'Brien."

"Yes, hello." He stepped aside and the unexpected gang shoved their way into the foyer. The young men spun around in a circle, exclaiming. Light oak panels lined the walls. The spiral staircase climbed to the second floor. Doorways opened off the massive foyer, leading to the library, the formal dining room, the parlor, and countless other rooms he wasn't sure if he'd even been in. The opulence impressed them, just as he'd hoped—but for the general, not the entire Rebel force.

He directed them into the formal dining room and offered them seats before ringing the bell. Ellie shuffled in with a rustle of skirts. Head covering tilted, hair sticking out at odd angles, she curtsied. "Y' rang, Massa?"

"Yes, Ellie. I need you to bring dinner for our guests."

Ellie twisted her head and gaped. She moved closer. "Mr. O'Brien, beggin' y' pardon, but I didn't make enough food to feed this many people."

He would not be embarrassed. "Then go back to the kitchen and cook enough to feed this many people."

"But, suh—"

"I don't care if you have to empty the cellar! There will be enough food upon this table." His hoarse whisper scratched his throat, but it was worth it. He couldn't have people believing him poor.

"Yes, Massa." Ellie dipped low before shuffling away.

He pasted a smile on his face. He would need to entertain his visitors until Ellie finished preparing the meal. No telling how long such a feat would take. He just needed wine, and conversation that didn't give away his nervousness until he figured out the true reason for the general's visit.

The general leaned back in the chair and patted his stomach. His gut protruded over his belt, making him resemble a man who had swallowed a whale rather than dining modestly on simple fare. He took a pipe from his coat and added a pinch of tobacco. "A mighty fine meal, Mr. O'Brien."

"Yes. Thank you." He feared it would be his last for awhile.

"My compliments to the cook."

He nodded. Ellie had performed decently, considering the circumstances, but he wouldn't be thanking her.

"I assume you desire to get about our business?"

He clasped his hands. Finally. "Yes. That would be nice. You see, my wife is ill and having company in the house makes her a tad nervous."

The general cocked a brow, but didn't question the revelation. "I see. Be assured this won't take long. There are but a few things we need to discuss."

"Yes, of course." A few things? Not thc single, simple matter of him attempting to break into the silo? O'Brien's heart began to beat faster.

"First, I understand you are curious about the silo."

He gulped. After all this time, he had hoped the young man hadn't mentioned him to his commanding officer. Now his hope vanished. What could he say in his defense?

The general nodded sagely, smoke drifting from the bowl of his pipe. "I understand your concern. What man in your position wouldn't want to know the weapons available to defend his vast holdings?"

"What?" He was flabbergasted; the need to defend himself had just vanished.

"I mean, I understand. You being the owner of every establishment in the town of Wheeler's Landing puts you in a certain predicament. With the Confederate Army in the south, you want to know that we can protect your investments. Let me assure you, we are more than capable of protecting your buildings and your other properties."

The general drew from his pipe, then released a puff of smoke. The other soldiers left one by one, as if some unspoken cue had been shared. One soldier dipped his head toward the general and whispered in hushed tones. The general waved him away, focusing on his host. The front door clicked closed behind the last Rebel soldier.

"Now that we're alone, I would like to give you permission to check out our storehouse."

"Truly?" This was too easy.

"Of course. Why not? You appear to be a fine, upstanding citizen. You have more than a vested interest in this area. I think it only fitting you know the army's capability of defending your property."

"That would be comforting." He fought the urge to rub his hands together in delight. All that time, all that money, wasted on trying to search the silo, and here it was being offered to him on a silver platter. It mattered little that Herrick no longer sought the information. Perhaps he could use it to his own advantage at a later date.

"I'm glad you're pleased."

"Oh, I'm very pleased. And honored."

The general stood, hitched his pants, and pulled his coat tighter around his circular frame. Several buttons remained undone, giving the man an unkempt air. If O'Brien had genuinely hoped he would save the town, then he would have been more concerned. As it stood, he couldn't help the relief that flooded over him.

"In the morning you may come to my tent beside the river and I'll have someone escort you to the silo. Then you may inspect everything within."

"Yes. That would be most acceptable." He could barely contain his glee.

The soldiers left, and he retired to his study. Ellie had left him a Scotch on his desk. The amber liquid sloshed in the glass. Maybe this news was too good to be true. The general had never stated *why* he'd wanted the meeting—if it had only been about the silo's contents, the general could have sent a note—and O'Brien had been so happy with the offer that he'd forgotten to ask. Had sharing the silo been the general's sole intent, or was there something more? Something more dangerous?

The house was quiet as he settled behind the worn desk. Worry gnawed at his gut, but he ignored it, pulled a stack of papers close, and pored over the town's financial records. The war and drought had affected his profits. Few people other than the soldiers had money or time to spend in the tavern. The only business producing profit was the store, and that was because of one person—Flint Hess.

Somehow, when everyone else's life had tanked down the outhouse hole, Flint and his family continued to prosper. Everyone knew Junior had avoided joining the military, claiming mental instability, but most of the townspeople knew better. The boy was fit as a fiddle, O'Brien was sure of it.

If the Hess family were a different sort, someone would have turned them in. But the family went out of their way to help the other farmers. Why, he'd heard that in the past, the Hesses had had too much open land for their cattle and had allowed other farmers the use of their property. Free of charge! And their crops just kept growing when everyone else's withered!

The Hesses also shared food and anything extra they owned. It tended to create loyalty. That loyalty, and Beauford's impending marriage, kept him from turning Junior over to the authorities. If the Rebel general caught the boy—

He pinched the bridge of his nose and rubbed his burning eyes. It wasn't good to stare at papers for too long.

He placed everything back into the safe and turned the key, then leaned back in his chair and propped his feet on the desk. Light bathed the ceiling. His eyelids drifted downward. Open and close, open and close, he struggled to remain alert. Then he heard—

# 23

Thick white clouds immersed in red and orange lay just over the mountain range, marking the sunrise. Tree limbs swayed in the breeze. What was the old phrase? *Red in the morning, sailors take warning.*

Dougal had sensed a storm when the family had visited Wheeler's Landing, but now he felt nothing. Was the sky's color a cause for concern or not?

He continued to the creek, undressed, and folded his clothes in a neat pile before stretching out on a smooth boulder. Love and need were the way most grays changed. But what about him? He wasn't most grays. He'd been born half-human, half-beast. Darkness had taken over his heart and he'd lived as a black gryphon for most of his life. Sacrifice had made him gray. Could he force the change? As a black, he'd whispered a few magic words Serena had given him and changed any time he wanted. But now… he didn't want to use the words. Maybe if he imagined danger or thought about love. *Yeah, that should work.*

Sucking in a breath, he squinted his eyes and gritted his teeth, willing the transformation to occur. He *needed* to experience the change, to test his abilities, to learn his limitations. He wanted to see himself.

*Pain.* Clutching his stomach, he curled over. Tingles, like his limbs were waking from a deep sleep, drilled into his body until he thought he would throw up. He'd never felt this way before. Why was it so painful? Was it to discourage changing without direct need?

Skin broke along his sides and he arched his back, biting his bottom lip to keep from screaming. The pain swamped him for long minutes. Finally it ended, leaving a dull ache radiating across his chest. He gasped for breath until that too subsided. Moments passed before he had the strength to walk to the water's edge. He drew in a deep breath and leaned over the glassy surface.

He stood close to seven feet tall, with gray fur, two almost human arms, full wings, and legs like the back of a lion. His face was sort of human, but with a short snout instead of a nose; thick hair above his eyes resembled eyebrows. Instead of claws, his fingernails appeared a little longer than a normal human's.

Entranced, he studied his arm. Among gryphons, the gray color was revered and considered beautiful. He'd never really understood why the outer appearance meant so much, especially not now, when he felt so different inside. He felt like a new person... or beast. Question was, what was he going to do about it?

One tuft of fur stood erect, out of place, and he licked his thumb and smoothed it down. He turned his head from side to side. The shorter snout was definitely the way to go.

He leaned back and stared over the slow moving water. Maeldun had wanted to know where Ailin, or Gregory, resided. Did this mean Ailin was nearby? And if so, did it mean he wasn't the only gray in Wheeler's Landing during this time period?

When Dougal had been young, he'd asked Cian questions. Cian had been the supreme authority on everything gryphon. For Dougal, keeping his alternate identity from the villagers hadn't been easy, and Cian had taken him under his wing, so to speak, and attempted to guide him. Dougal ultimately had refused the help. Humans had ostracized him. Why would he want to befriend them?

But Cian had assured him their behavior merely showed fear of the unknown. He hadn't listened well. That was when he'd met Serena, the village druid. She'd convinced him to leave the village in search of his real father, the father Cian had imprisoned. Yearning for revenge had twisted his heart and he'd left a potentially positive future to release his father. He'd succeeded. A sarcastic laugh escaped his throat. He'd found his father and as a result had had to sacrifice his own life. What a reward!

His gut twisted. His father could be here right now, terrorizing the people of this era.

He shook his head. No. He couldn't think about his father. He needed to concentrate. What had Cian told him? Black gryphons were like cockroaches. *If you see one, you have a million to deal with...* sort of. Not literally a million, but they never traveled alone. Also, they worked in a pack. Once you joined, you remained a member for life. Nothing could free you from the group except death. Cian, of course, had been the exception. He'd been the only one to successfully leave the pack alive. Cian had said, *"Because I should never have entered the group to begin with."*

Dougal ran his hands over his fur, jumped to his feet, and paced beside the water. The black gryphons maintained an organization. They followed Cahal, their supreme leader. He had started the group and no one questioned his authority, but the grays had always worked differently. They'd made a pact with the humans to protect them, and protect them they had. When a gray reached a certain age, he was sent as part of a group of twelve to an area village. Each village contained only twelve, never more, never less. Once in place, the twelve were on their own and never called for assistance from other grays. Dougal scoffed. No wonder the grays rarely won a battle. It was the worst military strategy ever.

The sun rose higher over the mountain ridges. Soon the whole family would be up and moving about. It wouldn't do to be caught in this form or in the act of transforming.

He closed his eyes. The pain as he shifted back to his human form was less, and he sighed with relief when the transformation was complete. He dressed quickly and settled back on the rock, burying his head in his hands. If Maeldun still lived and his father was close by, that meant the whole black gryphon army could be here as well. But why? What could be in this small Southern town in 1863 that would have value to an army of gryphons? Did it have anything to do with why he'd been sent back?

Stupid half dreams...

Mara approached the working men with the water bucket and allowed her eyes to rove over Dougal's shirtless frame. His shoulders rippled as he thrust the shovel deep into the ground. Today they were planting rose bushes for Ma, bushes they'd purchased during their trip to town. It was something Ma had always dreamed of, but they had never been able to afford. But this year their bumper crop had covered the cost.

Ma fanned herself. "No, that won't do. Place it just a tad more to the left."

"Now, LouAnn! Don't you start that."

"Flint! Don't you tell me what to do. I reckon I been waiting on these bushes for nigh on twenty year. I think I know where I want them to rest."

"Well, I reckon you do, but when you dun moved them about ten times our yard's goin' to look like a gopher's home."

"Humph." Ma crossed her arms over her chest.

Mara lowered her head and smiled. It wouldn't do for either of her parents to see that.

Dougal stopped digging and went to another location, just a few inches to the left of the last one.

"Now, that looks much better. Come stand beside me, Flint. Don't you see it? Don't you see how the light reflects off the roof and lands on the blooms? This is the spot."

"Well, it's good to know you've settled on a location. You're going to run Dougal as far away from us as he can get if you keep abusin' him this way."

Ma touched Dougal's shoulder. His muscles rippled in response and Mara held her hand to her fluttering heart. It was his voodoo magic. Ma touched him and she *felt* it. There was no other explanation for the strangeness.

"I just have to tell you how much I appreciate you puttin' up with my indecisiveness. It ain't often a woman gets to see one of her dreams fulfilled."

"LouAnn, why do you keep makin' such a big deal out of this?"

"Flint, you know why. My ma's name was Rose and she had a whole field of roses around our house."

"Sure did. They were the wildest and thorniest things I ever did see. The only reason she had them around the house was to keep everyone out."

Ma rounded on Flint and stomped. "You know that ain't true. My ma was friendly to you."

"Sure she was. Too friendly when I told her I wanted your hand. She followed me to the preacher with the shotgun over her shoulder and a wad of tobacco in her mouth. Why, she spit on my heels all the way to the church!"

Ma guffawed and shook her head. "That was me ma. Always takin' care of her children. That's why I want this bush. I want it to remember her by."

"Don't need no rose to keep from forgetting that ornery old woman."

Ma popped Pa on the arm. Envy washed over Mara. She would never have that because she had to act stupid.

Dougal cleared his throat, letting her know she'd stalled long enough. She carried the water bucket to him and set it on the ground near his feet, lifting the dipper for him. The shovel propped him up as he took the dipper and gulped deeply. Some water missed his mouth and dribbled down his chin. She restrained herself from reaching up and wiping it away. That was something a speaking person would do.

She tried to avert her eyes before he caught her, but she wasn't quick enough. While Ma and Pa continued their heated debate, Dougal grasped her hand and touched it to his chin, guiding her finger to one of the drops. As it trickled down his chin, he followed its trek with their joined hands. Then he let go, and Mara traveled with the drop of water down his chin and onto his bare chest. When she paused, her hand rested over his beating heart. Mesmerized by the rough, wild pounding, she flattened her hand and eased a step closer.

Heat radiated from him. Those ominous bronze eyes watched her. Magic floated around them; it felt as if the world belonged to them alone. No sounds of birds tweeting; none of creatures scurrying about. Not even Ma and Pa's argument. There was nothing but their breathing and their heartbeats.

She parted her lips. Words formed and she moved her tongue as she prepared to speak for the first time in ten years.

Energy surged around them. It felt like being caught in a wind tunnel. Dougal struggled to catch his breath.

Mara's black hair was tied back in a red ribbon. It tantalized him. His hands ached to filter through those glossy waves. His eyes devoured her well-defined features. His mouth sought to clamp onto hers. His gut clenched as she opened and closed her mouth as if to speak. If he moved, would the moment be ruined?

Her lips parted.

"Dougal! We've got it. This spot doesn't work. My ma, God rest her soul, would be disappointed if I didn't put the roses closer to the house. Flint and I decided to take them over to the front yard and stick one on either side of a walkway."

"Walkway?" He blinked, struggling to clear his mind. *Is someone else in the world right now?*

"Yes, a walkway. Now, don't get yourself in a huff. I know we don't have a walkway yet, but I thought since the farm is producing of late, you boys might make me a proper path, something to walk on up to the house. Then when we get off the wagon, we won't drag mud inside."

"But LouAnn, there is no way to keep dirt out of the house."

Pa had taken over the conversation. That was good, because he was struggling to focus.

"I disagree. I think we can dig down and have the boys shove rocks in the ground and make a walkway from the house to the barn—like cobblestones—and then you won't bring mud in."

Mara's head fell, hiding her face. The moment had passed. He wanted to bite his tongue in two. He wanted her to speak. If only he knew what had precipitated her silence in the first place, then he might have some insight into how to make her speak in the future. *If I stay around for the future, that is.*

He didn't know if staying was such a good idea. To hide and let his power grow seemed like the better option. Being out in the open would only cause trouble for him and anyone he stayed around. He could attempt to locate the nearest pack of grays and join their dozen. There was safety in numbers, even low ones.

Mara eased away, then turned and hurried to the house, vanishing inside. Her departure left him colder than ever.

For the remainder of the day, he and Pa moved the roses around to multiple locations, until Ma was finally satisfied. After they finished, he followed an exhausted Pa inside for dinner.

No one spoke more than a few words. The most said was "Pass the potatoes" and "These rolls sure are good." But other than that, the meal passed in silence. With everyone gorged, Pa pushed back his chair and headed to the front porch. On a night like this, with everyone exhausted, the girls would clean the dishes and then prepare for bed straightaway. Junior would go to the barn and lie down, which only left Pa and Dougal behind.

A thousand stars twinkled in the darkening sky as the sun finally collapsed over the distant mountains. The only other light came from Pa's lit pipe. He rocked in his chair as Dougal sat at his feet on the front porch steps. Tonight he was determined to get some answers. "Flint, do you mind if I ask you a question?"

"Sure don't. Although I have to tell you, just because you ask don't mean I'll answer."

He fought his smile at the pronounced sarcasm. He cleared his throat. "I have some questions about Mara."

"Oh."

"I know she hasn't spoken in ten years, but what I don't know is why. And another thing—how come she doesn't resemble any of you?"

"One of those questions I reckon I can answer for you. You'll probably think I'm tellin' you a fairy tale, but I'll swear it is the truth."

Dougal scooted to the edge of the step and held his breath. Which answer would he receive? Which question did he want answered more?

"I know you're a curious sort. So I'll try to keep to the facts as much as possible. And the plain simple fact of the matter is we found her."

"Found her?" So he was getting the answer to why she didn't favor the others. He'd take it.

"We found the wee thing." Pa looked around to make sure no one listened. "You see LouAnn, well, she was mighty distraught. We were expectin' ourselves, but it wasn't meant to be. The good Lord had other plans and she lost our child. About a month later, she was out walking around in her grief. Quite far from home she was, when she came across a storage house and heard a noise. She told me she felt mighty afraid, but the closer she got, the more she realized it sounded like a baby.

"Well, she knowed there was no way to sleep at night if she didn't check it out. Told me a horrifying story of how she stumbled in the waning twilight up to this creaky old door and pulled at the latch, but it wouldn't budge. Said she worked half an hour trying to get through when finally she spotted a large branch nearby. My LouAnn, a little weak woman, picked up the branch, wedged it in the door, and pushed with all her might.

"When the door popped open, she knew her speculations were correct. Afraid she might step on the fragile thing, she got down on her hands and knees and crawled around until she touched cool flesh. When she brought the baby out in the light, it was as pink as it could be. Full head of black hair and the palest blue eyes that looked like sparkling sapphires. So LouAnn brought her home. We named her Mara 'cause of the bitterness of losing our own young 'un. After all this time, though, I have to say we don't think of Mara as anything but our own."

Dougal's heart hammered in his chest. "Did you ever try to find her family? Or who left her there?"

"Nope. We never did. We're her parents and that's all there is to it." Pa took a deep breath. "Now, as for your other question, I can't answer that for you. One day Mara went to the creek. We didn't miss her for some time. When we found her, the child was huddled under a large tree with her eyes stuck open and all of her trembling from head to toe. For a while we were afraid to leave her alone with the other kids because of how she acted. One corner of the house became her sanctuary. She'd spend all day huddled in a little ball and lookin' around like she was expecting something to jump out at her. But she never did tell us what it was. She never did speak again."

So he'd received both answers. If he thought about everything, he knew then he had a pretty good idea what that *something* was that Mara had seen. Her fear when he'd been a gryphon had said it all.

Perhaps if he told Mara his true identity, then he could tell her that Maeldun would never find her again, that she was free. Free to be normal. Free to talk.

Free to love.

# 24

*The scream...*

At the sound, O'Brien's hairs stood on end. It so horrified him that he could barely catch his breath as he grabbed his cane and hefted it over his shoulder. If someone wanted to break into his home, then they were going to suffer the consequences. A wallop upside the head didn't seem like enough, but it would have to do until he could turn them over to the law.

He rounded the wooden desk and ran out the study door. He stomped up the stairs at a speed normally beyond his capability, but the scream had been so terrifying it drove him.

Ivy's door was ajar. Had Ellie left it that way or had someone else?

He peered through the crack. Ivy lay on the bed, holding out her hand as if to block something approaching. A dark, massive figure loomed over her. It was the single most terrifying thing he'd ever seen. The creature favored the look of a giant rat, with a long snout and a huge body covered in thick black tangled fur. Its legs bent inward at the knees and its feet clenched thick white claws into the wooden floor.

He moved in closer, accidentally hitting the door. The creature swiveled its ominous, repulsive head and cocked what looked like a hairy eyebrow. Then it snarled a wrinkled lip and sniffed. Bile seeped up O'Brien's throat and he swallowed it down. *Get control of your fear, man; get control. This is Ivy. She needs you.*

The closet. Secured inside was a small revolver with six shots. Could he reach it? He needed to try. Hand-to-hand combat wouldn't win him this fight. And the cane, while it might have been good to smash in some heads—well, he didn't think it would work in this case.

He scooted his left foot across the ornamental rug, keeping his eyes cast downward. The beast hadn't moved toward him, so maybe it hadn't seen him? He could hope.

"*Where do you think you're going?*"

Stricken with terror, he froze. The creature did see him and it could speak. Ivy had been telling the truth the entire time. Either that or he had joined her in her insanity.

"I asked where you're going. If you do not answer, you will force me to do something drastic. I don't think you want me to do something drastic, do you?"

The mere mention of the word *drastic* sent a stream of warm fluid down his leg. It wasn't the proudest moment in his life.

The creature twitched his nose and frowned.

*Be brave. Think of Ivy.* "I need to go to the closet."

"And what do you need from the closet?"

"My gun."

Ivy leaped from the bed then fell backward, landing in a mass of tangled limbs and chiffon. She struck her head against the bedpost. The crack reverberated through the room. His heart almost stopped. But he couldn't move. His courage was abandoning him.

"That didn't sound good. Would you like to check on your *wife*?" It sounded as if the beast spat the last word.

His head shook as he nodded.

The creature stepped back and placed its hand before its chest, as if gesturing for O'Brien to come forward. It acted like a gentleman. O'Brien found it hard to dislike, even if the creature was terrifying.

He reached Ivy's still form and started to crouch beside her. But the creature's hand closed around his neck and effortlessly lifted him several feet off the floor. The dislike was coming easier now.

The world faded to black, then he was dropped with an unceremonious *plop* beside his unconscious wife. O'Brien shivered. "What do you want?" His throat burned.

"What does every man want?" The beast's voice was almost a purr.

"I don't know." He lied. He knew—*power*—but he didn't want to give the beast any ideas if it had a different answer.

The creature thrust its head back in uproarious laughter. "You don't know. What an answer, coming from you."

The smell of sulfur burned his eyes and tears streamed down his face. But moments passed with no new torture, no new laughter or words. Finally O'Brien lifted his head. The white gauzy curtains billowed into the room. Ivy and he were alone.

He jumped to his feet and ran to the open window. The creature was nowhere in sight. It was like it had vanished. Freed from his terror, he rushed back to Ivy and held his curled fingers under her nose. Air breathed across his skin.

He slid down the wall and leaned over his bent knees. Stars danced before his eyes. Ivy remained pale and unmoving. Where were Elijah and Ellie? Hadn't they heard her screams?

"Help!" His voice shrieked. Embarrassed, he cleared his throat and tried again.

No one showed. Again he had to do everything. He struggled to his feet and pulled the bell. Seconds later Ellie rushed into the room and fell at Ivy's feet. He rushed downstairs and woke Elijah. "Fetch the doctor."

Elijah raced from the house. Finally left alone, O'Brien fell into his desk chair and clasped his head between his hands. What was that thing? What had it been doing in his house? And what did it want with Ivy?

O'Brien wrung his hands and paced before the office window. Doctor Frances Hyrem had arrived and gone up alone to examine Ivy.

The whiskey burnt his throat but he continued to drink. If Ivy awoke and told the doc what she'd seen, he might drug her with so much opium she couldn't move. Should he tell the doctor he had seen the creature as well? It would be the gentlemanly thing to do. It would defend his wife and her good name, but it might make him look crazy, as well. There was no way for him to win. And he had to win; he'd given up too much to lose now.

Knuckles rapped against the study door. "May I enter?"

O'Brien pushed the whiskey glass away and straightened. "Of course."

Doc Hyrem entered, his face full of concern. "I've checked Mrs. O'Brien. She does have quite a nasty bruise on her head, but other than that, she seems fine. I would suggest plenty of rest and lots of fluids. Of course, she needs to be watched, as well."

"Of course." He nodded; so far so good.

The chair creaked as Doc Hyrem shifted. "Did she say anything to you about *seeing* something?"

O'Brien shifted in turn. "Uh, no."

"Hmm. Well, I will return in a few days, and I'll talk to her again at that time. Unless you have something to add?"

He swallowed his bile. "No, I have nothing to add."

Doc Hyrem stood. "Then I'll see you in a few days. Call for me if there's any need."

"Yes. Of course."

The doctor glanced at him several times while making his exit. From the study window, O'Brien watched the young man board the wagon behind Elijah. The doctor pointed at the house and talked while Elijah flicked the reins.

O'Brien narrowed his eyes. The two men seemed mighty friendly. He should pull out his gun and shoot them both. What right did the doctor have to talk to his slave about the goings-on in his home? Why, none, that's what. Next time he saw the doctor, he'd tell him in no uncertain terms that if he had a question to ask him, then ask it and refrain from speaking to the property!

The curtain dropped back into place. It was past time to visit his wife. He had some questions to ask.

Sleeping, O'Brien stretched his arms over his head and curled his legs to his chest. The lounge barely held him. He envisioned weeds, sarcastically called Queen Anne's lace, dancing in the breeze. Crickets chirped and birds sang to their young. It helped him relax.

He awoke to whimpering, rubbed his eyes, and sat up. Ivy fought her covers and rolled from one side of the bed to the other. For a moment she froze, then wails rent the air.

O'Brien raced to her side and smoothed damp tendrils of hair from her face. "Shh, you're all right. I'm here."

"Barry, don't you see him? He's there—in the corner."

Grabbing the lapels of his dressing gown, she entreated, "Please help me. I'm scared."

Ivy's words brought fear to his heart. Slowly, he swiveled and looked over his shoulder, but the room was empty. He glanced back to the bed. Ivy was curled into a ball, rocking back and forth.

What did her cries mean? Had the grotesque beast really come into her room before? Ivy had acted strangely for the last *seventeen years*. Her previous physician had chalked up her behavior to losing their baby, but now O'Brien wondered. If he questioned her about the past, would she be able to express the real reason for her behavior in a way that would now make sense to him?

He clasped her hand, so tiny and frail. When had she become so lifeless? "Ivy, has the creature been here before?"

She pulled away from him and rolled off the bed. Tiny and frail, yes, but she jumped to her feet and slipped past him with her old natural grace. Tapping a finger to her chin, she strolled to the window, parted the curtains, and looked out into the night. "Yes. I told you so."

He swallowed. "What does it want?"

In a monotone voice, she said, "He comes more and more. Sometimes I see him perched on the tree here, outside my window. He sings to me songs of love and beauty. For a long time he wouldn't let me see him. I begged, but he refused. He said he feared scaring me. But I told him I wouldn't be afraid, because even if something appears hideous on the outside, it can still be beautiful on the inside." She turned and stared past him, her eyes distant as if in the land of memory. "But he told me he harbored ugliness there as well. I didn't believe it. Anyone who could sing with such beauty could not be less than wonderful."

She crossed to the bed, glancing back over her shoulder at the open window. "Then one day he flew inside. I retreated. I couldn't help myself. I saw him for what he was, a hideous beast! When his hand reached out to touch me, I fainted. When I woke, he stood above me. I told him to go away and never come back." Ivy stood before the mirror and lifted her hair, studying the bandage upon her head and neck. "What happened here?"

"You screamed. When I came in, the creature stood above you. Then you fell and hit your head."

"I screamed? But why?" She blinked.

"I don't know. I thought the creature hurt you." Hadn't she just admitted to being scared?

"Maeldun wouldn't hurt me."

"Maeldun?" She'd named the creature?

"That's what he is called." She smiled crookedly. "All he wants is to smell me."

"*Smell* you?" He gulped.

"But of course. Why else would he be here? He says I have a certain aroma that appeals to his senses. He wants to take me to his tribe. I've told him I cannot possibly leave because I'm married. He said not to worry, he would find a solution."

"What solution?" His palms sweated. Her revelation didn't sound good.

She massaged her temples. "Perhaps it was his plan that scared me and caused me to scream. Oh, my head hurts. I must lie down." Ivy sank into her plush armchair.

O'Brien knelt at her feet. The creature planned to get rid of him so it could take his wife and now *her* head hurt! "Ivy, you must tell me what it said. How does it plan to get rid of me?"

"Oh, that wasn't the plan. It was something else, much more sinister. He doesn't have a big plan for *you.* After all, it would be simple enough to rid the world of your presence. You travel back and forth to town, so what is there to plan? But no, something else entirely consumed his mind."

O'Brien was aghast at Ivy's nonchalance. The discussion of his death truly meant nothing to her? Perhaps his wife was disturbed and he had ignored her need for help for too long. In the next town over there was a mental hospital. Tomorrow he'd seek admittance for her. Yes, tomorrow. Maybe he'd send Elijah with a request tonight.

# 25

Dougal rose before dawn and began milking cows, hauling water to the irrigation channels, and doing other menial chores. The kinks in his back were fast becoming a permanent part of his everyday life. Pausing, he clasped his hands and stretched his arms over his head. Why should a creature with his vast talents subject himself to such degrading torture? The answer was that he shouldn't. Merely existing to work was quickly growing old. Besides, he'd put all that work into courting Mara so she would speak, and still he had nothing to show for it.

Disgusted, he left the barn and stalked to the well. As he hauled bucket after bucket of water to the thirsty animals, the cows and horses and pigs, he thought about the night before.

In all honesty, life on the farm could be rather boring. There was no television, no video games, no night life, and no forms of entertainment; of course, most of the time the entire family, himself included, was too tired to worry about entertainment and went straight to bed, so it didn't matter. But on the rare occasion when the work was completed early and the family sat around the fireplace before the sun set, like last night, then Pa would pull out a big book, flip it open, skim the words, nod his head up and down like he'd gotten a feel for it, then shut the book with a thud. Last night's story had been especially interesting.

*Pa leaned back in his chair and closed his eyes. "There once was a beautiful place. It didn't have no weeds to pull. There were no bad creatures or things to worry about. A body didn't have to worry about not havin' enough food or not havin' enough clothin'. It was perfect. There were all the animals you ever did think to see. There were elephants. There were frogs. There were fish, birds, and every kind of bug you could imagine. But they never ate the fruit or harmed the plants.*

*"The creator of this perfect place wasn't satisfied, so he added somethin' else. First, he made a man. But then he saw the man poutin' 'cause he was lonely. When the creator realized this, he made a woman. They were perfect. They were meant for one another."*

*"Just like you and Ma?" asked Junior.*

*"Yup. Just like me and Ma." Pa clasped Ma's hand and squeezed.*

*"What happened next?" asked Maude.*

*Pa returned his hands to his lap and leaned forward. "Well, you see, their place was perfect, except they couldn't eat this one fruit. And because they couldn't have this one thing, it made them want it all the more. Instead of bein' patient and just listenin' to the creator, they took what they couldn't have. That caused a whole slew of problems. Why, they lost their home. Then they had to go live in the desert with the weeds. The creator forgave them but after what they did, life was never the same. And that is why we have to work hard today. The end. Now, hurry up to bed so we can get up and work."*

*From his chair near the wall, back where no one could see him through the shadows, Dougal quirked his brow upward. What kind of encouraging story was that? He put on a fake smile, refusing to let the family know what he really thought. Surprisingly, love for each of them had taken root in his heart. He would never hurt their feelings, but he didn't know if that love was enough to make him stay. Even the feelings he harbored for Mara were starting to dim in the face of her disinterest. She had seemed so fascinated with him in the beginning. If only he could find what held her back and get rid of it...*

A rooster crowed and Dougal woke back to the present. Grabbing a pitchfork, he scooped fresh hay into each stall for the horses, but his mind continued wandering. The interruptions during every encounter he'd had with Mara hadn't helped his wooing. Maybe if he whisked her away to some secret location, where nothing could distract them, then she would open up. The thought of a private rendezvous set his blood racing through his veins. *Private... oh, yeah.*

Mara—the little orphan girl. He had asked Pa if Mara knew about her parentage and Pa had admitted they'd never told her. Her curiosity about where she had come from or why she looked so different from the other family members was nonexistent. He had found the revelation a little disheartening, as he had pegged her for a more curious sort. He'd pegged her as a match for his own curiosity, in all honesty. It hurt to realize she wasn't.

Last night after the story, Pa had dismissed everyone to bed, but Dougal couldn't sleep. He'd left his bed and crept outside, to the water's edge. The moon had bathed the pond in light. He'd skipped a pebble across the surface and distorted the serenity. He felt like the water. Being here was like a pebble skipping across his life. Cian had informed him of his responsibility—which he couldn't remember completely—so he wasn't sure if he'd fulfilled it, but he hadn't been whisked back to his own time nor returned to the white tower to live out his days. So why was he waiting around? Mara didn't want him and he didn't want to spend the rest of his life as a work mule.

Perhaps if fate wasn't going to snatch him back then he would make his own decision.

Wandering. It's what's for breakfast.

He dropped the pitchfork back into its place and looked around the yard. The other family members were busy with chores, so he snuck back to the house. He fashioned a hobo sack from one of his homemade shirts and stuffed it with his own pair of long johns and his extra shirt.

Strangely torn, he cast one last glance around the room. Did he really want to leave the only home he'd ever enjoyed? Did he really want to leave Mara after the electricity that had flown between them? The answer to both questions was no. But could he stay and risk exposing her to his dark side? He never wanted her to know him like that. Did he want to see the terror in her eyes when she realized he was a gryphon? No, it was better to leave while she held a good opinion of him. And while he had a choice. And maybe Cian wouldn't be able find him.

Heart both heavy and light, he hitched the sack over his shoulder and stepped out onto the porch. No one was around, no one watched, as he slipped between the corn stalks to the road and set out walking.

No destination came to mind. One foot in front of the other

eventually would lead him somewhere. That was the way he preferred it to be, or so he insisted to himself.

The sun climbed fully over the mountaintop. Light hit the clouds from behind and gave them a pale gray cast, reminding him of a certain pair of animated eyes. Pa said Mara's eyes were sapphire blue when she was young, and now they were slate gray with a hint of blue. They were unique in color as well as in shape, slightly slanted upward at the edges, giving her an almost oriental look.

But he had to stop thinking about Mara. Their nonexistent relationship was over before it could begin. He had done his job. Well, at least it seemed as if he had, since Maeldun had failed to return. Now it was time to live a little, right?

Town wasn't close and on foot it would take half a day to get there. He hadn't passed a soul on the road and the best he could tell, the Rebel soldiers weren't hiding out in the weeds any more. Guess they thought there wasn't much to protect, not when it was only him. But no one tried to stop him, either.

Approaching the town, he heard the revelry before he saw it. Although it was early in the morning, the tavern was already in full swing, and he wondered if it had closed at all overnight. His belly rumbled. Since he'd left before breakfast, he'd not eaten since the night before. Money. He'd need some, and quick. Guess he'd have to get a job.

"Hey, feller. Do I know you?" Outside the tavern, a young man wavered on the steps, staring at Dougal with a wrinkle between his brows.

He started to say no, then he recognized the speaker. The drunken man staring at him happened to favor one of the boys who had tried to assault Mara in the woods. Dougal smiled when he remembered this particular one's run-in with the tree.

"I do know you. Get away from me!" the man screamed, then turned on his heel and ran from town.

Typical welcome. Some things never changed.

He sauntered further along the street. None of the shop windows posted advertisements about work. On the general store's porch, a shoe shiner watched him with genuine hope upon his brow. "Need a good shine, sir?"

Dougal found he hated disappointing him, which was weird. "I'm afraid not. I'm looking for a job."

"Humph." The shoe shiner spat, a good long one that splatted into the street several yards away. "You and everyone else.

All the farmers done hightailed it out of town, so the only work around now is the army."

That was an idea. Joining the army would provide clothing, food, shelter, and a bit of money. Plus movement up the ranks would be swift for someone with his various talents.

Gray-clad soldiers lounged on almost every street corner. Surely one of them would know where a young man could sign up to support the war effort. Never mind that they might question why he hadn't done so already or that they were on the losing side.

His sights zeroed in on one soldier in particular, an older man who looked both kind and wise, and Dougal headed his way—only to be waylaid by a familiar voice.

"I have work for you."

He couldn't quite place the voice, although he recognized it from somewhere. But hey, someone already knew what he needed and offered it freely. He changed directions, from the kindly old soldier to the corner of the bank nearest the hotel, from where the voice seemed to be addressing him, but pulled up short when a new voice answered.

"And *I* have work for *you.*"

Dougal didn't like that voice at all. Smooth and oily, it personified everything he didn't like in a man. Besides, the tones of both men's voices made it clear they weren't speaking to him at all, but to each other.

"Now, that's a new one. What is it you want in return for helping me?"

"There's this *thing*, a *creature*. It stalks my wife. I want to know why."

*A creature...* Catching his breath, Dougal slipped to the building's corner and froze.

There was a guttural laugh from the first voice's owner. "And you think I can help you? May I ask why?"

"No offense, but I've seen the characters you associate with. Surely someone with your expertise knows what this *thing* is. I don't care if you have to hire someone to stake out my home. I want you to find the *animal* and interrogate it. I want to know what it *wants*."

Dougal rolled his eyes. Some people didn't trust you to know which words were important. Oily voice seemed to fall into that category.

The first voice's owner didn't sound insulted. "Do you know

anything more?"

"My wife—" The oily voice paused. "I know it sounds crazy, but she claims the creature wants to *smell* her."

Dougal froze.

"Smell her? Very interesting. Does she smell good?"

"Herrick, this is serious! I think the beast has plans to *do me in* and take my wife as his own."

Amusement returned to the first voice's owner. What had Oily Voice called him? Herrick? "Why would such a being want a human wife?"

"I don't know. Why do you think I'm asking *you*? Listen, I have permission to enter the silo. I'm supposed to meet with the Rebel general today for a personal tour to satisfy any concerns I might have for my town's safety. I'll tell you everything you need to know tonight. But you have to help me, too. I can't lose my wife."

"Is this because you love her?"

"Of course I love her. But there are other reasons. Now, will you help me or not?"

All amusement vanished from Herrick's voice. "My assistance with your endeavor is not part of the deal. As I've explained, the information about the silo's contents is no longer needed. The attack will happen according to plan regardless. But if you wish to share the information in return for your cooperation, you will receive Rahab's reward. Nothing more was promised."

"I know. Myself and my family will be saved."

Outraged, Dougal peered around the corner. A rotund man with a cane, the guy who'd bothered Pa at the pond during the picnic—that mayor guy; what had his name been? O'Brien, or some such?—ran an agitated hand over his balding head. A tall, weathered man in worn civilian clothes leaned against the bank's wall, staring down at the mayor with undisguised contempt in his eyes.

O'Brien said, "But what good will life be if I have no one left to live it with? You have to help me."

Herrick's lip curled. "I will consider it."

"Fine, consider it! I'll see you this afternoon at my office. Just tell one of the girls to bring you up. They'll be expecting you."

"As always." The man's feral smile displayed a row of perfectly white teeth, flashing in the sunlight. Kind of odd for this time in history, but maybe not impossible.

Dougal slipped around to the far side of the hotel and huddled against the wall, out of sight from the alley. O'Brien had just made a deal with this Herrick. Although Dougal hadn't seen either man very well, he knew O'Brien's identity. He was the father of Maude's betrothed.

Pa hadn't had a high opinion of O'Brien. He'd called him all sorts of names. Everyone in town knew the man's possessions had been practically stolen. His marriage to Ivy Wheeler had given him ownership of the town. From the looks of things, O'Brien had taken full advantage. Every building carried his name.

Regardless of Flint's opinion of the man, if Dougal wanted a job, then O'Brien was probably the first place to start. Besides, nothing of what O'Brien had said while hiding in the alley seemed overly sinister. A creature visited his wife. The woman probably held an overactive imagination. Then again...

He sucked in a breath. Could it be one of the grays, one of the very ones he'd wanted to meet? Could he have been right and a dozen of them were in the area? Or might it be a black? Cahal, perhaps.

He needed to find out what he could and return to the Hess farm. His newfound family could be in danger. A visit to Mr. O'Brien had just topped his list of things to do but now for an entirely different reason.

# 26

Mara whistled as she gathered eggs. A smile teased her lips. Dougal had given her an egg as a gift. It had been a little strange, but thoughtful. He was like that—strange, but yeah, kind of thoughtful. But he hadn't conjured the egg up with his voodoo; he'd just taken it forcefully from Junior. That was good.

She leaned her head back against the barn's rough wood and inhaled. Dandelion scent tickled her nose and she sighed. All was right with the world. The beast had stayed away and Dougal continued to woo her. Even the fact that he had voodoo couldn't dissuade her.

Carefully balancing the basket of eggs, she skipped to the house. Skirts twirled around her legs as she danced inside. Oops—she was late. Everyone already sat at the table. But there was no food, and sullen expressions covered their faces. That seemed strange and not good, and her stomach clenched. Something was wrong. Where was Dougal?

Ma lifted her head, showing tear-filled eyes. Junior, Pa, and Maude studied their clasped hands and kept silent. There was only one answer. Dougal had left. She hadn't been enough to hold him. And she didn't have the ability to even ask questions!

That stupid monster had taken everything from her—her past, her present, and now her future. Dougal had wanted her to talk and she had refused. That was why he'd left—because of her vow.

She needed to get away so she could scream, or at least

pretend to scream.

Setting the eggs aside, she flung dirty laundry in a basket. Sorrow oozed from her family's pores. She could feel it. They always felt sorry for her over something. She was never allowed to be a success or have anything good for too long.

Forgetting breakfast, she hoisted the basket onto her hip and fled, fast-walking to the creek. Slamming the basket of laundry down, she settled on the usual boulder seat and sifted through the clothing. Dougal had left nothing behind; that was probably for the best. To touch his clothing would be too much like touching him.

Even the woods smelled like him. He'd smelled of pine, fresh water, and something else. *Restrained power...*

There was so much about Dougal she hadn't explored. All because fear had kept her silent. That had to be why he'd left—he got tired of waiting. She couldn't blame him really. Circumstances dictated what she did. Why should she torment herself? There was no way to go back and change her actions. No way to go back ten years and not be curious—or be a fool.

She threw a pebble into the creek. It disappeared beneath the murky surface like Dougal had disappeared from her life. If speech had been an option, what would she have said? Would she have mumbled words of respect, joy, or words of love?

What did it matter? He'd left. He'd abandoned her. He didn't care about her. Had he ever cared?

O'Brien met the general's man at the silo, as planned. The aide, another young officer, gave him a grand tour of the outside, and the aide described in great detail every weapon within, every nick on every old rifle and the serrations on each Bowie knife.

Finally he stopped, a pleased smile on his face. O'Brien cocked a brow. That was it? "Excuse me?"

"Yes?"

"I was under the impression I would be allowed entrance."

"I'm afraid not."

"But the general—"

"Oh, you spoke with the general?"

"Yes, I did. In fact, he came to dinner at my home—" O'Brien puffed out his chest "—this past evening, and he invited me here today to *see inside* the storehouse."

"I'm sorry to hear that. You see, I have strict orders not to allow anyone to enter the silo." The aide crossed his arms over his chest.

The kid looked haughty. Was he trying to be haughty? "I understand. But the general—"

"Nope, can't do it. Like I was saying, we have twenty-eight Fayetteville rifles, one hundred and ten Richmond rifles, one hundred fifty-two Burnside carbines..."

The aide prattled on and on about stockpiled weapons that were of little consequence to him. Blood pounded between his ears at the wasted time. Even though Captain Herrick declared he no longer needed the information, O'Brien wasn't going to stop until he knew what was in the silo. If he fulfilled Herrick's initial request, then hopefully he wouldn't be required to complete another. And if Herrick had wanted the information so badly in the beginning, then it might benefit O'Brien to know why.

The aide's words trailed to an awkward stop. Without glancing at him again, O'Brien spun on his heel, stalked to his horse, and climbed awkwardly astride. If he wanted to, the baffled officer could stare at his retreating backside. He was going home and devising another way to get inside. He always got what he wanted—and right now he wanted Herrick off his back.

Dougal scoured the town for Mr. O'Brien. He would ask for work and complete his investigation in the process. And then he'd...

He didn't know what.

By day's end his belly and his search for O'Brien had come up empty. How could it be so hard to find a man whose name was on every building in town? Especially when the town wasn't that big? And when he'd just been in an alley talking to someone named Herrick. Maybe the guy had invisibility powers. It would figure Cian sent him back in time to a place with beings stronger than him.

He dropped onto a bench outside the tavern and palmed his chin. Raucous howls and music came from within. Maybe he should enter. He could easily swipe something from a plate and maybe even ask about O'Brien first. Besides, they might have fried chicken.

He was such an idiot. He'd had a bed to sleep in, food to eat, people who cared, and he'd left it. Maybe he should return to the farm. Maybe his job wasn't finished yet after all. He could tell the family he'd snuck into town to surprise them.

Yeah. That was what he'd do.

Rising, he dusted off his breeches. The new boots had left blisters on his feet. If only he could fly back—but there was an extraordinary number of soldiers hanging around and no place to transform without walking a ways first. Maybe if he soaked in the creek first, then he could make the walk.

The creek was further out of town than he'd thought and by the time he reached the bank he was hobbling. Gnarled tree roots formed a perfect chair. He settled into it, pulled off the boots, and slipped his red, aching toes into the cool, clear water. A sigh parted his lips as he leaned back. The soldiers had kind of thinned out as he'd walked, and he hadn't seen any for the last ten minutes. Maybe after he dragged his aching body off the ground, he could try changing. The thought of wind beneath his wings made his heart soar.

But as he imagined it, a flash of reflected sunlight blinded him. He squinted. Where was that coming from? Narrowing his eyes against the glare, he looked harder, peering between trees. A house? He didn't remember seeing that on the way into town, but he hadn't been looking off to the side.

Should he transform and return to the farm, or should he check out the house and see if they knew anything about O'Brien? The people in town hadn't known where he was or if they did, they weren't sharing it with a stranger, but someone out in the sticks might not mind telling him. The Hesses could be in danger if more gryphons were in the area. His pulse deepened and picked up speed at the thought. Here could be his opportunity to pay them back for their kindness.

Pulling his feet from the water and putting on his boots was one of the hardest things he'd ever had to do. Each step rubbed another hole in his instep or heel. He gritted his teeth as he hobbled along the driveway. Next time he was flying. He didn't care who saw him.

Finally he reached the huge white farmhouse. The wrap-around porch sported four white rocking chairs and a round table. Chickens ran between the house and a barn on the east side, clucking and pecking at the ground. Two goats munched grass, actively ignoring the chickens. He could hear horses neighing and cows mooing, but he couldn't see them. He also didn't see any humans. But the house didn't look empty or abandoned. The flowers were tended and the white paint gleamed.

He listened, and beneath the animal sounds heard the unmistakable *thunk* of splitting wood. Another *thunk* as he walked around the side of the house, and as he rounded the second corner, a shirtless man, his back riddled with pink scars, hoisted an ax over his shoulder and brought it down into a positioned log. Ribs poked through his skin. Dougal frowned. The guy was too skinny to be working so hard, as if he'd recently been ill. Maybe this was his chance to get a meal and some information, but looking at the young man didn't give Dougal much confidence on the meal.

"Excuse me?" Hopefully the fellow didn't have a gun nearby.

He lowered the ax and shielded his eyes. "Howdy."

Dougal cleared his dry throat. "I-I was wondering if I might be able to help you chop wood for a bite to eat."

The man scratched his head. The black curls gleamed with collected sweat. "I don't know. I can ask the massa."

So the young man was a slave, and the knowledge brought a weird sort of cringe to Dougal's innards. With those scars, he should have realized. He still planned to be polite. "I would be obliged to you."

"I'm Elijah."

"Nice to meet you, Elijah. I'm Dougal." He held out his hand, but Elijah didn't take it. Dougal lowered his hand. He understood.

Elijah leaned the ax against the woodpile and pulled his shirt on. The cloth's edges were ratty, but it was clean. "I'll go ask the massa." With a clean stride—no shuffling—Elijah strode away.

Watching him go, Dougal kicked at the dusty ground. What if massa said no? Would Elijah be willing to answer his questions about O'Brien? Or would he consider it beyond his duties? Elijah didn't seem like someone who could be conned or bullied. Too self-contained, too certain within himself. That such a man could be a slave seemed utterly wrong.

His stomach growled. Food-type smells drifted through an

open window, tantalizing his senses and setting his mouth watering. He wasn't going to make it. He just wasn't.

Then a side door slammed. Elijah bounded down three steps. "The massa says y' can help in return for one meal."

"Thank you."

Without waiting for another word from Elijah, Dougal lifted the ax and swooped downward on the waiting log. The wood split in two and fell to opposite sides. He didn't plan to waste any time.

In between ax swings, he stacked wood and positioned the next log to be cut. Sweat beaded on his forehead and ran into his eyes. Not having a bandana, he wiped it with his shirttail. Ma would be furious when he returned home. *Home.* He liked the idea of having one.

Again he set the ax aside, propping it against the massive slice of log that served as a block. Straightening, he rubbed his back and paused for breath. Strange how the exercise had cleared his mind.

A line of trees surrounded the property, the same line he'd peered through earlier to see the house. He hadn't used his gryphon abilities much since being sent to the past. If he thought about it, he wasn't entirely certain which abilities he'd retained. Did he still have that super distance vision? He couldn't remember if he'd tried that out or not.

Now might be a good time to see what he could still do. He squinted and the woods' hidden secrets came into focus.

A multitude of soldiers marched behind the trees, long untidy lines stretching away. If only he could see more, like the color they wore. Were they Union troops or Rebels? Should he worry about them or not? Did they endanger Mara and the Hess family?

A hand touched his shoulder. He jerked upright, whipped around, and came face to face with Elijah.

"The massa would like to see y'."

It couldn't be good that he'd been caught standing, doing nothing. "I hope he hasn't decided to take away my food."

Elijah heehawed. "No, suh, I don't think so."

"Then by all means, lead the way."

He'd not had time to question Elijah about O'Brien. Maybe he could do that after he ate. Elijah seemed like someone he'd like to get to know better.

He followed Elijah through the side door and into the hallway of the grand home. It was one of those plantation houses a person might read about in history books. The foyer floor was pure marble. Grecian columns reached for the ceiling. A winding oak staircase led to a sprawling second floor. Portraits of past family members lined the pristine walls. A parlor had been filled with richly covered furniture. Lace curtains hung upon the grandiose windows. Even in the future, he'd never been inside a place quite as extravagant.

A mirror. He hadn't really looked at himself in ages. But at the sight, he cringed. His attire was clearly unbefitting such a place and sweat matted his hair to his forehead. Hardly his most charming look. But he couldn't change now. Elijah pointed to a cracked-open door and he slipped inside.

A man sat in a large leather chair behind a desk, with his back to the door; only strands of thin black hair covering a balding head showed over the chair's back. He seemed familiar but Dougal couldn't quite place him. Then the chair swiveled around.

*Barry O'Brien...*

# 27

"Have you anything new to report?"

"No, sir. I'm afraid the silo is still unopened." O'Brien's inability to perform the simplest of tasks played into his hand so well.

"Why is the man so incompetent? I grow weary of waiting. There is a world to conquer."

"Aye, this is true. But the world will be much easier to conquer if we get what's in the silo." The statement was true, which was why he would secure the item for himself.

"I say we storm the blasted thing and take the weapon by force."

"Sir, you must not forget what the old woman said. We can't touch it. Only a complete human or a Jotunn can." He didn't believe the woman, but if the leader did that was all that mattered. It played into his plan perfectly.

The leader knocked over a table. "I know what the old woman said! I was there. I was the one who forced her to speak with her dying breath." He sighed. "What about Ailin? Has he been found?"

"No, sir." Ailin had kept his patrol out for too long for him to still be on the blacks' side. Why could the leader not see this?

"Well, of course not. That would make this too easy." He ran his hands through his fur. "How long has it been? The time must be soon."

"Yes, sir. The time is coming. Seventeen years have passed." He knew well the time. He'd watched and waited. He would be ready to enact his plan when the time was right.

"We have very little time left. The grays know the same things we know and they will come. They always come."

"Have you anything new to report?"

"No, sir. I'm afraid the silo is still unopened."

"Why is the man so incompetent? I grow weary of waiting. There is a town to conquer."

"Aye, this is true. But the town will be much easier to conquer if we get what is in the silo."

"I say we storm it and take the weapon by force."

A sense of *déjà vu* rushed over Herrick as he listened to Colonel Hastings, his earlier conversation with his other leader still running through his mind.

Hastings turned. "Have you heard anything more from O'Brien?"

"No, sir." He failed to add that he'd called the attack dog off.

"This is ridiculous. By now I could have raided the silo and taken everything within. We could have conquered the town and commandeered all the farmland in the area. Waiting is a bad idea."

"But sir, I have already spoken with O'Brien and he assures me the town will be ready. The Rebel soldiers will not fight back." Herrick didn't know how O'Brien planned to keep his Rebels from resisting, but he didn't care. Hastings wanted it done, his other leader wanted it done, so that was what he'd do, only in his own way.

"Well, it doesn't matter." Colonel Hastings leaned back in his chair.

"What?" His heart raced. If the colonel changed direction now, it could ruin his plan.

"I am no longer in charge of the operation."

"I don't understand." Herrick was baffled, and that didn't happen often.

"Headquarters has assigned the operation to another. If my theory proves correct, Mr. O'Brien is going to wish he had accomplished the task a whole lot earlier."

Herrick frowned. Which task did the colonel refer to? Retrieving the information from the silo or subduing the Rebel soldiers in town? Did that mean he needed to enact his own plan sooner rather than later?

Probably.

"Come, sit."

But the young man hesitated, so O'Brien tried to speak more reassuringly. "Don't worry for the furniture."

The boy clasped his hands and walked forward, perching on the edge of a plush chair. O'Brien thrilled to see the fellow who had lived with the Hess family for a while sitting across from him in his own office. If he hadn't been able to talk to Flint Hess earlier, now he'd been given a second chance.

He steepled his fingers but smiled so he'd appear non-threatening. "I take it you enjoyed your meal."

"Not yet."

"Oh, you haven't eaten?" Ellie should have fed him before sending him in. He wanted the young man buttered up and ready to share.

"No, sir."

"We shall rectify that." He stood and tugged the long braided rope.

A moment later, Ellie shuffled in with a tray of food and placed it on the boy's lap, which caused him to scoot further back in the chair. Despite his reassuring words, O'Brien cringed at the mud and sweat on his upholstery, but it would be worth it. Once he owned the Hess farm, he could take all the profits and buy new chairs.

He opened his mouth to tell the man to eat, but he needn't have bothered. The first biscuit was halfway to the boy's mouth before Ellie made it out the door.

"I take it that it's good?"

The boy nodded.

O'Brien clapped his hands and let a smile tilt the corner of his mouth. "Wonderful. Now, let's get down to business. Are you looking for work?"

Swallowing deeply, the boy replied, "Not exactly."

"Oh. Hmm, I thought Elijah said you wanted to chop wood and help out for food." He did add the helping out part, but it was to serve his purpose. He needed someone to discover the contents of the silo. What better person than a friend of Flint Hess? He was sure he could work that to his advantage in the future, even though he didn't know how at the moment.

The boy sopped his second biscuit in gravy. "I wouldn't be opposed to working a few days for some more food, and maybe some boots. My feet are killing me."

O'Brien clapped. That was what he'd wanted to hear. "Good. You see, I need a job done. And there seems to be no one in this town who is capable of doing anything. Such a shame." He shook his head. "But I digress. If you are willing to do this tiny favor for me, then I'll gladly purchase you a new pair of boots and feed you while you're here."

The boy lowered his fork. Was he thinking about the offer? "I guess it depends on what you want me to do. And just so you know, after I've gotten my new boots I'll be moving on."

"But of course. Few people make this area their permanent residence. That's one reason the train station is so popular." He crossed his fingers in his lap beneath the desk. He may have just gotten Herrick off his back at the cost of a pair of boots.

"I'll have to hear the details before I give my answer."

He needed to describe the job perfectly so the boy didn't get scared off. He inhaled, thinking fast. "I have some friends, important friends, who want to know what is inside a certain building. I seem to be having a hard time finding the answers they seek. Do you think you could help me?"

That earned him a long stare. "So let me get this straight. All you want me to do is tell you what is inside a building?"

"Precisely." The boy understood. That eased some of his burden.

The boy shrugged. "I don't see why not."

"Excellent." He clapped. Finally his luck was changing.

# 28

Mara broke beans and snuffled. Dougal was still gone. She'd held out hope for the first couple of days that he'd return, but going on day three, it was looking bleaker.

Dishes rattled behind her. "Ma, I can't stand it. Mara mopes around all day. We know she ain't supposed to be normal, and she don't feel things, but there has to be a way to help her."

"Maude, we can't help her. She has the love sickness. Poor child." Ma patted her head and Mara withheld her visible cringe.

"Why did Dougal leave?" Maude sat at the table and palmed her chin.

Ma collapsed beside them and started shelling peas. "Who knows? Maybe he wasn't meant for farming. Though I would have thought the boy would have had enough decency to say goodbye. But maybe it was just too hard for him."

"Well, when I see him, I think I'm going to give him a piece of my mind." Maude slapped her hands on the tabletop and Mara jumped.

Having Maude rise to her defense felt decidedly odd.

"Not if I get a hold of him first." Junior entered the cabin carrying a load of wood.

"Now what?" Ma paused, her hands cradling unshelled peas.

"How could he leave Mara like that? Pa gave him permission to woo her and then he just ups and leaves! He better be far away, 'cause if'n I see 'im, he might not survive." Junior stacked the wood by slamming it into place in the firebox. She was glad for his protection even as she felt bad for Dougal.

Ma shook her finger. "Now, Junior, don't go spouting off at the mouth. Let's just keep workin' and eventually Mara will forget she ever met 'im."

The dining room chair formed to her backside as she dropped the last peas into the bucket. Sometimes they forgot that just because she couldn't speak, that didn't mean she couldn't hear.

Tears coated her eyes. She closed them and prayed that she could hold in her emotions. Her mother was wrong; she would never forget Dougal. With his coal black eyes and hair and his voodoo charm? He could have been the only person who believed she had the ability to communicate, that she wasn't a complete dummy.

Her throat closed on a sob. She needed to get out. She couldn't stand the pity.

She pushed her chair back and stumbled from the room.

The barn wall scratched through her cotton dress as she leaned back against it and lifted her eyes skyward. The secret she carried, the vow she had made, that was what had done this. If only she had opened her mouth and spoken to Dougal, then perhaps he would have stayed. She knew he would.

She closed her eyes. Ten years. She had been young and curious and decided to skip down to the creek. Barefoot, she had stepped into the water. Cool liquid had washed over her legs and baby tadpoles had tickled her toes until she giggled with delight. Shiny scales had reflected blue in the summer sun. She had used her hands for balance and stumbled along the smooth rocks in hopes of touching the colorful fish.

Then a shadow had fallen over her. A reflection of two legs had rippled across the water's surface. Curiosity had gripped her. She'd never known a bad person in the small farming community of Coal Creek, so she'd thought surely it would be all right to introduce herself. She had kept her chin down as she rose to her feet and plastered a smile on her face. But when she'd looked up, a gasp had left her mouth and she'd fallen backward. The tug of the creek water had jerked her downstream right as a clawed hand whipped out toward her neck. But the water hadn't been moving fast enough and the giant beast had caught her. He had lifted her at the waist with his furry hands. The sun had been blocked by large wings.

And then it spoke.

*"You," he growled.*

*"Me?"*

*Gruffly and breathlessly, he said, "It cannot be."*

*Hanging from the beast's claws, Mara lifted her lip at the corner and shifted her hands to her hips. "I don't know who you are looking for, but I'm certainly me."*

*"I can't believe it."*

*"You can't believe it? What do you think about me? What in the world are you?" She tilted her head and studied the creature. He didn't seem so scary from her current angle. Although he was big, kind of like a bear, only with wings. Did bears grow wings? She should ask Pa.*

*"I'm a gryphon."*

*She drew her brows together and twirled a strand of hair around her finger. "A what?"*

*"I'm a gryphon. Actually, I'm a black gryphon."*

*Mara shrugged. "I can see that. I learned my colors a long time ago."*

*He released her and she wobbled until she got her balance. The water was bone cold, but she wouldn't shiver and let the bear-gryphon think she was scared.*

*"You mean you do not know the significance?"*

*"I can't say that I do. Should I?"*

*"This is very odd." An appendage resembling a finger tapped at his forehead.*

*"You're tellin' me. I was just comin' down here to skip pebbles and I wasn't expectin' to see no flyin', talkin' creature. I'm still not sure you're real." She stepped forward and poked him. He sucked in his abdomen before releasing it with huff.*

*"Then you are not afraid of me?"*

*"I am a little bit. Let's face it, you're kind of scary."*

*He grasped her by the collar of her wet dress and hauled her into the air. Her feet dangled over the water's surface and her heart pounded. The creature breathed deeply and a noxious odor drifted to her face. "You will listen to me."*

*Lip trembling, Mara nodded. Like she had a choice.*

*"You will go home and you will not speak a word. If you speak, I will know it and I will come back and kill your entire family. Do you understand?"*

*"Of course I do. You don't want anyone to know you're out here flying around. I got it."*

*Her head lolled back and forth as the creature shook her roughly. "I don't think you do. You're going to promise me. This is our little secret. If you ever speak and I hear you, I will come. And you don't want me to come back and visit, do you?"*

*Mara shook her head until it felt like her brains would fall out.*

*"Good."*

*Her breath whooshed out as the creature dropped her. Tears streamed down her cheeks. The creature stepped from the water, spread his wings, and flew away. She waited a few moments before jumping to her feet and sprinting home.*

*Words formed in her head about how she would explain to Ma and Pa what she had seen. They knew she never told a lie, so there was no doubt in her mind they would believe her. But as she ran into the yard and saw her family on the lawn laughing, speech stuck in her throat.*

*The sound of beating wings rushed to her ears, and she looked up and around to ensure she hadn't been followed. She slowed her steps and eyed her favorite tree. Greenery hung from the wooden branches, almost touching the ground. Slowly, she approached, parted the vines, and stepped inside the enclosure. With her back against the trunk, she pulled her legs to her body and rocked.*

A shovel clanged against the barn wall on the inside, the sound jarring her. She blinked as present day set in. She had promised to keep the gryphon's presence a secret because speaking could have put her family in jeopardy. And she'd not broken that promise.

Looking back on her decision, she had no regrets. This group of people, whether her blood relatives or not, was all she had. Dougal had been a passing fancy. She'd made the right decision to maintain her silence. To risk her family for him wasn't worth it. His leaving had proven that.

# 29

In three days Dougal had gotten everything he'd hoped for. O'Brien trusted him and he'd been fed. Now he just had to do this one job. He'd gather the information that he hoped would help the Hess family, and then he'd return to the farm.

The directions were so simple that any idiot could have followed them, so why Mr. O'Brien had so much trouble finding someone to do the job baffled him. But he wasn't one to spend too long questioning. Everything had worked out in his favor, so he was going to roll with that.

An updraft carried him high above the silo. It felt good to fly, even if he'd had trouble transforming. Grays didn't change easily, and he'd had a hard time convincing his body that transforming now would protect his person. There were always those magic words Serena had taught him, but he couldn't bear that; it was in the past. And deep down he knew what he found inside the silo would help Mara—even if he didn't yet have all the answers.

A sentry stood guard in front of the silo, just as Mr. O'Brien had predicted. The guard glanced upward as he descended, fists clenched. It was perfect timing. The sentry widened his eyes and crumpled into a heap. Dougal hadn't even touched him.

He tucked his wings to his side and nudged the guard with his claw. The guard didn't move. At a guess, Dougal had about ten minutes before the kid came to. Hey, he'd have stories to tell his children and grandchildren for years. Hopefully the poor fellow wouldn't be in the loony bin for those stories.

Dougal strutted to the silo door. A board barred the entrance, but with his gryphon strength, he lifted the slab and set it aside with minimal effort. Ducking through the doorway, he entered the dark interior.

Light bleeding through the cracks and the open door didn't help much. He lit a dark lantern from the bag hanging around his neck and carefully positioned the shutter to prevent wandering sparks; chances were he'd run into some gunpowder and he'd rather not blow himself up. What he wouldn't give for a flashlight! He missed modern conveniences.

Rusting rifles leaned against a tower of wooden crates. He pried open a lid. More rifles were layered inside. He backed away, bumping into another crate. Inside was a haphazard assortment of Colt revolvers.

"This is stupid." What could Mr. O'Brien hope to find? How was this knowledge going to help the Hess family? It was clearly a storage facility for their primitive weapons. He'd just wasted his time and let the Hesses think he'd left for good. No, there had to be something more.

In the middle of the room, hidden among the piles of crates, a dusty blanket huddled atop... something. He lifted the covering and stared at what it protected. Could that be what O'Brien was looking for? The weapon he saw was a big deal. It could kill a lot of people, including people he was coming to love.

He backed out and closed the silo door, peering intently around to make sure no one watched him before he took flight. The hour was late, too late to return to the plantation and meet with Mr. O'Brien. Besides, he didn't want to go there. He wanted to go home—to the Hess farm. O'Brien could get the information about the silo from someone else. He wasn't going to be the one responsible for telling someone outside of the Rebel army about *that* weapon.

Twilight descended as he studied the valley spread out below him. Two houses sat on opposite sides of a thick mass of trees, and as he stared at them, it all became clear. He could have slapped himself. The O'Brien farm bordered the Hess farm. That had to be why O'Brien was willing to let Maude marry his son Beauford. Since he owned the town of Wheeler's Landing, his plan could only be to eventually take over Flint's property and all of Coal Creek as well. With Maude and Beauford's marriage, all the land would combine and O'Brien could expand his holdings.

Now he was definitely not sharing what he'd learned with O'Brien. He knew what was in there, so he could protect the Hess family. That was enough.

He landed at the edge of the Hess property. Lights winked in the cabin. The family was probably sitting down to Pa's evening reading. Dougal had a sudden urge to peek in the window and share in the nighttime ritual. It had been the only time he had been part of a family, and he had given it up to feel free. Was the sinking feeling in his stomach regret? Probably.

He transformed and angled his stride toward the cabin.

"What are you doing here?"

*Maude.*

His gut clenched. Had she seen him transform? He faced her, letting a grin take over his face. Charm always worked on the ladies. "I thought I would check on Mara."

She planted her hands on her hips. "She doesn't need you to just stop in and check on her. She's fine."

Dougal didn't believe her for a second, but he'd give her the benefit of the doubt. "Maybe I'm not fine."

"Who cares how you feel?" She lifted her lip in a sneer.

At least she was being honest about her feelings. It was a blow to his ego that his charms seemed to fail him when he needed them most. "All right. I guess I deserve that."

"You sure do. And worse. If Junior sees you, he's going to rip out your entrails and feed them to the hogs." She crossed her arms. "I think you should leave."

Rip out his entrails, huh? That didn't sound pleasant. "I respect that. I'll leave, but will you tell Mara I stopped by?"

"No, I won't. It would only cause her more pain." Maude turned on her heel and stalked toward the house.

Well, that reunion hadn't gone quite as he'd planned. He probably should have just waited until Mara came out and then revealed himself. She would have been more receptive—he hoped. At the same time, he didn't feel hopeless. He'd had too good, too solid a relationship with the Hess family for it to have evaporated over one day's absence. So they were mad at him. That would pass.

He returned to the cover of the trees and changed. The pain of transformation seemed greater than normal, agony tearing through his bones, and he forced himself not to scream. Being a gray definitely had its disadvantages.

Again he looked around, this time with a sigh. Where could he go? He'd slept under the stars before, but he didn't feel like doing that tonight. The Hesses were going to need time to trust him again. Town didn't care for strangers right now—and there was the matter of money.

Since he had nowhere else to go, he'd just return to the O'Brien farm. Maybe Elijah could put him up without telling O'Brien he'd returned. Yeah, right. Now he really was living in a dream world.

Mara peered out the upstairs bedroom window, hidden in the shadows, as Maude dismissed Dougal. To her astonishment, he dropped his head and walked away. He didn't argue or question. What on earth was he thinking? He could take Junior in a fight! Why was he giving up so easily?

Mara collapsed on the bed. Tears stung her eyes and she angrily swiped them away. Was that who she wanted to be? Did she want to remain a timid little girl frightened by the shadows she hid in? Did she want to look back on her life with regret? Could she really let Dougal just walk away? Her head said yes, but her heart said no. Dougal was the one. She had to go after him, even if he'd bewitched her with his voodoo magic. He was worth it.

She jumped from the bed and rushed down the creaky stairs. The family barely glanced her way as she dashed past and slammed out the front door.

Panting, she stopped beneath a copse of trees. Dougal had been headed in this direction. Where had he gone? Determination, anger, and fear all swirled within her.

More shadows fell, hiding her in their depths. Her stomach clenched. She held her hand to her chest as she peered upward. A giant bird-like creature circled over the cabin. Something inside her tore. She ran for home, flailing her arms and screaming.

The family tumbled onto the front porch. "Mara?" Pa's brows formed a single bar over his nose.

She grabbed his arm and tried to tug him off the porch. But he wouldn't budge. She'd already screamed; it was too late to pretend otherwise. Awkwardly, her mouth formed the words she needed. "Pa, we have to hide."

But still no one moved. Shock froze them in place. Mara swallowed. Her voice sounded strange and foreign, but there was no time. They had to leave!

"Are you listenin' to me? We have to get out of here. The creature is back." Words she'd hidden for too long burst free. "Listen, I tried. I really did. I've not spoken for ten years, so you know I tried. But now I have to talk. I can't stand it no longer! I want to be normal and have a normal life. I want to talk to Dougal and you, my family. But none of us will live long enough to talk about anything if we don't get out of here!"

They blinked; their mouths opened and closed with no sound. She ran her hands through her hair and tapped her toes against the ground. It wasn't working. Forget it! She'd try running, and hopefully they'd follow. Whether they did or not, she would use the weapons in the barn herself. She was no longer afraid.

The ladder to the loft was old and rickety, and the loft above lay buried in darkness. The rungs threatened to snap beneath her meager weight, but still she climbed, wondering how Junior managed the feat every night. Finally she reached the platform above, panting and dizzy. The world spun and stars flashed before her eyes. She stretched out her hand and staggered forward. Somewhere in front of her waited the piled haystack where Junior slept each night, with the shotguns buried inside.

She brushed the barn's windowsill and then there was nothing beneath her.

Wind whipped through her hair as she fell. Shocked, she wrapped her head with her arms. Every bone in her body would break, and she braced for impact. But it wasn't what she expected. The ground felt warm—almost hairy.

She opened her eyes. Treetops whistled below. Terror returned. This wasn't good. Did the creature have her?

What had she done?

Dougal had been on his way to the O'Brien farm when he felt Mara's distress. Hearing her scream as she tumbled from the barn's loft opening had been bittersweet. She needed him after all, but the terror in her scream ripped through him.

Saving her had been easy; knowing what to do with her afterwards, not so simple. When she opened her steel gray eyes, she stiffened, and his heart broke. With her fear of Maeldun, how could he ever tell her the truth about himself? It was best he left and let her go. Maude had been right.

Finding a spot not too far from the farm, he landed and set her on her feet. Hoping to calm her, he backed away several paces and held his hands upward, palms flat. He thought he looked non-threatening, but he was formidable regardless so it was hard to be sure.

She hugged her middle. That gesture would do little good against a black gryphon, but he had changed, and seeing her trying to protect herself—from him!—broke his heart.

And then she spoke. "What do you want from me?"

His soul soared with joy. She sounded... *right*. The lilting tones reminded him of a warm summer's day, and he closed his eyes and soaked it in.

"Are you listenin' to me? I know you aren't the one who threatened my family so many years ago. You're different. But just because you're a different flying beast doesn't mean you don't want somethin'. So what do you want?"

She was feisty. He liked it. "I know not what I want."

"What kind of answer is that? How can you not know what you want?"

"I have a task to perform. Nothing more." At least that had been Cian's orders for Nuada, but Dougal didn't know if he cared any more. His life, what he really needed to take care of, was standing before him.

She blinked. "A task?"

"Yes. Once my work is complete, I'll be called away." At least he thought he would be.

Mara chewed her bottom lip, causing tingles to shoot down his spine. He took an unconscious step forward, his hand outstretching toward her soft cheek. But her face twisted and she took a step back. "Don't touch me."

He dropped his hand to his side. This was not going as he'd planned. Speech was supposed to be their only obstacle; now it seemed there was another, and maybe more.

"I must leave. You're close to home. Go in safety."

"But—"

He didn't give her time to argue before he took flight. He'd told the truth; he did have a task to complete. He would finish his business with O'Brien, if only so he could discover why the man was curious about those weapons, and then he would return to the Hess farm and beg forgiveness. Now that Mara was speaking, he'd make it work. He would just never change again. It was that simple.

He arrived at the O'Brien home in a few minutes. All the candles were trimmed, and everyone had bedded down for the night.

Darkness and shadows hid him from view as he transformed and approached the house on foot. Whether to bang on the door and wait for someone to answer or to just enter and find the master of the house was the question. No alarms or security bells would go off if he opened the door, although he might get hit on the head with a broom or a frying pan by a household slave.

He decided to err on the side of caution and knocked. In a few minutes, the door opened. O'Brien himself answered, arrayed in an embroidered dressing gown and slippers. He'd not expected that.

"What are you doing here?" O'Brien drew his brows together.

That was no way to talk to someone doing a favor. The meals hadn't been that good. "I have the information you wanted." He should have added, *But I don't know if I'm giving it to you.*

O'Brien opened the door further and then led him to the study. Dougal took the same chair as before, careful to sit on the edge, while O'Brien settled on the corner of the desk. "What did you find?"

"Right to the point, I see." Dougal crossed his legs. Let the man stew. He deserved it.

"I don't have time for games. This is important to a—a partner of mine. What did you find?"

*A partner?* It had to be the guy from town, the one he'd overheard speaking with O'Brien. Apparently returning here had been a good idea, after all. "The place was dark, but I saw Confederate rifles, Colt revolvers, some Ketchum grenades, and some boxes of ammunition."

"Was that it?" O'Brien's voice rose in a squeak.

"Impatient, aren't we?"

"Don't try me. Get on with what you found."

The guy had *fed* him, nothing more. Food had to be worth a lot more during the 1860s. "The only other thing was covered."

"Well, man? What was it? You did look, didn't you?"

"Of course I looked. I'm nothing if not thorough." Dougal

leaned back in the chair. He would have whistled, but it seemed a little inconsiderate. Well, okay, even more inconsiderate. When O'Brien narrowed his eyes in impatience, he finished. "A Gatling gun."

"What?" O'Brien widened his eyes. *Guess the man's surprised.* He'd been, as well. The Rebs must have stolen it. He didn't remember them having the capacity to make such a gun. But history wasn't his favorite subject. That would be women. He loved women.

But the image in his mind wasn't just any woman.

He waited, but he might as well not even have been in the room. O'Brien paced and talked to himself for the next twenty minutes. Finally, bored beyond reason, Dougal rose. O'Brien continued to ignore him. It seemed like a good time to slip out.

Feeling free for the first time in weeks, he made his way to the kitchen. A loaf of bread sat on the counter, and he pulled off a piece and popped it into his mouth. A large silver moon filled the night sky. Cool air seeped around the wooden window frame, bringing in the vague hint of honeysuckle. Memories swept over him. Mara sitting on a rock beating old clothes. Mara bringing him water. Mara smiling at him. Mara watching him. Mara's pulse beating wildly at his touch.

Women, yeah. There appeared only one answer for his future and now that he'd finished sharing his information, he was going to collect on his future. He'd deal with Maude and Junior.

"You're sure?"

They'd met in O'Brien's room at the hotel. Around them, Wheeler's Landing bustled at a lower pitch. Most of the farmers had left the valley. All that remained were the townspeople, the soldiers, the few farmers not bankrupted by the drought, O'Brien and Ivy, and of course the Hess family. The town wasn't silent—even through the solid window, a wagon rattled as it passed—but it had been diminished, and no one could deny that.

O'Brien nodded. "Yes, I have it on the best authority. They're hiding a Gatling gun."

"Nothing else?" Herrick's hands clasped in his lap, twisting viciously.

Was he expecting something more? Wasn't a Gatling gun enough? He'd been horrified since he'd heard. With that gun, many lives would be lost for the North. It might ruin his chances with his *friends.*

"The usual collection of rifles and revolvers, the same stuff they've been using. But this is big news, right? This is what you've been searching for?"

The disappointment on Herrick's face wasn't promising. But he said, "Of course. Thank you." Then he drummed his fingers on his thigh, as if distracted.

"Is everything still set for two days hence?" Maybe they'd changed their minds. He hoped so. The town wouldn't be ready for an invasion force and the Rebs wouldn't be ready to stand down if it were any sooner—he'd just started his plan of action.

"Yes. Will you be ready?"

"But of course." What else could he say? *No, I won't be ready, so please postpone your invasion.* He didn't think such timidity would be well received.

"Good. Now I'm going to leave you. Remember our deal."

"How could I forget." His sarcasm prevented the words from being a question.

The door clicked closed and he turned toward the window. Even at the lower tempo, Wheeler's Landing moved along just fine. The train ran on schedule. The bank had opened. The store boasted a few purchasing customers. Yes, everything was working like clockwork.

O'Brien removed his golden watch fob for the thousandth time. When would the moment arrive? Would he be looking out this very window in two days when the Northern army entered and overran his town, or would he be at home snug in his bed, pretending to be none the wiser to the town's predicament? If he had a choice, he'd rather be in a different country. As mayor, he might be called on to make decisions. Telling the people to roll over and let the Union take their town didn't sound like it would be well received.

The train whistle jarred him. He spun on his heel and strode down the hotel stairs, along the boardwalk, and to the tavern. Stools sported the morning usual of soldiers in gray. The night before, the tavern had graciously offered all Rebel soldiers a night of free drinking. They could consume all they desired, plus have a free night of rest in one of the rooms above. It was the only way to make sure every soldier within a mile radius would stay alive. If they were included in the revelry for the next two days, then there was no way they could fight back.

Even now some of the men lay against the wall, liquid dribbled onto their already stained uniforms. His hope was that they would be too drunk to fight and thereby reduce casualties.

Sunlight blinded him as he left the building and stepped into the street. He covered his eyes, peering toward the train depot, and his heart skipped a beat. A soldier arrayed in a blue uniform held his sword aloft and shouted a war cry that echoed along the narrow street.

What was happening? It was too early. Two days! He'd been promised two more days! The soldiers were not nearly soused enough. Would they fight back? Would there be a battle in the middle of his town?

Horses' hooves thundered down Main Street. Townspeople scurried out of the way, some grabbing their children and pulling them to their sides. Soldiers in blue seemed to multiply, scurrying around like ants. The leader of the invasion force stopped in the middle of the street. O'Brien hid his smile and searched for a familiar face. Although he had mainly dealt with Herrick, there were others in the Union army he should recognize. He drew his brows together. He recognized no one. It made no sense.

The leader shouted, "Find every Rebel soldier you can and bring them back to camp. Then burn the town."

Burn the town? What?

O'Brien's heart thumped rapidly against his ribs as he ran in front of the lead horse. He opened his mouth, but a riding crop slapped his face and sent him spinning to the ground. If not for the patrons of the store nearby who dragged him to safety, O'Brien would have been trampled underneath the pounding feet of the dancing horses.

The roundup of the Rebel forces took less than five minutes. Jolly laughter could be heard from the blue-coated Union troops over how easy it was, taking the soldiers and the town. Jokes passed back and forth about their drunken state. The Rebel soldiers were tied together and led staggering down the road as prisoners. The Union soldiers lit torches and threw them at the foundation of each building. The people who were inside rushed out by every available exit.

O'Brien watched in horror as the legacy he had built burned to the ground, and he realized he was the one responsible for making it happen.

# 30

Volunteers came from nearby farms to assist, but it offered O'Brien little solace. Everything was destroyed.

The bank lay in ruins. The vault, which had been a poorly constructed wooden apparatus, had burned, too, turning all the money inside to ash. The tavern roof had collapsed, smashing tables, the stage, and priceless bottles of spirits, which had helped the town burn all the hotter. The general store's inventory had been demolished and bits of charred fabric floated through the air. The hotel had toppled like an ant hill stomped by a child. The only building intact was the train depot, well separated from the rest of the town, and it sported a few sooty patches.

The fires had just burned out. Townsfolk sifted through the rubble, picking out what little they could salvage. The sun of a hot August day knew no mercy and it beat heavily upon their backs.

As the men and women worked, O'Brien mulled over the disaster. Somewhere he'd gone terribly wrong. All his planning, all the scheming to make his holdings grander, to give himself more land, and for what? Everything was gone. He just didn't understand. Captain Herrick had promised the Union soldiers would do nothing more than take over the town and commandeer the weapons from the silo. After their raid, he was supposed to be placed in charge of the land taken by the army.

Herrick had some explaining to do.

He cast a glance over his shoulder before clambering astride a handy nag ground-tied outside the town's remains, lazily picking at the grass.

He nudged the horse with the heel of his boot. He'd return it later. The owner was probably so busy sorting through his belongings, he'd never notice its temporary absence.

Herrick and his men camped not far outside of town. He'd find out what had gone wrong and he'd be in control once more.

O'Brien galloped into the camp and hauled on the reins before colliding with a tent. He dismounted, hitched his pants higher, and shuffled to the grinning captain. "Herrick! What is the meaning of this?"

With a nonchalant shrug, the captain replied, "What do you mean?"

"We had a deal!" He could hardly breathe. Herrick was acting like they'd not worked together.

"Yes." Herrick crossed his arms over his chest and tilted his head.

"And you broke it by burning the whole town!"

He shook his head. "Not I."

"Are you trying to tell me you had nothing to do with this fiasco? I gave you everything you asked. I was to be rewarded!" He was yelling but he didn't care. Everything had been ruined.

"As well you shall be."

"How exactly am I going to be rewarded? Everything I own lies in shambles. There's no money left to rebuild. If the people ever find out I'm responsible, I'll swing from a tree!"

"Then don't tell them."

He huffed a breath and fisted his hands. "I didn't plan on telling them. But someone will have to take the blame. And you know what I think? I think it should be you!"

He didn't even have time to inhale. He was thrust against a tree trunk and held there with one arm across his neck. Herrick clenched his teeth. "Never threaten me."

Panicking, O'Brien struggled to breathe. Finally Herrick released him, and he fell to the ground and massaged his raw neck.

"You will tell the townspeople that Dougal Lachlan is to blame. He told the Union commander of the town's vulnerability."

"Dougal? You mean the one who retrieved the information about the silo? And why would they believe him responsible?"

Herrick's plan seemed flawed, but it was better than him taking the blame.

Herrick patted his shoulder. "Does it matter? A good rumor is all that's needed. I'll plant some of my own men in town. They'll insist they witnessed Lachlan orchestrate the entire event."

"But what did he have to gain?"

Herrick sighed, impatience thick in his tone. "I tell you, it doesn't matter. He is your scapegoat."

"Yes, of course. But what about my property? What about the town? They burned everything. What is the plan now?"

"Don't you worry. Leave everything to me."

He muttered, "That's what got me into this in the first place."

# 31

Mara worked in the fields alongside Maude, pulling weeds and hauling water to the irrigation channels. Wagonloads of people passed the farm throughout the day. Pots swinging from ropes clanged against the wagons' uneven sides with each horse's step, drawing their eyes again and again.

She arched her back, stretching it the other way, and wiped sweat from her brow. Something had happened in town. Why else would so many more people be leaving?

About noon, a wagonload of wailing children and ragged parents stopped at the driveway. Before she could take a second glance, Pa had already laid down his hoe and made a beeline for them.

The father climbed down, his hat in his hands. "Begging your pardon, but could we bother you for some water?"

Maude grabbed the bucket and ran to the well before the sentence was finished. The man and his family drank greedily, and she found them an extra bucket to carry on the road with them.

Pa shoved his hat back on his head. "Would you like to come in for a spell?"

The father shook his head. "No, thanks. We're getting out of here as quick as our poor old horse will take us."

Pa narrowed his eyes. "Did something happen?"

"Sure did. Union soldiers done came through and burned the entire town to the ground."

Mara held a hand over her heart. It thudded beneath her palm, strangely hard and loud.

Pa blinked. "But how? The Rebs are everywhere. And they got all those weapons."

"Weapons? What a joke! The silo was raided because the Confederates didn't have but one youngster guarding the thing. I could have robbed them blind!"

"How did they know where to look?"

Mara felt sick. Who could have given up his countrymen so easily?

The father shrugged. "Some new feller."

Everyone tensed.

"Who?"

The father scratched his head. "I think they called him Douglas, or something like that."

Mara gasped.

"Douglas, or Dougal?" Pa's arms dropped slack to his sides.

"Dougal, that's it."

No, that couldn't be right. Dougal couldn't possibly have had anything to do with this. There had to be a mistake. He would never lead soldiers to Wheeler's Landing nor allow them to destroy it.

Mara ran. No one followed. Maybe they still thought her daft; it didn't matter. She needed solitude, and there was only one place she could find it.

It had taken days, but by retracing her steps, she'd found the cave, the one she had shared with Nuada. It wasn't quite as easy to get into without wings, but after close inspection, she'd found the crevice she'd used for her escape. The opening was just big enough to squeeze through if she flattened herself as much as possible.

She slid in. The sun was high in the sky and light poured through tiny holes in the ceiling. Yellow and silver flecks glinted off the smooth rock walls. Ahead, a distorted voice echoed, distant and lonely. She stopped.

"I'm such a fool. I had it all! Everything I ever desired, right there in my hands, and I threw it all away. For what? To have a false sense of freedom. Now I'm a suspect! They'll never accept me now.

"Cian, do you hear me? I want out of here! Do you understand? I'm done. I'm finished. I've done everything you asked. And if I had any other directives, I don't remember them."

The floor vibrated and she fell against the wall. For a moment, raw terror closed her throat.

The voice wasn't finished. "Why won't you speak to me? I need a dream. A memory. Something... anything. Please help me!"

The floor shook again, shaking her out of her terror. She should probably turn around and go home. Whoever was shouting was strong, if he could shake solid rock. He also seemed like he wanted privacy. Her intrusion might not be well received. But no, her curiosity wouldn't be denied. She had to see. She had to know who it was, because... yeah. The voice sounded so familiar.

Carefully, she peered around the corner. Someone knelt on the floor, head bent, hands together. The light in the room wasn't bright enough for her to make out any features, though. She needed to get closer.

But her foot slipped in the loose dirt. She yelped. Suddenly she was flung to the ground, the wind knocked from her. Crushing weight fell on her, and she had no more air for yelping.

Above her, he growled, and she trembled. Her fear was back with a vengeance. Whoever he was, disrupting his yelling might not have been the best idea.

"What do you want?" the man's voice rumbled.

The voice was even more familiar now that she was close. She inhaled. The smell of pine teased her nostrils. Reaching up, she cradled the rough cheek. It felt familiar, too. Could it be? "Dougal?"

The pain in her ribs dissipated as the weight lifted from her. With a jerk, he whirled around, away from her, and leaned against the far cave wall. "Go away."

"Dougal!" It really was him! He hadn't left town. Although that meant he could be responsible for what the stranger claimed—but she didn't believe it. He wouldn't do such a thing. Sure, he gave eggs for gifts and he had some kind of voodoo magic over her feelings, but giving up a town to be destroyed was not one of the things he would do. Despite his order, she started toward him.

"Mara, please go away. You don't need to be here."

Suddenly unsure, she paused. "But why are *you* here? What's happening? People are sayin' you helped burn the town. Then I find you in here talking to yourself."

Dougal faced her, self-loathing evident in his rigid being. He stalked toward her, yanking off his shirt and casting it aside.

Next, he kicked off his boots and ripped his breeches from his legs. His power and beauty mingled, sending tingles of excitement through her limbs. Her throat constricted. He was gorgeous, but what on earth...? Why was he undressing?

Then she realized. With each step, a new change occurred. Fur sprouted over his exposed body, claws descended from his fingertips, and fangs protruded from his lips. Wings fanned to his sides. His legs stretched and changed until a monster towered above her.

Terror won. She dropped to her knees. She was going to be sick. But she couldn't stop the words that poured from her. "I'm so sorry. I said I wouldn't tell. I said I wouldn't speak. And I've not done so for ten long years. But I had to talk now. I had to. Why? Why did you do this to me? Why did you torture me and lead me to believe you would kill my family if I spoke of you? Why did you show up at the farm pretendin' to have lost your identity? What do you want from me?"

He grabbed her hand and lifted her to her feet, turning her face toward him. "Mara, I'm not Maeldun."

"What?" His fur was soft as a newborn kitten's. She could rub it all day, and it seemed perfectly natural for her to do so.

"I'm Nuada, remember? Remember, I helped you when the other gryphon was chasing you?" He ran his hand over his head. "And I think I was sent to protect you."

"You think?" This was more and more confusing. Sent?

"I know it sounds crazy, but Cian, the leader of the gray gryphons, sent me from the future." He drew in a ragged breath. "It's hard to explain. I don't even understand it myself. All I know is I was sent to protect you from Maeldun and that's what I've done. Now I think I need to go home. To my own time."

"How have you protected me from Maeldun?" She needed to keep him talking. Had Nuada harmed Dougal? They couldn't always have been the same. No, it was another voodoo trick. Or maybe she hadn't had enough sleep. Or maybe when the earth shook, she'd hit her head. That was the most logical explanation.

"I killed him."

She shook her head. "No, you didn't."

His thick brows knitted together. "Yes, I did. I slit his throat."

"Then he must have a twin, because I've seen him. He visited the farm."

Nuada gripped her upper arms. "That's not possible."

"I'm tellin' you, he came back." Nuada didn't listen any better than Dougal. Maybe they *were* the same.

"That must be why I'm still here. You're not as safe as I thought." He massaged his chin.

"I guess not. Does this mean you'll come back to the farm?" Was she crazy? She was actually asking a flying monster to come home with her?

He squeezed his eyelids tightly closed. She hurried to continue. "I know this may sound strange, but I want to get to know you. There's something about you that draws me. Of course, I do know some things about you, but not near enough. I've been dying to speak this whole time. Do you know how much you've tormented me? I mean, gettin' within a hair of touchin' my lips and then withdrawin'? Why, I don't think I've ever experienced more torture in my entire life."

She pointed at his chest. "And I personally think you have some explainin' to do. How did you think you were goin' to continue to live on the farm and not tell me about your secret? I'm not very happy that you tried to hide your identity from me. Why, I almost fell from the barn and done killed myself 'cause of fear. But you did save me. I think you have done that quite a bit. Saved me, I mean."

She massaged his hand. "Even though you don't want to, I hope you'll stay around and save me a few more times."

Dougal's heart pounded. Mara had spoken. She'd spoken to him. Finally. It was the sweetest sound he'd ever heard and now he needed her to leave.

She trembled in his grasp. Did she even know what she was doing, how she tortured him? And when had he embraced her? He had no memory of taking her into his arms, and yet there she was.

He brushed a strand of hair behind her ear. She turned her face into his touch, rubbing her cheek against the back of his hairy hand. Surprising that with her fear of Maeldun, she hadn't run from him in a panic.

"Before I agree to return with you, I need to discover more of my mission."

She nodded. "You're going to make me leave, aren't you?"

"For now."

"What if I don't want to?" Cheeky woman.

"You must until I prove my innocence." And there were other things to contend with. Like Maeldun. How had he survived?

Mara pulled back in his arms and stared at him without moving for what felt like a short forever. Her gaze locked onto his, then traced the lines of his face, down his neck, across his furry chest, down to her eye's level, where his heart pounded beneath her stare. Then she smiled, brushed her fingers across his lips, turned, and slid back out through the too-small entrance.

Leaving him panting as if he'd just run a mile, or flown a thousand.

He followed Mara and watched from a distance, flying from tree to tree, until she was safely inside the cabin. Then he returned to the cave.

The warmth he'd enjoy in the future was missing. And with Mara gone, it seemed even colder. He needed answers, but first he needed rest, so he lay down and tried to sleep.

But sleep didn't come, probably because all he saw when he closed his eyes was Mara, her beautiful, nonjudgmental face as she'd examined every inch of him. After all she'd been through, those ten years of enforced, terrified silence, she was still willing to know him. She'd begged him to return with her, even. It was a miracle.

The top of the cave was fascinating, with its flecks of shiny rocks amid the granite, but not this fascinating. Besides, sleep was overrated. He might as well go out and start his hunt. Cian wasn't going to help him.

He flew from the cave, found a mountain perch, and sat, pulling his knees to his chest. The valley beyond the trees rolled into the foothills. The sunshine blazed down, wilting the greenery. Ripening fields of wheat fluttered in the afternoon wind. Chirping birds filled the air with song.

He lifted his short snout. Fall was in the air... and something else.

Each gryphon had its own unique odor. The black gryphons smelled like rotting garbage with a hint of sulfur, each with his own disgusting mix. The gray gryphons smelled of wood and sandal oil, foliage and nature. This scent was a mix. Not quite disgusting, but not entirely pleasing, either.

No time to hide. A whoosh of wind and the shadow of a large creature roared overhead. He flattened onto his belly and peered through the rocks he'd been sitting on.

Something heavy landed nearby. "I know you're there. I could smell you a mile away."

A gryphon other than Maeldun landed before him. Was he friend or foe? Guess he would need to find out. "What are you doing here?"

"Me? You question me? I'm Ailin Colin."

Dougal laughed under his breath. Gregory, as the black gryphon would be known in the future, was currently using his gryphon name. *Handsome and virile.* How time would change for him.

Ailin continued. "You will not ask the questions here; I will. Where are your brothers?"

"What?" He should pay better attention.

"There are always twelve, are there not?"

"So I've heard."

"So where are the other eleven? Are they hiding to try and attack me? It won't work. If you know anything about my kind, you know we travel together as one."

Dougal hurried to remember what Maeldun had said. They were looking for Ailin and here he stood, alone in all his black glory "True. But I also know you're currently estranged from your fellow blacks."

A rush of air escaped Ailin's throat. "How do you know such things?"

"I have my sources." Impossible to keep some smugness from his voice.

"Humph." Ailin changed to his human form. With grace befitting a ballerina, he settled his tall, lithe frame on a downed log.

Astonished, Dougal rose and shook out his fur. Had Ailin whispered an incantation? He hadn't heard it. And since when could Ailin change into a human anyway?

Ailin frowned. "Why do you look at me like that? Surely you can change forms?"

"Yes, of course, but—"

"Then please change and come sit with me. I believe we have much to discuss."

Huh. "I don't understand."

"Of course not, but you will. I've been looking for you."

# 32

Dr. Hyrem sat across from him, his face grave. "I'm afraid Mrs. O'Brien can take no more shocks to her system."

Sick to his stomach, O'Brien ran his fingers through his hair. "What am I to do?"

"She must come with me."

"No. I can't do that. The will states—" He clamped his mouth shut. Not the smartest thing he could have said.

Dr. Hyrem cocked a brow and adjusted his rounded spectacles, but didn't follow that line of thought. "I assure you it is for her benefit. Mrs. O'Brien's mental state has deteriorated further than I anticipated. She now needs constant care."

"Ellie is here. She can look after her."

"I don't think you understand. Without better supervision *and* medication, I fear your wife will descend into a mental breakdown from which she may never recover."

He crossed his arms over his chest. "Then I will stay with her and give her the medication and loving care she needs."

The doctor didn't even blink. "Sir, I must insist. She speaks of flying creatures coming into her room at night and whispering to her. She says the creature wants to smell her. Do you not think this is odd?"

O'Brien gulped. Why had she told a complete stranger about the creature? "Yes, that is odd."

"I fear for her sanity."

"As do I. Perhaps if our son returned from the war, it would help her." That, and maybe if he stood up for her, but he couldn't be seen as crazy. Who wanted a crazy man for mayor?

"Perhaps. But you must at least consider my recommendation. I fear your wife needs more care than you can give her. Even a slave with her at all hours..." Dr. Hyrem sighed. "Very well, then. I will return in one week to check on her progress. If there is no improvement..."

The doctor's words faded away to silence. Relieved, O'Brien scowled. What would the man do? Would he have authorities step in and take Ivy away? Then what would happen to him?

But the doctor left, and with Ivy to care for, the days passed quickly. On day three O'Brien searched the roads from her window. News of the Gettysburg battle had reached the town. Heavy casualties were reported, yet no word arrived about Beauford. If anything happened to the lad, Ivy would never recover. And he needed for her to recover.

Money had exchanged hands on several occasions, money that was supposed to keep Beauford behind a desk or give him a post somewhere other than the front lines. However, his son's letters had told the grim tale. Despite his best efforts, Beauford remained in harm's way, putting all of O'Brien's plans at risk.

Letters had come describing war-torn areas, and he pulled them from his desk and glanced through them once again. The mounds of dead bodies that lay rotting in the sun, bloated and disfigured, was an image Beauford loved to share, whether because he actually witnessed the gore or because he wished to, O'Brien couldn't decipher and didn't care. He only wanted his son to return.

He planted his palms on the desktop and scrutinized Beauford's last letter. With an angry motion, he shoved it aside and re-read Mr. Landing's last will and testament for the thousandth time. His eyes blurred from searching for a hidden clause, something to save him from his predicament.

Nothing. As usual, he found nothing.

Before he could put the will away, tapping echoed from the cracked door. He controlled his surprise with anger. "How did you get in here?" he called, even before he reached the door and swung it open. He needed a guard. But shock stopped his voice.

Herrick leaned against the study door. "Is that any way to treat a guest?"

He fought rising anger. "Look, I've done everything you asked. You've burned down my legacy. You've destroyed my wife's mind. You've taken my son. What could you possibly want now? " Maybe Herrick had come to help, but he doubted it. And that sort of *help* he could do without.

"There is *one* thing."

Oh, indeed. "And what will you give me in return?" It popped out with only a small measure of guilt.

"Ah, there's the spirit. Always looking out for number one. That's what I like about you. You remind me so much of myself."

He cringed. Herrick was a monster. He didn't appreciate the comparison. "Go ahead. Tell me what you want. I'm very busy."

Herrick sauntered over to the desk, deliberately removing his black leather gloves and slapping them down onto the papers. "Ah, I see you're reading your father-in-law's will. What an interesting clause. *If anything happens to Ivy whereby she cannot stay in the family home, all property is forfeited to the town parson.* How interesting."

Heart pounding, he pushed Herrick out of the way and leaned over the document, blocking it from view. He knew every clause in the will and didn't need some monster telling him of the ruin he faced. "Where did you see that? I need to read it."

"Don't bother."

"But—"

Herrick laid a hand on his chest. Raw power thrummed through the touch, and a shudder raced through O'Brien.

"I said don't bother. What I have to say is much more important than a clause in some old piece of withered paper."

Out of options again, O'Brien collapsed into his chair and leaned back into the padding. Candlelight flickered up the walls. Herrick's shadow reared onto the ceiling, stretching into an outline of a monster in truth, and almost seemed to grow wings.

Herrick smiled, but it didn't reach his cold eyes. "There, you see, now you're relaxed. That's what I like to see from you. No worries." He rubbed his hands together. "Now, for the favor I have to ask and then your surprise. First, I would like to talk to your wife."

Ivy? What could Herrick possibly want with her? "She is unwell. The burning of the town has exacerbated her illness. I'm afraid your request is impossible." He tensed his legs to spring from his chair if Herrick decided to ignore his warning.

"Nothing is impossible."

O'Brien opened his mouth to interrupt again, but Herrick's upraised hand stopped him. "Now for what I am prepared to offer for just a few words with your *wife*."

He crossed his arms over his chest. He wouldn't allow such a conversation. "Nothing you can give me will change my mind."

"I can bring your son home."

"What?" He jumped from the chair, catching it with one hand before it toppled backward.

A casual shrug lifted Herrick's shoulders. "I know where your son is. He's in an army hospital in Virginia. From my understanding, he was wounded. Now, I have the ability to bring him home, or..." His voice trailed off.

"Or what? If I don't let you torture my already enfeebled wife, then you'll do something to my son. Is that what you're trying to say? What could you possibly want with Ivy? She's very ill."

"I know." Herrick's lips twitched.

O'Brien's knees shivered. He balled his fists and wished he were a stronger man. If only he dared... If only it would make a difference.

Perhaps there was another way to save Beauford. If he called in his contacts, or—or—Who was he kidding? Casting his lot with Herrick had brought nothing but trouble, but if there was even the remotest possibility of bringing Beauford home and thereby aiding in Ivy's recovery, he had to take the chance. Besides, what could Herrick say to Ivy in just a few minutes that would disturb her even more than she was already? Why, she might not even realize he was there.

"I see you're contemplating going at this alone. I don't recommend it. You see, your son is in a *Union* hospital, one where I happen to have a special relationship with the head nurse. The lady's willing to do anything for me. And shall we say, she owes me a favor. Besides, what's your concern with me speaking to Ivy? I've done so before."

His stomach clenched.

"In fact, I've done so on many occasions. You might say Ivy and I are practically best friends. Hasn't she told you?"

Heat rushed to his cheeks. "What are you insinuating?"

"Why, nothing, Mr. O'Brien." Herrick wagged his finger. "But hear me now. Either allow me to speak with your wife and I will release your son, or I will doom them both to an early demise."

# 33

Dougal stared at Ailin. So much of what he thought he knew was wrong. Every time he thought he understood the mystery, another, deeper one was revealed. In the not-so-distant future, Ailin would live in Ireland as part of the army of black gryphons. He would fall in love with Mairin, Arin's sister, and capture her. His failure to turn human would cause Mairin to find him hideous. She would trick him and, while he was gone, take her own life. This series of events would lead to a war that would end the black gryphons' reign for over a hundred years. But today—today Ailin sat across from him in human form. Ailin wasn't gray or black, but human.

And Dougal was so confused. "Why are you here?"

"I've been looking for you since the day you crashed in a field."

Ailin had been there? Why hadn't he helped him? Why had he been looking for him?

"Why do you stare?"

"Tell me, do all black gryphons have the ability to change?" He knew the answer; at least he thought he did. They needed magic to change. The darkness of the heart had taken away the ability to truly love and therefore change on their own. And most of the black gryhpons didn't care. They enjoyed living in gryphon form; that was why some of them chose that life.

"You do not know?"

"Let's just say I've spent more time on the human side of

things." And he wanted to hear it from Ailin's lips. If he could have changed in the future, then Mairin wouldn't have died and Cahal, his father, would never have been imprisioned.

Ailin nodded as if he understood. "Of course; you are gray. I wouldn't expect you to understand the complexity of being a black gryphon."

Let him believe what he wanted. Dougal leaned forward and clasped his hands. "Please tell me what you know."

Ailin lips twitched. "I know many things."

Dougal snickered. Ailin was a character. "I'm sure you do. But first, explain how you morphed."

Ailin shrugged. "Your level of shock comes as a surprise. But I will endeavor to enlighten you. The gray gryphons travel in packs of twelve. Ah... you nod your head, so this you know. Good. The grays, of course, have had the ability to change since the beginning of time, and their original purpose was to protect the Jotunn."

"The who?" He'd thought they'd been put there to watch over *humans*. Another strike for him. Being a gray seemed to be harder than he'd thought.

Ailin tsked. "Don't you know anything? I do not think we have time for me to start from the beginning. The sun has set. *Things* happen in the dark."

"Please." Begging wasn't in his nature, but he could use charm even on a guy when necessary.

Ailin lay back on his elbow and crossed his ankles. "When I found you in the field, I didn't think I would meet you later to discuss history. I must be growing soft. But for some reason, I feel the need to tell you." He shook his head and massaged his chin. "I guess I shall follow my instincts. The Jotunn was a race of beings with superhuman abilities, such as super strength. Rumors say they were derived from nature spirits, and were hideous. Claws, fangs, deformed features—the things monsters are made of."

Dougal kept his mouth shut. Didn't Ailin realize who he'd just described?

"But then another line of Jotunn emerged. They were beautiful and powerless. The gray gryphon was given the special job of protecting them. Twelve special warriors were chosen for each village. I was one of them."

Dougal gaped. Gregory—or Ailin Colin—would be searching out the key to the white tower as a black gryphon. How was it possible he'd ever been a gray?

"Again I have surprised you. But it is true, which is one reason you are still alive. I was an original twelve. We were to protect the fragile Jotunn from the black gryphons at all costs. For centuries, we lived in peace among them, until the ancient scrolls were found and shared at one of our group meetings. The scrolls said that if a Jotunn left the village, he would obtain limitless power. This knowledge caused an uproar amongst us. There was one who thought he knew better. One who didn't want to protect the Jotunn any longer. Betrayal ran through the ranks. Brother fought against brother, no one knowing for sure who had changed allegiance. As long as we were in human form, it was impossible to tell friend from foe. So in order to find the traitor in our midst, a contest was proposed. Three members of the twelve were unable to attend, thereby becoming immediate suspects.

"But before investigations could begin, a raid occurred on *my* village." A deep sigh escaped Ailin's lips and Dougal could feel his pain. "Without warning, the village was attacked. Everyone was slaughtered."

"Everyone? But why?" He scooted to the edge of the log.

Ailin ran a hand through his long blond hair. His sad eyes found Dougal. "Because the new leader didn't want to be challenged."

"I don't understand."

"Of course not. You don't even know that blacks can change."

He almost blurted that he knew blacks could change with magic, but he held his tongue. Let Ailin believe what he wanted. He had bigger problems, apparently known at the Jotunn.

Ailin stood and stomped around the area before plopping down again. "Don't you get it? One Jotunn can wipe out an entire army of gryphons."

*One?* That didn't seem possible. "But—"

"You see," Ailin's voice slowed, became dreamy, "there is a legend which tells that at the end of time, a Jotunn of the fire tribe will inflict the final destruction on the world. But there is another, a Jotunn of light, which will stand up against the first."

"Do these tribes live separated, each with their own group of twelve gray gryphon protectors?"

"That is a good question," Ailin regained his pedantic tone, like a school marm, "but the answer is no. The fire and light tribes *lived*, past tense, together in peace and harmony within the village walls. They didn't even know of the legend. Their powers and abilities were not discovered until they left the village, either by their own will or by force. Now do you understand?"

"Not really. I guess I'm failing to understand what the big deal is. If no one survived the raid..." Dougal shrugged. If he played stupid, maybe Ailin would continue.

"The big deal, you say? The big deal is, I'm... no, I shouldn't say. Perhaps we should leave—"

No such luck. "Now, wait just a minute. You can't tell me you were a member of the original twelve, tell me your charges died, and then just quit talking. I want to know how you changed to black. If anyone shouldn't be trusted, it's you, not me."

Ailin snickered. "You make a good point. Very well, I will continue. You see, not everyone in the village perished."

"But you said—"

"Yes, I know what I said. I may be hundreds of years old, but I'm not senile. While my brothers were under attack, I managed to rescue one Jotunn."

Dougal's jaw dropped.

"It's actually amusing. Believe it or not, I placed the babe in a wicker basket and floated her down the River Shannon. Ah! The blacks never suspected a thing. While they were busy annihilating the innocents in the village, the babe drifted right past them and off to safety. Of course, it was afterward that I was discovered." Ailin sighed wistfully. "I had a choice to make. They offered me a new lease on life if I would convert to their dark ways. Foolishly, I believed if I did so unwillingly, I would in my heart remain gray. Imagine my surprise when the leader slit his wrist and placed his black blood against my own. I've not been the same since."

"And the baby?" His head was pounding.

"Of course, the babe. Once I escaped the scrutiny of my new brothers, I rushed to a small bend in the river. As I suspected, the basket had caught in the reeds. The babe wailed. I drew her from the water, held her in my arms, and flew her to safety."

"Where is she now?" His heart hammered in his chest.

Ailin cocked a brow. "And why would I tell you such a thing? We've only just met."

# 34

O'Brien agreed to Herrick's terms, but he added a few conditions. First, Beauford would be within arm's reach before Herrick would be allowed anywhere near Ivy. Second, O'Brien would be present for the conversation. A nonchalant shrug was all the answer his requests received.

The date and time were scheduled, and today he would arrived. Pacing the entry hall for what seemed the thousandth time, O'Brien waited for his son. The lad had been seventeen when the war began. With a straight spine and stiff upper lip, he had stood in the parlor and declared his intent to join the Rebel forces. O'Brien remembered it like it was yesterday.

*"Father, I wish to prove myself."*

*"But son, you're already a great man. You have land and an inheritance coming your way. You have a betrothed. It would be a simple matter to have you released from this obligation to your country."*

*"Father, if I am to own this land, then I should defend it. Forgive me for any disrespect, but this is something I must do."*

*"But what of your mother? With the fragile state of her mind, this might have devastating consequences for her."*

*"Mother will be fine. It is not as if I shall never return."*

Even looking back through his memories, he could see the goofy grin on Beauford's face. When he'd informed Ivy of their son's decision, the shriek that came from her scared the animals in the barn.

The day Beauford had left, Ivy had captured his legs in a wailing embrace. Not wishing to hurt her, Beauford had reached down, pulled her erect, and patted her head, as if she were a wayward child. He'd promised to return, and then he'd walked from their house and their lives.

Three years had passed and still their son had not returned. But today, today he would be here. At last, he would come home.

O'Brien glanced out the study's bay window. Dust stirred at the far end of the drive. A group of horsemen approached the house. Emotion clogged his throat, heart-rending but otherwise impossible to define. For all the hardness of his heart toward everyone else, he held a soft spot for his son. Beauford meant everything. More so than the buildings in town or his role as mayor, Beauford was his future.

A thump from upstairs made him pause. Ivy didn't know of Beauford's promised return. He had feared if something prevented the homecoming, the disappointment would severely affect his wife's sanity. So even though he'd yearned to, he'd told her nothing.

In the fireplace, smoke drifted from the charcoaled remains of a burning log. The log's carcass represented all that remained of Beauford's future. He no longer had land or holdings to offer his son; all that remained was ash. Everything he'd worked for, everything he'd built, was gone, vanished, poof, up in smoke. The remains mocked him. Everything had been lost in his pursuit to garner more. Why had contentment not come with what he had?

But he knew. In his heart, he knew.

Heavy footfalls echoed on the wooden porch. O'Brien raced from the study, through the foyer, and yanked open the front door.

A shadow fell across the entryway. "Father?"

"Beauford?"

Beauford fell into his arms. Words formed in O'Brien's mouth, but nothing came out. There were so many things he wanted to say, but where could he start?

Embarrassed, he stepped back and swallowed, eyeing his son. The lad had grown, filled out, and then shrank, so that the gray uniform which had once fit so well hung raggedly from Beauford's now-thin frame. A sling held his arm close. Caked blood peeked out from a dirt-encrusted bandage wrapped around his head.

One side of Beauford's mouth hiked up in a good-natured grin. "It looks worse than it is."

He nodded. Emotion still clogged his throat too much to speak. He was a wreck—no, everything was. He shouldn't have let his son leave. He should have rescued him earlier. He should have—

"I see you two have become reacquainted." Herrick suddenly loomed behind Beauford.

He cringed. Herrick wasn't going to forget their deal.

And he was right. "Mr. O'Brien, I wish to speak with Ivy now."

O'Brien shot a glance over his shoulder. The way was clear. "I will accompany you."

A mocking grin covered the captain's face. "But of course."

Beauford slid between them, steady on his feet despite his injuries. "Father, what's happening?"

"Nothing." He needed a distraction, something, some errand—"Why don't you go to the kitchen and have Ellie fix you something to eat?"

Beauford didn't move. "Why does a Union captain wish to speak with Mother?" He peered up the stairs.

No, it was too much to explain. "Beauford, please, go see Ellie. She's missed you terribly."

"But I want to see Mother."

It was too much to bear. He patted Beauford's shoulder. The boy was so thin. "Soon. I promise."

Beauford obeyed, but sent a weary glare over his shoulder as he walked away. O'Brien's stomach twisted. Would Beauford tell his unit commander that a Union officer had come into their home and talked to his mother? Surely not. That would bring a lynch mob to their home and Beauford wouldn't risk their safety. Still, he would need to create a reasonable explanation—soon. But later.

He didn't speak as he led his unwanted guest upstairs. When they reached the landing outside Ivy's room, the door flew open.

"Barry, I heard voices." Ivy stepped into the hallway, her hands folded before her. If not for the food-stained gown that swathed her frail body and her wild hair, she might have passed for normal. How had her mental state deteriorated so quickly? Was Dr. Hyrem's prognosis correct? Did she need the long-term care of a dedicated facility?

Herrick stepped around him and engulfed Ivy's hands in his. He stroked the inside of her wrist, even as he led her back into her bedroom. A sigh escaped the captain's lips. *"Ivy..."*

To his surprise, Ivy didn't pull away. Striking a statuesque pose, she waited. O'Brien felt as if he were interrupting a private tryst. The thought didn't calm him. "Ask her what you want to know, and then leave."

"But of course."

Ivy rocked back on her heels and hummed, as if in a trance. O'Brien bridled. It was a very contented sort of trance.

"Ivy Wheeler O'Brien, do you know where you are?" Herrick's voice dropped to a crooning murmur.

"Yes. I am at home." Her voice sounded distant. Had Herrick hypnotized her?

"Do you know where you were born?"

"I was born in Wheeler's Landing."

"Were you born in this house?"

"I don't know."

"Ivy O'Brien, how old are you?"

A smile tugged at the corners of her lips. O'Brien's heart flipped; he hadn't seen such a smile in a long time and now he realized how much he had missed it. Unfortunately, she didn't smile at him.

Renewed vigor lit her sad eyes. "I don't think that's a question you should ask of a lady."

Despite the situation, he had to restrain his happiness at her cheeky behavior. Oh, he'd missed her spirit, and O'Brien's heart warmed.

Captain Herrick's lips twitched upward. "Touché."

In a hesitant voice, she asked, "Why do you want to know these things?"

*"I need to know."*

He heard the words, but Herrick's lips hadn't moved. O'Brien's pulse pounded—something wasn't right. Something—

As if the couple communicated through the air, the conversation continued, and by some esoteric means, he was part of it, whether he wished to be or not.

*"Ladies do not tell gentlemen their age."*

*"I have a gift for you."*

*"A gift?"*

*"Yes. But to receive the gift, you must give me some an-*

*swers."*

*"I like gifts."*

*"I know."* Herrick grinned, ignoring Ivy's frown. *"I need to know your age. It is important to me. It is important to you."*

*"Very well. I'm thirty-seven."*

Herrick frowned. For a strained moment, silence held them spellbound, even the air quiet.

*"You are not pleased with my age, I take it."*

*"No, I'm not."*

*"I'm sorry to disappoint you."*

*"It was not unexpected."*

*"Do I look so old?"*

*"Nay. You are the most beautiful woman I've ever seen."*

Red flooded Ivy's cheeks. O'Brien balled his fists against his sides. If Herrick didn't finish with his questions soon, it wouldn't matter; he'd finish it for him.

*"Was I supposed to be a different age?"*

*"I had hoped so, yes."* Herrick smoothed a strand of gray-blond hair behind Ivy's ear.

*"Do you have any more questions for me or may I have my gift now?"*

Herrick nodded. At that same instant, Beauford burst into the room. "Mother!"

Ivy ran to him. Tripping over the hem of her long gown, she fell directly into her son's waiting arms.

Herrick stomped down the stairs, anger and frustration clouding his face.

Ignoring the captain's obvious displeasure, O'Brien turned back to his family. They looked so perfect, with Beauford's arms around Ivy and her face lit by a brilliant smile. His own heart overflowed with joy and his eyes were wet. Everything would be fine now. It would all be fine.

# 35

Mara shelled peas at the kitchen table while everyone else sat unmoving.

Three days ago Pa had ridden into town and returned with the most astounding news. Beauford O'Brien had returned, wounded but whole! Maude fell into a complete tizzy. The house had to be perfect. Clothes needed washing. Windows needed wiping. The floor needed sweeping. A huge meal needed to be prepared. No word had been given on when the young man would come calling, but Maude was determined to be ready when he did.

But he hadn't come. Maude's dejection showed in her slumped shoulders and perpetual pout.

For two days Ma had made excuses for Beauford.

*"Maybe it's taking a while to get settled..."*

*"Maybe his ma wouldn't let him out of her sight..."*

*"Maybe he needs time to recuperate..."*

But no matter what Ma said, Maude had refused to be consoled.

Finished, Mara dusted off her hands and set the peas aside. If she left for a minute, no one would notice. They were too miserable for that. First Dougal had left—and no one knew he hadn't really except her—and now waiting to see Beauford... It was too much. Earlier they'd barely bothered to water the crops, and their wintering-over depended on that.

The cool morning air was a welcome respite after the heat

of the last few days. She lifted the hair from her neck and enjoyed the caressing breeze as she walked toward the creek.

It had been almost a week to the day since Dougal had made her return to the farm. She knew she had to, but waiting to see him again was sweet torture. Now that she had given in to the urge to speak, all she wanted was to sit and talk with him. There were so many things to discuss. A flying creature sent from the future to protect her! Just imagine.

She closed her eyes and raised her face to the sky. But something changed. She sensed the shadow, felt a rush of air. Dougal must have figured out her desire to see him and he'd returned. She smiled and opened her eyes.

It wasn't Dougal.

"Ah, there you are. I had hoped you were not the one, but I'm afraid I was wrong."

Absolute terror exploded within her heart. What was Maeldun doing here? He wasn't supposed to come back. She'd been talking for ages and he'd stayed away. Why had he returned? Her family; she had to protect her family.

She dug her heel into the ground and whirled, running back to the farm. Brambles tore at her dress; branches smacked her face. She held her hands out in front of her and charged through the thickets. What would Maeldun do to her family if he followed her there? Would he kill them like he'd promised? It would be all her fault. Somehow, she had to stop him.

A powerful arm wrapped around her middle. She screamed, but it lifted her off the ground. Tree branches grabbed at her as powerful wings pumped for altitude, and the underbrush fell away beneath them. If she struggled, the beast might drop her. Maybe she could convince him to let her go when they landed. Maybe—

Wind blasted her face as the flying beast whipped past trees and other natural obstacles. She closed her eyes tightly, refusing to look at him. That would happen soon enough.

Finally they touched the ground. The beast set her on her feet and grabbed her arm, steadying her. Maybe she should look now. Or maybe not until after she'd figured out where she was. A silo was behind her. Oh, no! What were they doing *there*?

The beast leaned close, hot breath stroking her cheek. "Get inside."

*That voice…*

It couldn't be! Could he really have been that close, watching her, protecting her? Heat rushed to her middle. "Dougal?"

"Get in the silo, Mara. Now!"

The power of his voice made her jump and hurry to obey. The silo's door was shattered, probably from when the Union soldiers had broken in and stolen the stockpiled weapons. The story had been passed all around Wheeler's Landing and had even made it out to the farm.

She leaned in. It was dark and smelled musty.

She bit her lip. Did she have to go in? But a glance back didn't help, for Dougal narrowed his eyes back at her. Looked like the answer was yes.

Carefully she eased over the threshold, into the depths of the dark, wove a path through rows of busted wooden crates, and settled on the ground against the back wall, wrapping herself into a ball.

The walls were thick and blocked all sound, but something about the silo's darkness seemed familiar. She closed her eyes. Was that a voice? It was low and almost sweet. It sounded as if someone was singing a lullaby. But why and to whom? Was there someone else in there with her? No. No, there couldn't be.

Dougal hadn't followed her inside. Again she bit her lip. When she saw him again, she was going to berate him for leaving her alone in the dark. Didn't he know she didn't like the dark…?

"You again?"

"Don't tell me you're not happy to see me." Dougal maintained his normal level of cockiness. He wouldn't let the black scare him.

Maeldun's derisive laugh echoed across the valley floor, and he restrained his anger. The beast could have just stayed dead and saved them both a lot of trouble.

"I'm not in the mood to waste time. Step aside and give me the girl."

"Never." He widened his stance and popped his knuckles as loudly and annoyingly as possible.

Maeldun shook his head. "Why must it always be this way? Why do you grays never listen?"

"Guess it's in our blood."

"Humph. Stand aside. I do not have all day."

"Neither do I, so let's make a deal. Leave the girl alone and I'll allow you to live."

"You're funny. But it doesn't really matter. The girl is mine. She has always been mine. She will always be mine."

"How do you figure?" He couldn't wait to hear Maeldun's reasoning.

"Cahal gave her to me."

The name stopped him and left him stunned. How many times had he said Cahal would never control him again? But at the mention of his father's name, his pulse raced and he felt frozen. All he'd ever sought was his father's approval. Seeking that acceptance had caused him to do terrible things. Now an opportunity to rectify the situation presented itself. Redemption was at hand and he was taking full advantage of it. Dougal crouched lower. "Cahal can give you nothing."

"You do not know of whom you speak. Cahal is the leader. I'm his devotee. Cahal can give or take as he wishes."

"I think not. Mara is not for you. She has another purpose."

"I know well her purpose. That is why she will be mine."

"No."

"Yes."

A stalemate.

Had it just been moments before that he'd sat calmly in the valley talking with Ailin? Without warning, his heart had raced. Sweat had beaded his brow and unrestrained power had coursed through his veins until he'd been unable to keep still.

Without needing any evidence, he'd known Mara was in danger. Words had tumbled from him as he'd explained to Ailin, and then he'd flown away. He'd hoped his potential ally would follow, but so far no luck.

Maeldun lowered his head and smoke drifted from his long, ugly snout.

He felt weaker than before, but he was still smarter. "I don't wish to fight. Maybe we can resolve our differences another way."

"I doubt it." Maeldun relaxed enough to stand straight, a touch of swagger in the shift of his massive shoulders.

"What do you want with the lass?" Maybe he could buy time until Ailin arrived. Maybe Ailin would bring the cavalry and he wouldn't get creamed.

Maeldun knit his brow in confusion. "You do not know?"

"As you said, I'm fairly new. I don't know much."

"You speak correctly." Maeldun sniffed. "Very well. You wish to know what I want with the girl; maybe after you hear, we can work together."

Dougal didn't comment—he knew better—but he waited. And as he'd expected, Maeldun told pretty much the same story as Ailin, the story of the Jotunn, but he added a new part.

"Mara is the last. A gryphon tricked Cahal and stole her away. I believe it was Ailin, Cahal's newest convert, but he doesn't believe me. But it doesn't matter. She was stolen and brought here. Since the Jotunn tend to age slower than humans, we've been watching the wrong woman. But now I know for sure. Mara is the one we sought all along."

"That still doesn't answer the question of what you want from her." Dougal held his breath. He wasn't going to like the answer.

"It should be obvious. The lass is strong. *Very* strong. Strength beyond imagining. And when she wields the secret weapon of the Jotunn, she will be unstoppable. With Mara by my side, the black gryphons will rule the world and I will be the supreme leader."

So Maeldun wanted to be the leader. That made sense. "And if she picks the opposite side?" She had to pick the other side, right?

"That is not an option."

"But let's just say she decides not to help you. What then?"

Maeldun shrugged. "Then she will die."

# 36

Ailin's patience was at an end. He'd taken a great risk, leaving Dand and the other members of the black gryphon patrol alive as he reached out to the gray named Nuada. The black gryphon, even though he was Ailin's second in command, could easily inform Cahal of his treachery. But something about that day in the field, when they'd seen the young man sprawled as if he'd fallen from the sky, kept haunting him. He'd known he was supposed to help. He'd known the gray's presence was about the girl. Now the girl needed real assistance and the ones destined to protect her were sitting in a circle around a glowing fire, arguing about whether they even believed in the Jotunn.

"Let's say we believe you," said the leader, Tomas. "What would you have us do?"

"Help the girl!" Ailin ground out through gritted teeth.

"But—"

"There is no *but*. There is no time. She has hidden amongst the humans for seventeen years. Maeldun knows about her. Discovery of the *object* is next. If the lass is taken by the black gryphon, all is lost. Have you not fought your whole life to protect this valley? These people? How can you sit idly by now and wait?"

Another gray shrugged. "The Jotunn are a myth."

Ailin slammed his fist into his palm. "No! I tell you I was there."

"But you're black. How can we believe you?"

Ailin's imploring eyes turned on the younglings. "You must. You have no other choice."

Tomas turned away and poked the fire. "It was a legend, nothing more."

"I will explain. I was one of the twelve assigned to the Jotunn village of fire and light." He'd revealed his secret twice in one day. He should be careful or it might become a habit that could get him killed.

"Impossible," breathed the second gray. The ones farthest from the fire rustled like a disbelieving breeze.

He breathed deeply. Every time he told the story, his fall from grace was deemed impossible. "Not impossible. When the blacks raided the Jotunn, my brothers were killed. I alone survived. Converting to the black's heathen form was the only way to save the last child. They believed they had killed them all, but I saved her. I brought her here. I hid the weapon, too. Now she has been discovered. The lass was never meant to be a warrior. The Jotunn males were the ones who fought and killed. But with the last drops of Jotunn blood flowing through her veins, and the village no longer surviving to hide and protect her, she was chosen. Yet without the instrument, her powers could be limited. We *must* protect her until she finds the weapon."

"What say you, leader? Should we go to her aid?"

Tomas tapped his finger upon his chin. Ailin waited. Frustration gnawed at him. Why had he not approached the council sooner? Sure, he'd known they would be hard to convince because of his color and his dark heart, but he should have tried. If he'd warned them sooner, perhaps by now they'd believe him. Perhaps—

"Aye." Tomas rose and shook out his wings. They flared behind him, their shadow thrown by the fire looming against the rock wall.

Following his lead, the twelve stood to their lion-like legs, spread their wings, and together they took flight. Relieved, his heart pumping in rhythm with his black wings, Ailin followed. He just hoped they weren't too late.

In the deep dark of the silo, Mara squatted behind broken crates until her legs cramped. How long was she expected to wait in this dank place? It made her skin crawl. And she *hated* the dark. Who knew what dirty, creepy-crawly things it hid?

Finally weary enough to risk touching something, she sat back and laid her head against the wall. From the corner of her eye, a blue light winked. She lifted her head. It vanished. She lay her head back again. It returned, a shiver of blue in the darkness.

She should just leave it alone, right? This was the Rebel's armory, where they'd stored their weapons. It had been raided when the Union soldiers sacked the town, but what if something harmful had been left behind? She didn't want to risk touching something that could kill her, did she?

The light winked again. Maybe it wouldn't hurt to just look.

When she reached out, her hand met rough wool. She tugged the thick blanket aside. A flash of blue arced through the air.

She scrambled back, sliding on her bottom. She shouldn't, she really shouldn't. But something about the blue fire called to her. Her hand shook as she eased forward. This time when she yanked, the cover fell away completely. An eerie blue glow danced around a sword from tip to hilt.

Entranced by its beauty, she brushed her fingertips across the glossy surface. Beneath the blue fire, the metal gleamed in the dark as if polished only moments ago. Shivers raced down her spine, but she didn't stop. She couldn't. It was so lovely, she thought she could stroke it forever.

Then the blade hummed. The words of a lullaby came to her, as if someone sang softly nearby.

*Sweet baby girl, savior of the world, take this sword in hand, protector of man.*

Not exactly the words she'd learned to that tune while growing up.

A woman wearing a gown of purest white appeared, her dark hair flowing over her shoulder. More astonished than scared, Mara scooted back toward the silo's wall and curled into a ball once more. What was happening? Apparently she hadn't learned from her previous mistakes; curiosity could kill you. She needed to stop talking to strangers and stop touching strange objects. Maybe it was a voodoo thing.

The specter held out her hand. "Do not be afraid, my child. This is your destiny. Grasp the sword."

She shook her head. No way. She didn't believe in ghosts and she wasn't doing anything one of them told her to do.

The ghost smiled. "Do not be afraid. I'm with you."

She blinked. "What?"

*"I'm with you."* The apparition faded away with the last syllable.

The specter, the voice, the lullaby, they were all so familiar. Her heart ached. But the sword continued to hum, as if calling to her. It had a point. Old-fashioned it might be, but the sword was a weapon and flying creatures were trying to attack her. She should take it.

On the thought, she grabbed the hilt and raised the sword. The blue light flared, lighting the silo's dark cavern almost to day.

The door flung open. One of those horrid winged creatures stood in the opening. "No!"

Calmness flooded her. She clutched the hilt tighter. Just let him try to attack her now. She was ready.

The earth rumbled...

Power coursed through her body. Fear retreated and Mara was overwhelmed with confidence. It was as if everything had been wrong or tilted in her life before, and suddenly the problems were all fixed and she could do anything now. She strode toward the door and Maeldun scrambled back, stumbled, righted himself, and took to the sky. Wings pounding a desperate rhythm, he disappeared over the distant mountain peak.

That had been much easier than she'd expected. Now she needed to find Dougal and they could go back to the farm together. With the black gryphon afraid of her, she no longer had to worry about her family being harmed.

But across the clearing, near the first grove of trees at the forest's edge, a huddled form lay collapsed in the withered turf. It wore the tattered remains of Dougal's shirt, one of the ones Ma made for him, but the color was wrong. Slowly she approached, trying to figure out what was wrong. Nuada lay on his side, and the ground around him was stained, too, darkened and red. Her confidence wavered. She rushed to his side. His grey gryphon form was beautiful, in spite of his fading color and the bright red stain across his chest and side.

She pressed her hand to his wound, a deep one under his arm and too near his heart, yet the blood refused to staunch. Tears formed in the corners of her eyes. "What can I do?"

His voice was raspy and low. "Nothing. It's too late."

"No! There has to be something I can do. I'm somebody. I know I am. I'm a protector or something. This sword means something important." Not to mention the specter told her so, and a ghost had to know what she was talking about.

He grabbed her hand, his blood slick between them. "You *are* special. Ailin will explain."

"Who?" She didn't want Ailin, whoever he was; she wanted Dougal. Or Nuada, if it came to that.

"Don't worry. He'll find you."

"I don't want Ailin to explain. I want you to explain. You will not die! I won't allow it."

The sword hummed louder, as if approving her words.

"I don't think we have a choice. Maeldun—he's too strong." Nuada coughed, sending out a fresh stream of blood.

"There has to be something I can do. There has to be." Ignoring the blood, she placed her head on his chest, her tears flowing freely.

With her head on his heart, one hand holding the sword and the other his hand, memories flooded her. She was a babe. And yet despite her age, the conversation between her mother and older brother had resonated in her young ears.

*"They are coming."*

*"Who, Mother?"*

*"The destroyers. They want us to leave the valley."*

*"But why?"*

*"To harness our power. But do not despair. The gray gryphons will protect us."*

*The cradle rocked side to side, bringing her comfort. It seemed as if time passed.*

*"Mother, the grays! They are all dead!"*

*"But how can that be?" The rocking stopped.*

*"I don't know. Only one remains. He will take our babe and save her. There is nothing else we can do."*

*"I will never part from her." Lifting her from the cradle, her mother hugged her to her chest.*

*Her brother's voice trembled. "But we must. She is the world's only hope."*

Her mother's hands had let her go. What had happened after that? But no matter how much she concentrated, she couldn't remember anything else.

The sword hummed in her hand, the vibration rumbling

through her from her fingers to her heart and mind. It was trying to tell her something. She had to save Dougal; there had to be a way. She needed him.

With one hand on the sword's hilt and the other on Dougal's wound, Mara concentrated.

"Any news to report?" Cahal asked.

"The traitor has been taken care of." Maeldun forced his voice to remain calm.

"Very well. And what of our brother Ailin? Has he been found?"

"No, sir." He didn't care whether Cahal found Ailin, his new best friend. They had bigger problems. Much bigger.

Cahal paced. Ragged breaths escaped into the morning air, causing smoke-like tendrils to float from his fanged mouth. "You understand I am not happy with this situation."

"Aye, I do." Yes, indeed, he understood that. Cahal was never happy.

"You are sure the traitor, this Nuada, has been taken care of?"

"Yes." That wasn't a lie.

"You understand if he is allowed to escape, he will surely contact the council of twelve."

"That may be. But what can they do in the face of our army?"

"They can do much, if they have the girl. The *right* girl. Have you discovered her identity?"

"Yes." Maeldun maintained eye contact. The leader mustn't know of his cowardice. No one could ever know that he'd flown away as fast as he could from a girl with a sword. She hadn't even looked big enough to hold the thing properly, but she had. Oh, yes, she had.

Cahal glanced aside at him. "Where is she?"

"Unknown."

Nostrils flared. Tendrils of smoke with an odor of brimstone filled the room. "Your answer is unacceptable."

"As I knew it would be." He clasped his trembling hands behind his back. Cahal must remain ignorant of his true plans to use the girl for his own purpose. If only that fool O'Brien had retrieved the sword earlier. Or if he hadn't been so foolish as to believe he could retrieve it without human assistance. The old woman had been right after all. He wasn't happy about that.

Cahal paused in his pacing and cocked a bushy black brow. "We must take the girl, find the sword, and force her to work for our side. Otherwise all is lost! Do you understand? The Jotunn are the only beings who can defeat us. The grays may try, but with only twelve of them to hand, they will never succeed. And these foolish humans—they unwittingly help us at every turn."

A harsh laugh echoed through the tent, making it sound large and cavernous. "Imagine them thinking we're part of the Union army. Suggesting I take Colonel Hastings' place for the raid was pure genius. And burning the town was icing on the cake. They give us the power over them!" He turned away. "The grays will come and try to halt our progress. But it doesn't matter. There's always someone like O'Brien willing to give us anything to further his own advancement."

"Yes, my master." Maeldun bowed his head. What else could he do? Obedience would keep him alive until the time was right.

Cahal rounded on Maeldun, trembling from head to toe with unrestrained rage. "I do not want your excuses! I want you to get me the girl."

"Of course. There is, however, one problem. I don't think she possesses the sword." Could Cahal tell he'd lied? Since Cahal had become the leader of the black gryphons, he'd stayed away from fieldwork. Any investigative skills he might have once had were no more. So Maeldun should be safe.

Should be.

"Then find it! Do I have to tell you everything? Have you been around the humans so long that their laziness seizes you? I will not have it amongst my ranks. Do you understand?"

"Yes, sir." Maeldun dug his nails into his palms to keep his secrets his own.

"Get out of my sight." Cahal waved him away.

Maeldun bowed and left the tent, lifting his eyes to the darkening sky. His lies had come easily enough. Cahal didn't need to know about the young maiden finding the sword nor how he'd panicked when he'd seen her with it.

The raging pulse, fluttering heart. He'd run away like a skittish deer. Cahal's army could be in trouble. Few of the soldiers within Cahal's ranks could overcome such fear.

He lifted his nose toward the sky. A storm was coming. The burning town had merely been the beginning. War was on the way. Epic battles would be fought, on the ground and in the sky.

Ailin led the council of twelve to the silo. His gut clenched as they sifted through the dirt inside the structure. The sword was missing, the woolen blanket crumpled atop a splintered crate. For seventeen years, the sword had remained hidden, untouched and unnoticed. Now it was gone.

Their only hope was that Mara had found it. If the blacks had it, they would be able to keep it from her reach. And that would have devastating effects on the world.

# 37

Mara's shoulders burned as she bore the burden of Dougal's weight back to the Hess farm. The trek was excruciatingly slow. Every few steps, he had to stop and rest. Yet it was a miracle he was alive, so she probably shouldn't complain.

They stopped again. His shoulders heaved as he panted. "I can't make it. Leave me."

"Your wound no longer bleeds. You just need to rest." But he kept panting. She grimaced. "Perhaps we should stay here for the night." They were getting closer to home, but not close enough. Curiosity burned within her, but she couldn't ask now. He was too weak. But he had to know something. He turned into a furry beast and she was a savior of some sort. He couldn't be ignorant of the details she yearned to know.

He shook his head. "We're too exposed and you need to get home."

"And what will my family do against an army of black gryphons?"

"Trust me when I say they are better off with you close by."

The sword hummed at her side, its vibration thrumming within her. She'd fashioned a sort of holster for it with some cast-off rope and strapped it to her waist. Did he think it would help them? If he thought her able to wield such a weapon, he was more delusional than she'd feared. It was heavy and cumbersome. And it shocked her with every touch. Sure, she felt as if she was supposed to have it, and she'd put on a good enough show to frighten Maeldun, but that didn't mean she would ever figure out how to use it.

He staggered back up and again they moved on. Dawn threatened to break before they made it home.

"Perhaps we should stop here. We can go to the cave or—"

He shook his head "No, we must get you to your family."

"My presence will only put them in more danger. Or don't you remember that Maeldun is after me?" Back at the silo, Maeldun had run like a scared chicken, but that had been one instance. The rest of the time, whenever they'd met, he'd flung her around like a ragdoll.

"Just the opposite. The black gryphons might keep their distance if you are with them."

"Are you sure?"

"No."

Wonderful. He wasn't sure, but he wanted her to return home and perhaps bring a race of big, scary, powerful flying creatures with her for a visit. Did he think Ma would invite them in for coffee?

The edge of the Hess property was surrounded by a thick line of trees. They pushed through them and into the open just as the sun crested over the nearest mountain. A sigh of relief escaped her. Their night filled with terror was coming to a close.

Coming home brought new worries. Maybe they should just stay nearby, watching over the family but at a distance? If he was spotted half dead, then the family would ask questions. Junior might even help finish the job. It was probably best just to stick close by. They'd go to the barn, and then she'd warn everyone before bringing him in. She could convince them to let him back into the fold. She was sure of it.

They made it into the barn's shelter, among the horses and cows restive from the smell of blood, but Dougal passed out as she let him fall onto a haystack. In a way, it was a relief. Now she could deal with her family and come back for him. But before she left the barn, she remembered the sword humming at her side. She'd hide it so the family didn't see it. A blue flaming sword wouldn't be well received.

She slid it into her secret hiding place in the barn, then glanced in on Dougal once more before straightening her gown and leaving the barn. Bright morning light poured over her when she stepped from the barn's shadows, but no one seemed to have started chores yet. The trek across the yard was eerily quiet. Dark forms moved behind the windows as she bounded onto the porch. She froze at the window and peered in, hiding behind the lacy curtains' edge, half expecting to see Maeldun looming over the stove flipping griddlecakes.

Not Maeldun.

Pa patted their visitor on the shoulder. "We're happy to have you home, lad. Didn't think we would ever see you again."

"Pa!"

"Sorry, Maude, but it's the truth. So many of the boys who left haven't come back."

"I'm afraid you're right, Mr. Hess." Beauford's voice lowered.

Beauford! Mara's pulse accelerated. He'd returned after all!

"How were you so lucky?" Pa leaned forward and leaned his elbows on his thighs.

"I was wounded when a cannon shell burst too near our position and pieces of shrapnel lodged in my arm and shoulder. Another piece conked me on the head and I was left on the field for dead. Union soldiers got to me before my boys figured out I was still alive, and they took me prisoner. While I was in the hospital, I believe my father arranged for my release."

"Good for you, son. Good for you. So when's the wedding?"

Maude winked and pink infused Beauford's cheeks. Still hiding behind the curtain outside, Mara shook her head. The poor fellow was being put on the spot first thing.

"Not sure, sir. I wouldn't mind getting married now but I'm afraid the army may call me back."

"No!" Maude rushed to his side.

"Now, dear, I have to go if I'm called. Did you know I was promoted to lieutenant?"

"That's wonderful! You're so brave!" Maude grabbed his arm and leaned into him. Mara had to squelch her jealousy. After all, Maude deserved to be happy. And doing so with Beauford meant she wouldn't be after Dougal, which was a good thing. No way Maude could handle being attracted to a flying creature. She was struggling with it herself, but mostly in her private moments, which had been few and far between.

Beauford cleared his throat. "That means if my boys come this way, I'll need to join them. I can't let them fight without me."

"But—"

"Listen, my father has already tried to deter me. But my mind is made up. Especially after what them blue bellies up and did to our town! I can't believe it. If I ever see that Dougal feller who sold us out, I'll wring his neck with my bare hands!"

Pa's mouth opened but no words came out. Frozen in shock, Mara continued to stare through the window. Pa's lack of defense on Dougal's behalf made her angry. Dougal had been their guest. And if not for him, their crops would have failed and they'd have lost the farm and starved like everyone else. If Pa didn't have the gumption to defend Dougal, who lay in their barn close to death because he'd tried to save her, then she would do it.

Even though Pa didn't know Dougal was there.

Furious, Mara shoved the front door open and burst into the room. "Pa! Don't just sit there and let him say those vile things about Dougal! Especially when you know they ain't true."

Pa squirmed in his chair. "Now, lass, don't get your knickers in a wad. We don't need to be correctin' our guest."

She stomped her foot. "Well, I'm going to correct him."

Beauford widened his eyes. She stared him down. Let him be afraid. She was going to tear him limb from limb if he said one more cross word against her protector.

Mara rounded on him, her hands on her hips. "You've been gone for three years. We've had no word from you. Why, Maude believed you found another woman and up and married. Now you have the audacity to blow in and start accusin' people without understanding a bit of what actually happened. I won't have it! Dougal is a good man. He had nothing to do with burning the town."

Beauford glanced nervously back and forth between Ma and Pa. He pointed a shaky finger. "She can talk?"

She slapped her forehead. Of course that would be the man's greatest concern. "Yes, I can talk. And I'm tellin' you right now, Dougal had nothing to do with the fire."

"But—"

Pa's restraining hand settled upon her arm, and he drew her aside. "Mara, we shouldn't be accostin' our guest." He turned. "Beauford, you'll have to forgive the child. Dougal stayed with us a wee bit and he helped around the farm. In fact, we did well while he stayed."

"He left?" Beauford leaned forward as if excited. She stiffened beneath Pa's restraining hand. If Beauford thought he was going to catch Dougal and bring him in, then he had another think coming. Dougal could rip him to shreds and she wasn't sure she would try and stop him.

"Sometime back, he left for parts unknown. We have no knowledge of the lad's involvement with the fire other than a few rumors. But frankly, I can't see him doin' such a thing."

"Hmm. Perhaps I judged him too quickly. Forgive me, Mara."

She didn't want to. But forgiveness... well, it was a good thing, wasn't it? Reluctantly, she dipped her head and acknowledged his apology. Good thing or not, it was all he'd get from her.

Maude's face glowed.

Ma clapped and shoved up from her seat at the table. "We been up all morning jawing. Who's hungry?"

Hands rose and in no time the table was covered from one end to the other with food. The heavenly smells made her belly rumble. Laughter echoed in the tiny room. Even while Pa blessed it, Mara eyed the breakfast. Poor Dougal waited in the barn, hopefully resting, but surely hungry. Beauford's presence would keep her family from noticing when she skipped out.

She lifted a biscuit from a passing plate and hid it in her skirt pockets, then followed that with some bacon and cheese. Beauford started talking about the war and everyone's eyes glazed over. That must have been why they hadn't noticed earlier that she wasn't around—because he'd been there and telling war stories. For now it worked to her advantage. Before the meal was fully over, she left the table, her pockets full, and no one seemed to even care.

Groans emanated from inside the last stall, where she'd stashed her protector. She slid the door open. Atop the haystack, Dougal was curled into a ball.

"I brought food." She tugged the door shut.

Dougal buried his face in the hay. "I'm not hungry."

Now that wasn't like him at all. "But you gotta eat something."

"They think I burned the town."

"What? How did you know—?"

A sigh left his lips. "I heard them."

"You did?" If he could hear conversations from such a distance, make people smile randomly, and do all the other things she'd seen him do, then she knew he had to know all about her. Voodoo magic had to be really impressive.

He didn't seem impressed with himself and kept his face buried. "One of my many talents."

What if he could see through walls? Heat flushed her cheeks. "Have you—"

"Have I what? Listened to other conversations? What would be the point? Your voice was the only one I wanted to hear and you never spoke." Sadness filled his black eyes as he rolled over and pressed his hand to the wound at his side.

"Does it hurt a terrible lot?" She dropped beside him and pulled out the biscuits and bacon. Maybe the aroma would make him hungry.

"I've had worse."

"What can I do for you?"

"You could kiss me."

More heat struck her cheeks. If she got any hotter they could roast a chicken on her face.

A wicked grin teased his lips upward. "You don't understand. If you touch me, the healing process goes faster."

"Oh. But that makes no sense. I carried you all the way here."

"Hmm, true. But we need skin-to-skin contact."

"So if I place my hand upon your skin, then it should help?" Her heart rate increased. Pa would be appalled at her boldness. And she wasn't sure she believed Dougal at all.

With his eyes, Dougal followed the direction of her palm as it moved closer. He licked his lips. When her hand touched his naked side, a jolt shot through her. It stung and she jerked back, unable to maintain the contact.

The air blurred, the barn seemed to shiver around her, and his wound closed. What was happening? That hadn't been her; she was sure of it. It could only be his voodoo magic.

He leaned up on one elbow, wrapped his arm around her waist, and pulled her close. His lips crushed hers, taking her breath. She felt beautiful and loved as he placed kisses upon her eyelids, the tip of her nose, and each cheek. They rolled down into the hay together. His hands splayed on either side of her face and brought their lips back into contact.

Warmth infused her body. Heat flushed her cheeks and she snaked her arms around his neck. Each time his lips broke apart to kiss other places, he whispered words in another language.

*"Is tú mo ghrá, a chuisle, mo chroí."*

"What are you sayin'?" Why was it so hard to catch her breath? Had he stolen some of it with his kisses?

"What?" He still embraced her.

"You said something. What was it?"

A hint of pink tinged his cheeks. "Nothing." He pulled away as if trying to escape.

She held on. "No, you don't. Get over here and tell me what you said."

Leaning back upon the hay, Dougal clasped Mara's hands in his. He stared into her eyes as if he peered into her soul. *"Is tú mo ghrá, a chuisle, mo chroí."*

"Yes."

"It means," he paused, "I love you, my pulse, my heart."

# 38

O'Brien watched from atop his horse as his Rebel soldiers shuffled through town in chains. Boys in gray, uniforms sagging off their emaciated bodies, straggled between the burnt-out buildings. The recent loss at Gettysburg had been a turning point for the Rebel army, and the destruction of his town hadn't helped. Now all the boys coming home would be prisoners. Guess it was good he'd allied with both sides.

He whipped his horse around and dug in his heels, aiming for home. Times weren't going to get better. Too many soldiers from both sides were entering the valley. And what about Beauford? The young man hadn't been still since his return. Within three days of coming home, he'd gone to see his fiancée. The lady in question was ready to be married at a moment's notice.

But Beauford had nixed the idea. Probably because he was mentally mounting a rescue to save his fellow soldiers, the ones who were being held captive; or because he was going to join the ones coming to free them. Either way his distress could not have been greater. After O'Brien had given in to Herrick's demands, his son intended to go right back into the fray. Outrageous!

A feeling of worthlessness overwhelmed him. What was left for him to do? Over the past decade, he'd poured his life into the tiny town of Wheeler's Landing and now the train depot was all that remained, and even though the depot still stood, the train was dead on the tracks. No one would ride the rails to a broken-down town. Why go beyond Wheeler's Landing when the entire South appeared basically the same—broken?

Somewhere between the dead town and his mansion, he and his horse crossed the battle lines. In town the Union soldiers held sway, but as he approached home, the boys in gray he spied between the trees no longer wore chains. His pulse quickened. That close; they were that close. And then—

"Where are you going?" A young Rebel officer on horseback barred his driveway.

He pointed. "I'm going home."

The officer raised his eyebrows. "Might want to hurry. I'd get my family and hightail it out of here if I was you."

"Whatever for?" Sweat beaded his brow, not necessarily from the heat. Where had he put his handkerchief?

"The Union army is on the way." The boy's face turned grim. "We're preparing for battle."

"Where?"

"Right over there."

He was going to be sick. "But you can't! That's my family land."

"Can't be helped. We have to have a flat, raised spot to dig in our cannons, and that hill's the best place for miles around. Now gather your family and get out."

"Can't we stay in the house?"

"Is it that big white building over yonder, beyond the hill?"

A sinking feeling dragged down his gut. "Yes."

"Afraid not. We've already taken your home as our head-quarters. But we promise to take good care of it."

"But you can't!"

"Yes, we can."

"But—"

With a sudden sharp thrust of his spurs, the officer surged his horse closer. Knee to knee with O'Brien, he curled his lip and snarled, "I know what you did. The whole Rebel army knows what you did."

"What?" His heart hammered with fear. Had Herrick told anyone he'd helped the on-duty soldiers get drunk? He'd only done so to protect them. If they'd fought back, they would have all been killed. This way they were only taken prisoner.

The hammering lengthened, slowed, as his innards turned cold. Beauford would be devastated if he heard.

"The men in that town swore to defend you and you incapacitated them. Your town would have been safe, but you had to go and make a deal with the devil. Now you'll see what happens."

"But it wasn't me. It was—"

"We know who did the deed. Now get out." The officer jerked the reins and his horse backed up a few snorting, dancing steps. "That's the only warning you'll get. And just so we're clear, the only reason you're gettin' a warning instead of a gunshot is because of your son. I hear he's a real hero."

The officer turned away and left O'Brien gasping. Impossible to gather his wits, so without thinking, he kicked the horse's flanks and raced home.

Ivy crouched on the lawn, her head buried in her delicate hands, rocking back and forth. Her skirts trailed in the stamped-down flowerbed. Agonizing wails of grief poured from her.

He truly had lost everything.

Herrick peered through the spyglass. The blue coats were on the move and lining up along the field. A little further north, O'Brien had just turned toward his home. Dust kicked up behind his galloping horse. So the man was in a hurry. He should be. The war was coming to his front door. When he'd told Ivy he had a means to make her troubles go away, he'd meant it.

"The men are in position." The black gryphon soldier looked the part of a young military officer. One day they would rule and would not be forced to hide behind such hideous forms. But for now, the human body was useful.

"Good. Perhaps the battle will bring out the one we seek." He rubbed his hands together. He was ready to get this over with and escape before Cahal learned of his plan to take control—before the real battle began.

# 39

Reluctantly, Dougal agreed to hide in the barn until Mara thought it prudent for him to show himself. Personally, he wanted to hide indefinitely or leave. He'd heard Beauford's comment about taking him out with his bare hands. He didn't want to have to kill Maude's future husband. Well, maybe he did want to kill the jerk. No, he didn't. No matter how he felt about it.

Mara, however, held some foolish notion that with time, the family would welcome him back. He doubted it. In his experience, mistakes weren't easily forgiven.

"They know you didn't do it."

For her sake, he didn't roll his eyes. "But how?"

"Because I told them and they believe me. If you heard Beauford the first time, surely you heard him the second time, when he apologized for assumin'."

Oh, yeah, he'd heard him. The sarcasm had oozed from Beauford's tone, but sweet Mara hadn't heard it. "I still don't think this is a good idea."

"Well, I do. And I want you to—well, I want you to—"

"Yes...?" He batted his eyelashes. What did the little sprite want? He'd give it to her, indeed he would, but not without baiting her first.

She wrapped a strand of hair around her finger. "I want you to ask to woo me again. Only this time, I want you to do it for real."

"A little forthright, don't you think?"

"Don't you like it?" Her voice caught. Aw, shoot, she really was worried.

He relented. "Actually, I do. From timid to bold, that's my kind of gal." A red hue tinged her cheeks. He liked that, too. "Have I embarrassed you?"

"Of course not. It would take much more than that to embarrass me." She lifted her chin.

He doubted her words, but he liked her haughtiness. Shoot, he liked everything about her. "Look me in the eye and say it. Because I don't believe you."

Mara raised her gray eyes to meet his black ones. A little electric shock shivered through him.

"You want the truth; I'll give you the truth. Every time you look at me, I'm embarrassed. Are you happy now? You've made a girl go and reveal her most private secrets." She studied a piece of hay, refusing to look at him again.

"I won't be happy until I receive a kiss."

His head dipped slowly toward hers. Her eyes slid sideways, and her face turned toward him. She licked her lips. Their heartbeats resounded in his head. Pulse quickening, blood rushing...

"What are you doing in here?"

Oh, rats, not again.

Before he could even think, she whirled around and planted herself between them, her legs apart. "Junior, I-I—"

Junior pointed over her shoulder, right at Dougal. "That man burnt down the whole town. What are you thinking? Do Pa and Ma know? Get over here and get away from him."

"Junior, let me explain." Mara didn't move, but he could see that her pulse fluttered in her neck.

"There ain't no need to explain. I know what he is. He's a traitor. Now get away from him."

"I won't do it." She crossed her arms.

"I'll yell for Pa and then we'll see what you do."

"Go ahead. They'll listen to me."

Brother and sister stared at each other, as if they'd forgotten he was even there. A wrinkle creased Junior's forehead, confusion rumpling his face, then he left and Mara's shoulders sagged.

Dougal clasped her upper arms and gently squeezed. "It's okay. I'm leaving." Apparently her family wasn't as ready to forgive as she'd thought.

She shook her head. "No, please, you can't go. That'll be proof that you're guilty. Besides, you can't leave me. I need you."

He rubbed her smooth cheek. A single tear slipped from the corner of her eye, and he swiped it away and cradled her face in his hand. "I won't be far. I promise."

"But I feel like I just found you. I don't want you to go." Her voice trembled.

"I don't want to leave, but it's for the best. If you need me, sing."

Her eyebrows shot higher. "Sing?"

"Yes, sing."

He released her face and left her standing. Outside the barn, in the drenching morning sunlight, he shielded his eyes and tried to think. Loud voices erupted behind him as he raced to the wood's edge. Once within the safety of the trees, he morphed and took flight.

For once, the pumping of his wings didn't thrill him. Where could he hide that would keep him close to his love? During the day he could watch over her from a high tree, sheltering from prying eyes in the leaves, but at night—

At night, he slipped down from the tree, tried to stretch out his cramped legs, and limped to the creek. The bed of grass, sheltered beneath a willow, was soft and comfortable, but a rock for a pillow wasn't. However, Dougal made do, even though he kicked himself for refusing the breakfast Mara had offered him. His belly rumbled with hunger as the sleepless night stretched before him. Would he ever rest? Finally, the sound of the rushing water lulled him into a deep sleep.

*"Dougal..."*

*"Yes."*

*"It's time."*

*"Time for what?"*

*"Time to come home."*

*"No! I can't leave now. Mara needs me. Maeldun is still alive. She isn't safe."*

*"The time is now. The end is at hand. You must return."*

*"No..." His voice in his head seemed to trail away to nothingness.*

Water droplets landed on his face, waking him from the awful dream. The willow's limbs above kept most of the rain at bay, but enough trickled through to wake him. Scooting farther under the tree's protection, he rested his head in his hands. Not now. He couldn't leave now. Didn't Cian understand the mission was incomplete? Mara didn't know her history, and she wasn't strong enough to protect herself.

But did he have a choice? The dream seemed to indicate no. The summons to return had been issued. But if he refused... Could he refuse?

The rain pelted his shelter. Water ran down the trunk of the ancient tree, fell onto his shoulders, and seeped into his thin clothing. He shivered. The cave would have provided more shelter. Perhaps going there now would be a good idea. A fire and a dry place to sleep would make everything better.

Before he could move, a branch snapped somewhere behind him. Sitting up straight, he scanned the trees for an intruder. But then pain radiated along the side of his head and blackness swam across his vision. It was too late.

Ropes cut into his raw skin, gouging tender spots that burned with every movement. Darkness surrounded him. Could he be in the white tower? Had his time travel back to his original time already occurred? He'd not been ready. Mara still needed him.

He blinked until his eyes adjusted. Moonlight filtered dimly through the worn canvas. Apparently he was prisoner in a tent.

"Welcome." The voice was deep and rough.

He struggled against his bindings, moaning as pain shot up his arms.

A chuckle. "Be still, my son. No need to struggle. You will not be able to free yourself."

"Who are you?" He knew. He didn't want to know, but he did. But he had to be wrong. His captor was a human, not a gryphon, or at least had taken human form. Did all blacks in this era know the spell and have the ability to change? Major unfair.

"Do you not know my voice? Everyone knows who I am, in some way or another."

The husky voice, the smell of brimstone and sulfur. *Cahal.*

He had called him "son." Cahal didn't know how correct he was. Dougal wouldn't be born for another fifty or sixty years, but still this vile creature would play a major part in the event.

"I know you." Dougal kept all emotion from his voice. He wouldn't give him the satisfaction of knowing how affected he was.

"Good. Then I assume you know what I seek."

The word dragged from him. "Power."

Cahal lit a lamp and flooded the tent with light, then leaned his head back and roared with laughter. "Power. Such a simple answer. You're correct—power is the ultimate goal, but for now, what I require is the girl and the sword."

"What girl?" His heart hammered against his chest. He'd seen what Cahal did to people he no longer needed—Serena's severed head floated across his memory. The thought sickened him, but determination flooded in behind that. There was no way he'd ever give Mara up. No matter what Cahal did to him.

A *tsk*. "Are you going to play dumb? This is not the best time for you to do so. I have you at a great disadvantage."

"True. But I still don't know what you're talking about." The ropes were tight, but if he could just loosen the knot, he should be able to slip free. The canvas tent would be nothing against his escape, but there would be guards. He would just need to make sure Cahal stayed safe. Otherwise he—Dougal—might not exist in the future.

Cahal settled into a seat across from Dougal and steepled his fingers. "I see you want to be difficult." He tapped his finger to his chin. "I know who you are. You are a gray gryphon. But you're not one of the twelve, I think. No, you're alone. There is no one to protect you."

Fear gnawed at his gut, but he wouldn't show it. Cahal could guess and be correct all day and he wouldn't care.

"The Jotunn wield the power of giants," Cahal continued. "The Jotunn will kill everyone in their path. Only I can save humanity. If you wish to survive, then you will tell me where the girl is."

"Some things are worth dying for." For the first time in his life, he really believed that. And keeping Mara safe was one of those things. Besides, Cahal was a proven liar. Why would he ever believe him, even if he was his father?

Cahal hauled him into the air by the scruff of his neck. Fierce eyes penetrated his face. "Do not mess with me, boy. I will have the girl. I can do it the easy way or the hard way."

Dougal struggled to draw a breath. "I guess you'll be doing it the hard way." His voice was hoarse. How could he rescue Mara if he couldn't break free from his father?

Cahal dropped him, let him stagger and find his balance, and then pulled back his fist. Dougal cringed as he prepared for the blow. It was going to hurt. The only time his father ever touched him, and it was going to hurt.

"Sir! Sir! Someone's coming." A young man slid to a halt at the tent flap, wild-eyed and panting.

Cahal flared his nostrils. "What do you want? Were you not told I wished to remain undisturbed?"

"Yes. Of course. But Maeldun insisted. It's urgent."

Snarling, Cahal swept aside the tent flap and stalked outside in a huff. Saved by Maeldun: the irony wasn't lost on Dougal.

He worked at the bonds, wriggling his hands back and forth to loosen the knot. Pain radiated along his arms from the raw spots his twisting enlarged, and he sucked in a swift breath. He just needed to—

Someone tugged on his wrist. He jerked. What was this new torment?

"Stay still before I cut you." Ailin's voice.

Dougal's heart soared. *Saved!* He felt the pressure as Ailin sliced the ropes, and he flung off the remnants and rubbed his raw wrists.

When he glanced up, Ailin was in human form and dressed in blue. A Union soldier? What was happening outside this tent?

Ailin didn't seem inclined to stop and chat. "We must hurry. Once Cahal realizes Maeldun didn't send for him, we'll be in trouble."

He was puzzled, but followed Ailin out of the tent and into a large, bustling camp filled with soldiers, all dressed in blue. What kind of crazy, mixed-up universe had he fallen into? Did Cahal have Union soldiers working for him or were these black gryphons in human form?

Ailin whispered, "Walk in front of me like you're my prisoner. Keep your hands behind your back and your head down. Don't look anyone in the eye."

Heart pounding, arms tingling with pins and needles as blood flow returned, he stared at booted feet, tent pegs, and horses' legs until they reached the camp's far edge, and then they walked some more. Finally, after what seemed like forever, trees surrounded them on all sides. The small clearing felt tight, like a cage. Surely they would need more room to fly away, if he could even transform and if he could get his wings to cooperate. After having his arms tied behind his back for so long, he wondered.

But beyond the little clearing, a field opened to the sky. Ailin transformed and took flight. Dougal's eyes followed the black gryphon as he gained altitude. He should probably do the same, surely Mara needed him still, and the stab of terror the thought aroused began the change. Within moments, he was airborne.

The cry of alarm sounded as soon as they reached the sky.

# 40

Mara remained despondent and moped around the farm, doing only the bare minimum—mainly hauling water to the irrigation channels, although she no longer cared whether the corn lived or died. Dougal had disappeared again! Even though he'd promised to stay close by. Close enough to hear her sing, he'd said.

The night before, she'd sat at the water's edge and sang until her throat ached. All she had to do was sing, huh? And what? He'd ignore her? Because that was what he'd done. She'd sung words that held no meaning. Words which barely went together, strung into a semblance of order, and sung loudly. But still he'd not returned.

Without Dougal, the world seemed half full. Of course, Maude experienced no such lethargy. Since Beauford's unexpected return, her sister was as happy as a lark. She skipped around, making wedding plans and grinning from ear to ear. Mara was happy for her, or so she insisted to herself. Maude had waited a long time for this moment and she deserved it. Well, maybe.

"Do you like it?" Maude twirled in her wedding gown.

Mara nodded. The white gown reached the floor. Lace formed a V at her neck and around her sleeves.

Maude continued. "I know Beauford said if the army comes back he would need to join them, but we're still going ahead with the weddin' while he's home. Don't you think that's the best idea?"

Mara nodded again. What else could she say? *No, wait.* That advice wouldn't be well received.

Maude didn't let her sister's lack of interest discourage her. "I wanted to get married here on the property. You know, take a boat on the river and show up by the lower field. I told Pa all I wanted was a white parasol to go with my dress and he agreed! But then Beauford told me his Ma wasn't feeling well and the only way she could attend the weddin' would be if we had it at the Wheeler house.

"I guess I'll just be happy bein' married and startin' my own family, no matter where it starts. Of course, even after Beauford and I get hitched, I'll live here until he's truly done with the war and he finds us a place. I told him there was no way I was livin' in the big house with him not being there. No way."

Mara folded clothes. Maude wanted to talk. She wanted to sing—for Dougal.

"Besides, I would be lonely and bored, for sure. I'd miss our talks and Ma's cookin' and even Junior's lumberin' around." She cocked her head. "Mara, are you listenin' to me? I've been talkin' for a month of Sundays and you haven't said one word! I know you're pinin' over Dougal." She put her hand on her hip. "When are you goin' to get it through your head? Dougal is no good."

Tears streaked her face and she turned away. How could there be more tears?

Maude kept talking. But she couldn't take any more. She dropped the dress and ran.

Downstairs, a hot breeze wafted through the house, almost but not quite bearable. She needed privacy and turned toward the creek, where she could be alone and sing her throat out. A large shadow flashed over her, then another... and another... and another. Cold fear drove out the day's heat. She swallowed and raised her head. Gryphons! Her pulse raced. She needed to warn her family.

She ran toward the barn—wasn't Junior cleaning stalls?—but her fear made her clumsy, and she stumbled and fell. Without pausing, she splayed her hands in the dirt and pushed herself up. Before she quite made it, a loud boom like thunder echoed all around. The gryphons vanished, leaving the sky crystal clear. However, a puff of smoke rose beyond the nearest hill, the one leading to the old Wheeler property. Was there a fire?

Junior ran into the yard from the corn field—he must have been irrigating—and slid to a halt, hauling her to her feet with one hand. "We've got to get Ma and Pa and leave now!"

He'd seen them, too?

"Mara! This is important. The Union soldiers are just over that rise. We've got to get out of here!"

So he hadn't seen the gryphons. If he had, he wouldn't be worrying about soldiers. "I don't know where Pa is, but Ma and Maude are in the house."

Junior didn't wait to hear if she had more to say. His feet slapped the ground as he ran toward the house. With a yell upon his lips, he raced inside and seconds later dragged the two women out. The noise must have alerted Pa, because he came running from the fields on her left.

Chattering in fear but working as a team, they hitched the horses to the wagon and climbed in the back. Once she was safely aboard, though, Mara paused. Uncertain, she glanced one last time at the barn, wondering if leaving was the right thing to do. Dougal might return... and what about the weapon? Couldn't it help them?

At the end of the drive, Junior pointed. A battle raged in the fields to the east. Pa slapped the reins down and the horses jumped forward. As the wagon lurched into motion, she made her decision and quietly dropped off the back, sliding into the underbrush and running back to the house. The family moved on, so busy watching the battle they didn't even notice her departure.

Well, she hadn't really been one of them. Had she?

The cannons fired again. The acrid smell of burning gunpowder filled the valley with dark, drifting smoke. The ground shook with each volley. Men screamed in agony as metal struck flesh. Then, for an eerie moment, all was quiet. Even the birds fell silent.

Step by slowing step, she approached the barn. Whether she should run as fast as possible or be stealthy, she wasn't sure. Was it possible someone watched her? Ultimately, reaching the sword was her only priority. After it was in her hand, the question would become what to do with it. She could run and catch back up with her family, or try to fight before returning to them.

The door creaked as she pushed it slightly open. She cringed, steeled herself, and slipped inside. With her back flat against the wooden wall, she crept around the barn until she reached the empty stall in the back, beside the one where she'd hidden Dougal. She dropped to her knees and swept away the hay and debris. Beneath the clutter was a loose board. She touched the edge and prepared to lift.

A thousand hammers slammed against the metal roof above. She dropped onto all fours, crouching in a ball, until the thunder ended. But it wasn't thunder. The sound was all wrong. What—

Again the crashing came. This time she covered her head and squeezed her eyes shut. Surely no army in the world had a weapon capable of producing such a sound? If it was a gun, when it was finished being used, there'd be no one left to pick up the pieces except the one man who'd pulled the trigger.

She should go outside and look. Slowly she began to uncurl.

A force as strong as that sound flung her into the wall. Pain radiated along the back of her skull and she slumped, stunned. A hand grabbed her neck and hoisted her upward until her feet dangled above the floor. She gasped for air. If she screamed, would Dougal find her?

Her assailant wore a ragged captain's blue uniform. A rapier hung from a rope tied about his waist. Dirt encrusted his fingernails, but he seemed fit and in decent condition. If not for the evil shiftiness in his eyes, the look of anger on his chiseled face, he might have been handsome, in a rugged way. And there was the matter of him trying to kill her.

With all her strength, she tugged at his hands, trying to loosen his grip.

"Where is it?" His perfect teeth ground together.

The room swam out of focus. Just when her lungs seemed ready to burst, he dropped her. Her feet slammed into the floorboards, crumpling her into the hay. Her bones trembled from the impact and she remained perfectly still, squelching her gasps of agony.

"You don't understand the pressure I'm under. I have courted you for *ten years*. This is my moment. Now, where is the sword?" he growled.

What on earth? No one had ever courted her, not until Dougal pretended to, and certainly not a Union officer. The man was delusional. Trying to decide what to do or say, she glanced down. The floorboard beneath her lay exposed. She pretended to collapse beside it and shifted the hay.

Even though she was unsure of what power the sword held, she had a feeling that in the wrong hands, it would cause something very bad to happen and she had no intention of finding that out for certain.

"I don't know what you mean." Putting a tremor into her voice took no guise at all.

He huffed. "So now you've decided to speak. I thought I told you years ago that speech was forbidden."

"I don't know you." Or did she? Had the air thinned? She was finding it hard to breathe, the terror closing her lungs.

Clothing ripped. The air seemed to darken as the man transformed. Unlike Dougal, the captain lurched and jerked, his bones twisting into an unnatural shape. A long snout, black fur, dark and powerful wings. Then he was there.

Maeldun glared at her, his fangs bared. But he seemed as afraid as she. "I will have the sword or I will slice your throat."

Slowly she rose, forcing her shaking legs to hold her. "Why do you want it?"

His fear seemed alive—but why? What on earth could frighten such a monster? "It's simple. Power."

She needed to keep him talking. "What kind of power?"

Again he huffed. "The power to rule the world, of course."

The only thing that could frighten a monster was a bigger monster. The answer clicked in her mind and Mara took the chance. "Don't you mean your leader wants the sword? You're just a flunky. You're nothing." She was reaching, but she needed to stall.

His fist struck her cheek. She stumbled backward and fell, reeling to the ground in a heap. Something within her changed, twisted like the changing beast's bones, and her anger ignited. He'd hit her. How dare he!

Maeldun pricked his ears and his head twitched.

"Mara..." Dougal. He hadn't left her! He was coming for her. Saved!

"Will the gray never die?" Maeldun snarled.

Rough hands grasped her around the waist and yanked her up. The stench of sulfur made her gag as Maeldun shoved her toward the barn door. Her legs shook with each step, but at least the sword was safe. He wouldn't find it, because he clamped one hand upon her shoulder and drove her before him as he opened the barn door and peered outside.

One claw poked into her neck, barely breaking the skin where her pulse beat a terrified tattoo.

Gray wings flashed and furled as gryphons landed around the barnyard. Dougal had come to rescue her, but he wasn't alone. A whole group of gray gryphons stood with him, and one black one. Would this band be enough to defeat Maeldun? Or would she need to help them? She didn't know if she was ready.

The Gatling gun fired again, bullets striking ground, trees, and flesh. Dougal's pulse raced in rhythm with its chatter. The Gatling gun was a terrifying machine. The six barrels, working together, could fire over four hundred rounds a minute. Only about twenty-five of the powerful guns had been used during the Civil War. Union General Benjamin F. Butler had used two of them around Petersburg, and a few were mounted on naval boats, but he knew the South had never possessed such a weapon. Had they stolen this one?

Beside him, Ailin cringed, and Dougal remember where he was and why. Twelve gray gryphons had accompanied him and Ailin to the Hess farm, flying high enough to keep the humans from seeing them. Black gryphons had threatened them en route, but not enough to make a serious fight. But it was only a matter of time. Cahal had a whole army of blacks. They couldn't avoid confrontation forever.

Tomas scanned the area. "Where is the girl? You said she would be here."

"She *is* here." The wagon was gone, but he knew Mara hadn't left with it; he felt her.

"I don't see her." Tomas frowned and shrugged. "We should go back."

Ailin frowned. "The girl is here. Can you not feel the presence of the Jotunn? Have you been so long from the mainland you have forgotten? May I never forget the feeling of their presence."

Tomas narrowed his eyes. He probably didn't enjoy being called out by an ex-gray turned black, no matter how or why it had happened, and Dougal smirked, wondering what Tomas would do if he only knew the whole truth.

With a shake of his wings, Tomas reentered leader mode.

"You, scout the perimeter. You, search the house. The battle between the humans draws closer. We must hurry." He shifted his gaze. "Are you sure, Ailin?"

"I'm sure. The girl is in danger, and she can save the world or destroy it."

*Save it... destroy it.* Dougal shivered. Were the stakes truly so high? There had to be something he could do, and he remembered that a gray was linked to the human he'd been sent to protect. Maybe he could connect with her. Closing his eyes and concentrating, he focused his mind on her face. A tingle raced along his spine. It felt as if he touched her soul.

"*Mara...*" It felt like it was dragged from his throat in a hoarse whisper. She was close; he could feel her.

Just like the first time he'd seen her, she appeared as if she were an apparition. Light streamed around her. The white cotton dress she wore enhanced the glow of her tanned skin. It was almost as if he could see through her. He sucked in a breath and admired her vast beauty.

With a tentative step, she moved out from behind the barn door.

He stepped forward with his arms open, then stopped. Something dark loomed behind her.

"One more step and I will break her neck."

# 41

Dougal's blood pumped faster and faster through his veins. Maeldun rested his claw upon Mara's vulnerable neck. Now they needed to remove her from Maeldun's clutches *and* retrieve the sword... no problem. An ancient need to protect overwhelmed him and all thoughts for his own personal safety fled.

"Step back!" Maeldun pulled her closer.

"Let her go." His voice was deep and booming, startling him.

Maeldun shifted his gaze and cocked a brow. "Ailin, I see you have returned. And associating with grays, tsk tsk. Wait until Cahal learns of this interesting development. Do you know I've yet to inform him of your treachery? Your prowess with women is his excuse for your untimely departure. Only I know the real reason you aren't with our forces, where you're supposed to be. Only I know you helped the lass escape the village raid."

So after rescuing Mara, Ailin had returned to Cahal's group and became one of his trusted advisors, at least until the debacle with Arin's sister. Cahal had never known of Ailin's first treachery, which explained why he'd lived long enough to help Maddie and Chase in the future.

Ailin looked relaxed even as his feet shuffled and kicked up dust. "Why didn't you tell him? Cahal would have ordered all his minions to search for me."

"Why should I tell him anything? I'm second in command. I can more than handle any situation on my own, including you."

"Then you have no intention of giving him the girl or the sword?" Ailin sounded shocked.

Dougal swallowed. That wasn't good.

Maeldun shrugged. "The thought might have crossed my mind."

Ailin relaxed his fists. "Why don't you come over to the winning side? Give up your wicked ways and your struggle for power. Let the girl go." Ailin motioned Maeldun forward, like he was inviting a friend into the group. The irony. Later they'd both do the same thing, all over again.

A maniacal laugh rolled from Maeldun. "I wouldn't go that far. In fact, I have a better plan. You will give the girl her sword and I will take over the world for myself."

The twelve grays fanned out around captor and captive. Dougal edged around the side of the barn, planning his own sneak attack. Other than Mara, he was the only one who knew the sword's location. Without the sword, how much power did Mara possess? Probably none. That was the way power worked—all or nothing. But she was out of her natural village, her proper place...

From that angle, he could see she trembled from head to toe. The closer he came to her physical presence, the more emotion he felt. The feeling of her terror was distracting. He blinked it away and sucked in a deep breath. He needed to focus, to concentrate. To rescue her.

Another boom. A billow of smoke filled the air as cannon fire rocked the ground. Maeldun lost his tenuous grip—

—and Mara scooted away! Maeldun tried to grab her again, but it was too late. She'd already run for safety and crouched behind Ailin. The grays pounced and Maeldun roared as they piled atop him.

Dougal didn't wait for the order. He rushed to Mara's side, swooped her up into his arms, and pumped his wings, flying her away from the melee. When he thought they were safe, he touched down in a clearing and released her. She clung to him, so close he could feel her heart beating, her breaths gasping.

"We have to go back." Her wide eyes stared into his.

"No."

She clutched his forearms. "We have to! The sword! If Maeldun discovers it, all is lost."

That didn't sound good. "Did you remember something?" He wasn't sure a black gryphon could wield the sword. Ailin's story pretty much meant that she had to be the one holding it, which was a good reason to keep her far away.

"Yes." Her voice lowered, like she was trying to keep others from hearing.

"Well?"

She bit her lip and her sigh shook her entire body. "I remember a beautiful village, everything green and lush. The mountains were tall enough to touch the sky. We were all happy. Then I remember a day of screaming and terror, and my mother telling me I wasn't meant to be a warrior."

He smoothed hair from her brow. "I would prefer that you never had to fight."

"I was just a baby then, but not any longer. I don't know how, but I know I have a job to do, and I'm going back to get the sword. And while I have no idea what I'm supposed to do with it, I'm going to figure it out."

No way would he would argue with her. Either he helped her, or she'd do it alone. She was that determined. "What's your plan?"

"Plan?"

"Yes. We need a plan. We can't just swoop in and demand Maeldun step aside so we can retrieve the sword, now, can we?"

"Do you think he can take on all those gray gryphons and survive?"

"I'm not sure. Maybe he has help that we don't know about." Most likely he did. Dougal scratched his brow. "There has to be something we don't know." Maeldun had seemed too relaxed, too confident. He'd gone against Cahal, hadn't he?

Battle sounds grew closer. The Rebels and the Yankees dueled for control of the country, while the grays and the blacks would soon be fighting for the world.

It was going to be a busy day.

# 42

After the Rebel officer ordered O'Brien to leave the farm, he rushed home. Ivy's grief over the battle raging on her land only slowed him down briefly. He gathered her and Beauford, and announced his spur-of-the-moment plan to take a trip. The Mississippi, he'd said; they'd make their way to the big river and board a paddlewheel, maybe ride it all the way down to the Gulf of Mexico.

Ivy perked up immediately. Her lucidity returned, if only for the moment, and she packed a valise full of clothes, then a second one. Ellie tried to help her, but O'Brien gave her different orders and so instead she busied herself by packing up the silver and other valuables. No matter what the Rebel officer had said, O'Brien didn't trust any army to protect his property.

While Ivy packed, he pleaded with Beauford. "You have to stay with us."

"But, Father—"

"Besides, those soldiers aren't yours." His frustration mounted. If Beauford stayed behind with *these* particular soldiers, then O'Brien ran the risk of personal exposure. Someone might tell his son he'd given them alcohol, and that couldn't happen. If he had to, he would use Ivy's instability to keep Beauford close.

"I'll stay until Mother is settled, then I'm returning to my command."

He'd never been so relieved. In a final rush, he sent Elijah out to prepare the carriage, Beauford with the luggage, and he personally led Ivy outside. But when they got there, Elijah and Ellie huddled together behind a Rebel officer—neither of them on the carriage.

Beauford loaded their bags in the back before assisting his mother inside.

O'Brien tapped his cane to the ground, but Elijah didn't move. "Sorry, massa, but they won't let us leave with you."

O'Brien faced the crowd of soldiers.

"The slaves are staying. We might have need of them." The young officer crossed his arms over his chest.

"My wife needs Ellie. Can't you see she's ill?"

"Too bad. And if you wait any longer, then you won't be leaving at all."

Reluctantly, O'Brien climbed onto the driver's seat and flung out the whip. He'd driven many years before and he could figure it out again. The horses naturally followed the tree-lined road, but once they were out of sight, he reined them off the road and behind two trees.

"Father, why did you stop?"

"We'll wait here for the soldiers to leave, and when they do, we'll go back."

"But why? I don't understand."

"I won't leave my possessions behind." And he didn't like being told what to do.

They waited at the bend, hidden behind the trees, until the soldiers trotted past. When the last one went by and vanished in the distance, O'Brien wheeled the horses around and urged them into a gallop. In front of the house, he jumped from the carriage and rushed inside, while Beauford waited with Ivy. Hopefully he wouldn't be long. He just needed to find Elijah and Ellie. Where were they? He hadn't seen them with the departing soldiers.

Gunfire rang out, too near. Now what was going on? Was the battle getting closer, or was something else happening?

He raced to the front porch. Smoke drifted over the nearest ridge. Beauford and Ivy climbed from the carriage and joined him, Ivy's face pale and drawn. Beauford looked ready to bolt, both angry and determined. Could he hold his son back if more than one Rebel soldier stood right in front of him? Probably not.

Dust billowed along the dry road leading to the house. It couldn't be the Rebs again; they had only just left. O'Brien stepped in front of Ivy and thrust out his chest.

A wagon rounded the bend, the horses going at a strong trot. He shielded his eyes. Flint Hess called to the horses and stopped his wagon beside the carriage. Maude jumped down and raced to Beauford's side. "We need to go! They're coming."

"No. You go. Take my mother and father. I must rejoin my men." Beauford tried to step off the porch.

But Maude held tight. "No! You can't. It's too dangerous." She tugged on his sleeve. For the first time, O'Brien liked her. He couldn't hold his son in place, but maybe his fiancée could.

Beauford cupped Maude's cheek and touched a brief kiss to her dusty brow. Tears ran down her dimpled face, creating one clean line beneath each eye. She twisted her hands in her gown. Beauford ran toward the barn and she reached out to his departing back. When he returned, he rode O'Brien's best saddle horse.

O'Brien's heart hammered as Beauford rode past without even acknowledging him.

Maude grabbed her skirts and ran after Beauford. Her pleading voice drifted back as she begged him to wait.

Flint Hess pushed his hat back on his head. "Mr. O'Brien, I reckon you should grab your household slaves and come with us. We're headed out of town, seeking somewhere to wait it out. The battle is too close for comfort."

O'Brien managed a nod—he had come back for that very reason—even if it bristled that Flint had had to remind him. All he needed was one more problem, and with the thought, Ivy crumpled onto the porch in a dead faint.

Before he could yell, Elijah appeared from around the barn, easily lifted Ivy, and carried her back to the carriage, settling her inside. Ellie tucked a pillow behind Ivy's back.

For a short moment he was tempted to stay behind and protect what little remained of his property. But the thought of Ivy lying alone on the carriage seat, his son astride a horse and headed back into the fray, caused him to bend at the waist and vomit.

Slippered feet appeared beside him. Maude laid her cool hand against his flushed forehead. Maybe she wouldn't be so bad for Beauford after all.

There was nothing more to be done. Junior helped him into the carriage, Elijah climbed up to the driver's seat, and Ellie hung on behind. He didn't protest. Right now he could use all the help he could get.

Reins snapped overhead and the wheels lurched into motion, shaking the last thoughts from his head. The interior of the carriage seemed smaller with Ivy inside; he'd grown too used to riding into town alone. With a sigh, she laid her head back against the wall and stared off, her face blank. Beauford shouldn't have left her again. She needed him, needed her son.

Cannon fire smacked the ground—*too close!*—and rocked the carriage. He wedged his hand under the bench and held on.

So Hess had been right. Danger was coming and they were in the middle of it. Even with the burnt-out buildings in town, they would be safer there than here. And if necessary, they could always continue on down that road, as far as they needed to go.

He lifted the curtain and peered out. Charcoal-colored smoke billowed into the sky. Trees splintered. Pounding cannons sent his pulse into overdrive. He was going to be ill again. Beauford—his son—had gone back into that? And for what?

A new sound pierced the air, a pounding chatter like a gun firing impossibly fast. His heart threatened to stop. It was the weapon from the silo. The Gatling gun.

The volley seemed to last forever. When it finally ended, the world was silent, as if he could no longer hear or all sound was gone. Then a wail of grief rose. He startled. It hadn't come from the battlefield, but rather from inside the carriage. He turned in time to see Ivy lift her head and fling the door open. She jumped out, screamed, and waved her arms like a madwoman as she ran toward the carnage.

O'Brien leaped from the moving carriage, shouted for Elijah to keep going, and ran after her. Before he reached her side, she fell to her knees and peered heavenward. Her eyes glossed over. Now he was really afraid. But he had to look. He had to know what she saw.

He drew in a deep breath and looked. A mass of huge black flying bats hovered overhead. Each had what appeared to be at least a twelve-foot wingspan and looked like fruit bats or flying foxes, only much larger and meaner, with sharp claws and bared fangs. But these were no fruit bats. They were like the creature he'd seen in Ivy's room, the one with human features. What were they doing flying over the battle?

Ivy trembled. "No!"

He grabbed her arm and tugged. They needed to move. The weapons fire was coming closer and they were out in the open. "Come, dear. We must return to the carriage." But she fought to pull away and he clenched his teeth. Could Junior haul her over his shoulder back to the carriage?

"Not safe. Not safe!"

"That's right. It's not safe here. We need to go."

Her eyes bulged wide as she gripped his arms tight enough to leave bruises. "I'm not the one. I'm safe. But she's not. What can we do? What can we do?"

He started to berate her, but she skulked back to the carriage, climbed inside, and shut the door, leaving him kneeling in the empty field. The next explosion of cannon fire sent him into motion, running after her. The Hess family eyed him as he jumped into the carriage. They would probably like an explanation for Ivy's strange behavior. If so, they would be waiting a long time. He couldn't tell them anything, because he didn't understand it himself.

She sat ramrod-straight on the seat, repeating in mumbled tones, "What can we do? What can we do?"

He ignored her and faced the window with his chin squared. Elijah set the vehicle into motion. Ivy repeated the same question, over and over again.

"Now we are alone." Ailin hadn't wanted things to happen this way, but the time had come to end it. The gray gryphons formed a half circle behind him, pinning Maeldun to the barn.

Not that that would hold him.

"We are indeed, and you can stop pretending. I know you wish to rule as much as I. Otherwise you would have allowed yourself to die with your brethren over seventeen years ago. Speak to the girl; have her give up the sword. We can work together, I assure you."

"Maeldun, your time is up. The girl is on the side of the gray gryphons. She will use her power to rescue the world, not destroy it." At least, that was what he'd hoped for the last seventeen years.

A laugh of derision rent the air. "You're delusional."

"Me?" Ailin could have commented on Maeldun's delusion,

that he had a chance of survival once Cahal discovered his treachery.

"How can the girl possibly think she can save the world? You know as well as I what is coming."

Just the reminder, the bare thought of what was coming, brought Ailin to a standstill. Fear raced through his heart. Fear of the future should bring him to his knees, but he knew he wouldn't be around to witness it. He would play a part in how it occurred, but he wouldn't be there for the end battle. He didn't know how he knew; he just did. But today none of that mattered. Maeldun was just trying to scare him, make him drop his guard.

He straightened his shoulders. "It may be coming, but not now. And we cannot force the happening any earlier than it should be."

Maeldun guffawed. "That remains to be seen."

"Maeldun, give it up. Let the girl go. Leave this place."

"All interesting possibilities, to which my answer will be no. Now, if you will excuse me, I have a girl to find."

Shadows descended. Again the ground shook, this time not from cannon fire. This wasn't good. He didn't need to look to know he and the grays were now surrounded by a multitude of black gryphons.

"Alas, reinforcements." Maeldun looked past Ailin and raised his voice. "Please take care of these *pests*. I have business to attend to."

Ailin finally looked.

"Your wish is our command." One of the many black gryphons stepped forward.

Twelve grays and him against a huge group of blacks—they didn't stand a chance.

The blacks attacked. The ground shook again. They were like a school of lampreys, jumping on the backs of the grays, their mouths open. They ripped and tore flesh, sucking out the life and blood. One of the grays screamed. The fight lasted no more than a few minutes before Tomas yelled the order to retreat.

Wounded, Ailin, Tomas, and two others barely escaped, ducking beneath the forest canopy and hiding among the trees. A gryphon healed with time, even with such wounds, but those they had to leave behind were too far gone. Now all they could do was retreat.

Peering from beneath the stout branches, Ailin scoured the land and sky with his weary eyes. Fortunately they were not pursued. If more blacks had come, they would never have survived. Weak from such a simple battle? He huffed. How would Mara be able to hold back these vicious animals? The idea that a sword and a small timid girl could save the world from such evil seemed preposterous. Yet the legends had to be right.

It was their only hope.

Mara buried her head against Dougal's warm, soft, strong chest. She could bury her fingers in his fur, rub her face against his wings, for eternity—if she didn't need to save the world, of course. The sword was her saving grace—she knew it. When they reached the farm, the gray gryphons could distract any blacks remaining while she retrieved the sword. It would be simple. Sure, like the rest of her life.

Dougal's gulp shot fear through her heart. She drew in a shuddering breath then glanced down at the farm. Dead, broken grays littered the yard. One of them smashed Ma's brand new rose bush. Black hunks of fur testified to a great battle. Were the blacks still around? If they were, Dougal would be in danger.

"Maybe we shouldn't land," she said.

"No, you were right. We need the sword."

"But what if the black gryphons…"

"Shhh, my love. I'll protect you."

Warmth flooded her body, and she clung to him as they landed as close to the barn as possible. She didn't look at the carnage as she rushed inside, lifted the floorboard, and grabbed the sword. There was no glow or hum, and something inside her froze, even in the summer heat. Did that mean the power was gone? Were they too late?

She shuffled her feet. Dougal blocked the light streaming through the door. Was he trying to protect her? But no, he moved aside, and she slipped through. The battlefield was even more devastating from this angle. Each sprawled gryphon lay in tatters, their features virtually unrecognizable. No amount of power could save them, and the sword offered none. She was as useless now as she'd ever been.

Bile rose in her throat. She covered her mouth and ran to the pond, then buried her face beneath the still water. When she rose, tears mingled with the water droplets.

Dougal was there, still in his massive beast form. He pulled her to her feet and drew her into a crushing embrace. The soft fur on his chest tickled her nose as she snuggled closer. If only this was what she had to do for the rest of her life. Saving the world seemed like a huge task.

"You have the sword."

"I do." She twirled his fur around her finger. "Retrieving it was easier than I thought."

"For some, yes." He glanced over his shoulder, back at the gryphons who'd died to give her the opportunity.

There would be no rejoicing, and no time for grieving. "What do we do now? We only planned to retrieve the sword, not what to do afterward."

"You didn't think we would accomplish the task, did you?" He smoothed hair off her cheek.

She smiled. "I hate to admit it, but I did have some doubts."

Dougal-Nuada sighed. "We should leave this place. The blacks may return."

"Yes, you're right." She wished she'd had the power to save the grays, but it was too late. She'd come too late.

Dougal swooped her up into his arms and took to the air, his pumping wings straining for altitude. Looking down made her dizzy, so she focused on him and not losing the sword. There was still no hum or glow. Maybe the power had been lost. Or she needed some magic words to activate it. Maybe Dougal's voodoo could help.

He landed them on a jutting precipice on the mountain's face, called Demon Rock. The cliff had a large mound of boulders where you could walk out and view the entire valley, tracing the railroad through the pass and watching the ant-sized farmers at their work. Demon Rock could only be accessed two ways—by hiking up the mountain for hours or by flight. It was the perfect defensive position.

She edged slowly across the rock shelf until she reached the edge. On the farmland far below, fierce fighting raged between Rebels and Yankees. Smoke pillars rose as cannon balls smashed the ground, sending dirt clods and blood spraying into the air.

She sat down and leaned back. Sharp rocks poked her

backside. She wasn't sure if any grays had survived, but if they had, they were probably too hurt to help her.

Dougal was it, all the help she had. He crouched beside her and studied the sky. Her throat seized. They could be the only things standing between the black gryphon army and world destruction.

Dougal watched her from his eye's corner. She was no longer the timid girl, the silent one. No, the fear radiating from her had disappeared. She sat on the cliff's edge, black hair billowing behind her in the howling wind, an aura haloed around her, her chin raised and eyes bold.

While cannonballs smacked into the earth below and the Civil War raged on, another battle shaped up between the black and gray. The gray protectors and the black destroyers—only one could win.

*Mara...* it had been her all along. The silo. The place of her discovery, the place that housed the sword of the last Jotunn. To think she was a superhuman, of a superhuman race, closely related to the gryphon, but not the same.

O'Brien had sent him to search the silo and he'd found the Confederate's simple, archaic weapons: guns with bayonets, lead balls, grenades, and black powder, even the Gatling gun. But he'd missed the true secret. He'd missed the sword.

With the sword, she was invincible. Her purpose, to lead the protectors to victory. With her power, the gray gryphons would be unstoppable. But first, she'd had to come of age. That had been the only reason the lass had been allowed to live—because Maeldun had needed her power, too. He'd admitted he wanted to rule the world. If he had killed Mara, his chance would've disappeared. No, patience had been the key to his future victory.

She rose and stood at the cliff's edge, the warrior princess. Her white dress billowed around her. The sword glinted in the afternoon sun. Did the armies notice her? Did they feel the charge in the air? Or was it just him? Dougal might have been looking at the sky but he still felt the electrical charge radiating from her. Could they not tell everything was about to change? That the end was near?

He narrowed his eyes. Someone was heading their way,

great wings sweeping against the sun and making it impossible to discern the color. At the last moment, the black flared his wings and allowed the wind to carry him to their position. Maeldun landed with a thud. Dust rose as he stalked toward Mara on his lion-like feet. In those few short steps, he morphed into a human—Captain Herrick of the Union army, standing naked in front of them.

"Herrick?" Dougal blinked. It was happening again? Blacks had to have magic. Where were they getting it? Was Serena around here somewhere?

A laugh of derision split the air. "Are you nervous?"

"What are you? How did you—?" He was babbling like an idiot, but he couldn't help it. Before the black annihilated him, he wanted to know how they all kept changing. Maybe if he asked every black he met, he'd figure it out. And if it was Serena... he couldn't do a thing, because it might damage his future. Going back in time wasn't easy.

"Did you think you were the only one who could change?"

"Uh, yeah." Not really, but he'd hoped.

Herrick narrowed his black eyes. "Well, you're not."

"But—" Now he was only killing time. Where was Ailin? He hadn't been amongst the dead at the house, so he could still show up and give them a hand. Crazier things had happened, and one of them stood in front of him now.

"I don't have time for this. I've come for the girl. Move aside."

"Never."

"You defy me?"

"Yes, I guess I do."

"Should I tell her what you did?"

"What?" Dougal's palms sweated. A glance over his shoulder revealed Mara listening to the entire conversation. What could Maeldun say to screw him?

"Should I tell her what you did when you ran away?"

He slumped. He'd run away and helped O'Brien. He'd investigated the silo, maybe for the enemy. That meant he might have had a hand in burning the town, just as they'd accused him. Knowing that might affect her opinion of him.

Her hand touched his fur-covered arm. "What you've done in the past doesn't concern me."

He grimaced. She might change her mind if she knew the truth. He had worked for the enemy, on multiple occasions.

Good thing Maeldun-Herrick didn't know his entire past. That could get real ugly.

Herrick crossed his arms. "Don't you want to know what he did before you decide it doesn't matter?"

"No."

"But Mara, I may have been the one to start all this." His voice rose an octave.

"No, you didn't." She waved her hands. "Not the fire in town. Not the war. None of it. This was our destiny." She stiffened. "Now, I suggest you go and help your brethren, Herrick. Because if you don't work together, you all are going to die."

Dougal risked a glance aside at her. The last of the Southern country girl melted away; not even her accent remained. She stood tall and straight, the sword held gracefully beside her, at the edge of the cliff as if she owned it all. She'd pronounced judgment on Maeldun and expected him to obey her.

But Herrick appeared unperturbed by Mara's declaration. His lips moved without sound. There was the magic he'd expected to see.

Skin melted away, replaced by thick black fur matted and smeared with dirt. Heavy, stinking smoke rolled from his mouth. His claws were bared, his fangs dripped a nasty yellow fluid, and his eyes took on a dark black shine. He was one of the scariest blacks Dougal had even seen, and that was saying a lot.

Maeldun bent on one knee, his knuckles resting on the ground as if he had punched it. Wings flared on either side. The figure he presented was imposing and fearsome. He resembled a football player standing on the line, waiting for the whistle.

A loud burst of cannon fire rang out.

Leaping off the ground like a runner at the starter's gun, Maeldun flew at Mara.

Dougal pushed her aside and stepped in Maeldun's path. They collided and tumbled to the ground.

A howl rent the air. Was that him? The pounding of blood between his ears drowned out all other sound. Pain in his side held all his attention. Maeldun pulled his lips back, exposing his long, jagged teeth as he shoved against Dougal's arms. The pressure mounted. His legs shook beneath him. It was too much and all he could manage was defense. The vein in his neck beat wildly. Maeldun's eyes seemed to focus on that one spot. He was literally going to go for the jugular.

With a burst of strength, Dougal thrust upward. Maeldun appeared surprised and fell backward, unharmed.

As one, they jumped to their feet.

Dougal grabbed his side. Three claw marks ripped his skin, but his healing was already underway. Fighting while his body worked the miracle only slowed it down. If he could get away from Maeldun for even a few moments, then he'd be in better shape. Unfortunately, Maeldun wouldn't comply with his needs. He was determined to destroy him and get to Mara, and if Dougal flew away to heal, he'd leave Mara undefended. Not acceptable.

Maeldun came at him with a frontal attack, wrapping his wings around Dougal and holding him helpless while pummeling him with hammer blows. He tasted blood and smelled iron. Constant pain wracked his body. Only moments remained before he wouldn't be able to move. Then what would Mara do? She was an untrained warrior. A girl, really. Cian had been a fool to send him back. Mara needed an army for her task, not him. He was nothing, just as he'd always been.

# 43

Battles raged on the ground, in the air, and right in front of her. Mara watched the sky over the battlefield. After the battle at the Hess barnyard, three grays had remained alive. With uncommon fierceness, they returned now to fight. Wheeling through the skies, they fought a legion of blacks, even though there was little hope of success. Always, they protected the humans.

The fight on the precipice pulled at her. Dougal was struggling to hold his own. Maeldun was clearly stronger, delighting in causing pain.

She stared at the rocky outcropping as they wrestled. A volley of cannon fire struck the base of the mountain, causing Demon Rock to shudder.

She spread her legs to keep from falling. In her hand, the sword hummed. Finally—the power had returned, perhaps from the cannonballs' pummeling. Around her, the battle noises disappeared, and the quieter sounds of nature returned. Wind whistled through the trees. Crickets chirped within the thick carpet of grass.

She closed her eyes and the sword vibrated faster and faster within her grasp; energy emanated from tip to hilt. Power surged through the blade and flowed into her.

When she opened her eyes, the world was different. The battle still thundered on, but now she knew what to do. One-handed, she hoisted the heavy sword into the air—she barely felt its weight—and raised it over her right shoulder. She slid one foot forward while the other braced in back, slightly turned. She twisted at the waist. She didn't know why she adopted the stance, but it felt right, appropriate.

The Gatling gun fired out a volley of bullets, echoing around Demon Rock. Sparks shot from the end of the barrel, caught and magnified by the sun, sending light around in a scattering sweep. One beam hit the blade of the ancient sword, sending out other shafts of light, and the blue fire flamed. One by one the gryphons paused overhead, as if fascinated by the dancing colors.

They hovered, watching, then changed direction. One by one, they came for her.

She held her position. Let them come. She was ready.

The first gryphon approached, slowed, edged within reach, all the while watching the sword as a moth watches a flame. She swung the sword down in a wide arc, landing a glancing blow upon the gryphon's forearm. It was barely a flesh wound and he must have realized it, because he poised for another attack. Then the look in his eye changed. A burst of light swept from the small wound in the gryphon's skin. Its scream rent the air as it burst into a million sparkling pieces and drifted away like ash in the wind.

He'd just exploded into light. And she'd barely nicked him!

Power surged through her. She faced the others with renewed vigor.

She hoisted the sword once more. Sweat clouded her vision and slicked her palms. The remaining black gryphons roared. Rage must have guided them because they flew in for the attack.

A twist of her hips, and she resumed the fighting stance. A flick of the sword caught the next gryphon in the leg; he exploded with a flash. Another came, no longer staring at the sword but claws and fangs out, and she pricked it. Another scream, and more sparkling light. On and on they came, each one trying to kill her. The sword grew heavier and heavier with each stroke, but still she fought, thrusting downward and forward, slashing upward and sideways. Her heart thumped like hummingbird wings, like an Indian beating a war drum.

The three gray gryphons that had battled the blacks in the air retreated out of sight. The fight became hers alone. Her arms felt leaden as she raised the sword above her right shoulder one more time.

She blinked sweat from her eyes. There were no gryphons left. Nothing remained of the ones she'd fought but tiny particles of dust floating in the breeze. She'd done it! She'd defeated them!

A roar of fury blasted the air.

A new gryphon landed on Demon Rock, the darkest black she ever seen, the odor foul beyond human understanding. It loomed over her like a mountain. Snarling, the beast stalked toward her. "What have you done?"

Mara didn't answer. She was too afraid. She'd just slain a hundred gryphons without effort, and the arrival of this one made her doubt it had even happened.

"You have annihilated my entire army!" He pointed a clawed finger at Maeldun. "And you allowed her to do it."

Scarred and gouged, Maeldun struggled free of Dougal's hold.

Dougal lay on the ground, wounded and panting. At least he was alive.

Maeldun hung his head, the devotee of the dark one awaiting punishment. She could almost feel sorry for him—almost.

"You have allowed her to defeat our entire army! Do you know how long it will take to rebuild? At least a hundred years! Do you hear me, Maeldun? Do you understand what I'm telling you?"

Mara remained in a fighting stance. Her muscles tensed with the constant exertion. How much longer could she hold the sword? Not much longer. Maybe the gryphons would give up soon, and the hope grew within her.

Dougal must have noticed the trembling in her arms, for he said, "Cahal, the great leader. You surprise me."

A growl erupted.

"I find it hard to believe you're willing to let such insolence go unpunished. Do you know Maeldun planned to keep the girl and the sword for himself? For over ten years, your *friend* here has worked to ensure *his* future, first by using O'Brien and second by terrifying a young girl.

"Once he realized Mrs. O'Brien wasn't the Jotunn, he knew it had to be Mara. What's funny is that he worked under your nose the whole time! All that curiosity about the silo, but he never gave you the information, did he?

"Both of you knew something was in there, but neither of you realized exactly what it was. The girl was hidden there, and then found by the Hess family. Only the sword remained behind. What irony! The means of your destruction lay buried under your nose the entire time. And Maeldun planned to mess you over! He never had any intention of giving you the girl, the sword, or the power."

A howl of rage rang over the mountainside. Cahal's hand shot out and slammed against Maeldun's chest, sending him tumbling to the rock's edge. With one gnarled hand, the black gryphon hung on. Then he let go, dropping into the air and taking flight. With a sneer, Cahal followed.

Mara blinked. Had what Dougal said been true?

Dougal hobbled on his quivering legs to Mara's side. She stood like a marble statue, as if she didn't see him. He approached in a non-threatening manner, lest the lass bring down the sword down on his head and he become like sparkling dust. When he reached her side, he touched her trembling arm and the sword clattered to the ground.

He opened his arms and she fell into them. Her hair hung in thick damp clumps. He brushed her hair aside with his fingers. A sigh escaped her as she collapsed against him.

Finally the battle was over; they'd won. It didn't sit well to let Cahal go, but they had to or he wouldn't exist, and that could put a real damper on his future.

They returned to the Hess farm. Mara rested inside the cabin while he morphed back into human form and found something to wear, then waited for her to awaken.

The sword lay next to her bed. It glowed and hummed in rhythm with the rise and fall of her chest. A smile covered her beautiful face. It was a happy moment, and they'd known too few of those.

The other members of the Hess family had yet to return. What had happened when they'd discovered Mara was missing? He could only imagine their panic. Surely they'd turned back as soon as they'd realized.

He left Mara upstairs in bed and stepped outside. With his back against the porch's wooden post, he focused on the crystal clear sky. The battle had ended. The dead soldiers littering the green valley would be collected and buried. Prisoners would be marched away. The Union had won yet again.

This battle and others like it would continue a trend from which the Confederacy would never recover. On April 9, 1865, Confederate General Robert E. Lee would sign a note of surrender in Appomattox, Virginia, ending the war. The war between the grays and the blacks would continue, though.

Dougal waited and watched, but Cahal and Maeldun didn't return. If the future foretold anything, Dougal would guess Maeldun would receive his just reward from his glorious leader. Neither Captain Herrick nor Maeldun was anyone he remembered from his own time. And since Herrick was the only one who knew of Ailin's treachery, Herrick's death must have occurred before he could inform Cahal of Ailin's treachery. Otherwise the black gryphon would have been ripped apart.

But now what? Would he stay in this time period forever? Loved by Mara, part of the Hess family? There had been no more dreams from Cian. All he could do was wait... something he wasn't very good at.

Days passed before the Hess family returned with the three O'Briens in tow. Their home had been destroyed by cannon fire and now it was nothing but a skulking hull. Beauford had survived the battle and managed to evade capture; while he grieved the loss of his men, he now had no command he could return to.

The O'Briens declined to stay with the Hesses and took the only remaining place in town, hastily repairing the old train depot and covering the windows with some of Ma's leftover cloth. However, that day Elijah, Ellie, the O'Briens, and the Hesses were all crammed into the Hesses' small home as Beauford visited his fiancée. Planks on two sawhorses in the front yard accommodated everyone at feeding time.

No mention was made of his past transgressions. Mara had been right—they had came around.

He sat across from her at the large makeshift table. Whenever he glanced her way, she dipped her head and hid a shy smile. A rosy hue tinged her cheeks as he continued to openly gaze at her with admiration. He didn't care how embarrassed she was; he wasn't going to stop looking at her until Cian took him away.

When Mara reached for a piece of bread, he did so as well—on purpose. That simple touch was electrifying. All around them conversation flowed about Maude and Beauford's upcoming wedding. He'd been confused before, but now he was ready. He knew what he had to do.

When the meal was finally finished, he rose from the table and held out his hand. "Would you walk with me?"

She grabbed his hand and smiled. He'd take that as a yes.

Wind rippled across the pond's surface. They stood at its edge, and it seemed as if the ghost of a young girl sat on the rope swing, humming under her breath, hoping no one would hear her.

He drew in deep breaths. Now that he'd decided on a course of action, he was nervous. Was he doing the right thing?

"What's wrong?" She caressed his shoulder.

She wasn't making this easy. "I have to leave."

"What? No, you can't." She clasped her hands.

"I don't have a choice. I'm not supposed to be here."

"I don't understand."

"I know. But I don't think I can explain it adequately."

Mara turned and walked away. He grabbed her and tugged her back. "Don't leave."

"But—"

"I know I said I have to leave, but I'm not gone yet." He rested his hands on her upper arms and rubbed up and down. "I want to stay."

"You do?"

"Of course I do. I love you."

Her knees sagged and she began to collapse. He jerked her up, into his arms, and plastered his lips upon hers. The roughness of the kiss conveyed everything he felt, all his yearning and wishes and empty, aching soul. And she kissed him back, exactly the same.

When at last he pulled away, her eyes were glazed. So he'd done something right. She hadn't slapped him.

Somewhere, people were yelling their names. Funny how he hadn't heard them during the kiss. Swallowing, he backed away, expecting to be whisked away at any moment. Why would Cian allow him to stay any longer, now that Mara was safe? Maeldun wasn't coming back and Cahal needed to rebuild his army. So what was left of his mandate?

Her steel gray eyes implored him. Would she ever forgive him if he was jerked away by an untimely departure? Probably not. Would it matter? He wouldn't be around to know, and that hurt most of all.

# 44

Weeks passed. The people of Wheeler's Landing returned and built small houses wherever they could. Life returned to its usual rhythm, and finally it was Maude and Beauford's wedding day. The surviving town folks arrived in multiple wagons until the Hess farm was full to bursting.

Dougal waited for Mara at the back door. Dressed in the best clothing Ma could design, he was to escort Mara to the bower. He was looking forward to it.

He was thrilled and surprised by his continued presence in the nineteenth century. How long it would last, he didn't know. But at the moment he anxiously awaited his cue. He had no trouble embarrassing Mara, but not like that.

He didn't even mind that he'd been relocated to the barn, because Junior had staunchly refused to give up his bed to a healthy man. And after all, the barn wasn't such a bad place, especially when privacy was considered. Within his own walls, there were more opportunities to sneak kisses with Mara.

He tugged down the hem of his jacket. Since Cian hadn't visited, he'd taken that as a green light to stay, so he'd proposed. Mara and he would marry in one week, even though Maude complained that Mara should have to wait as long as she had. Tingles raced along his spine. In a few short days, Mara would be his wife.

A guitar strummed a tune and Mara appeared beside him. He slid his gaze aside to the woman of his dreams and gasped.

She wore a pale blue gown, the sleeves resting right below her elbows. White lace lay delicately against her neckline. Her ethereal beauty stole his breath. As if to whisper in her ear, he leaned down—and nipped with his teeth at her neck, evoking a shiver that moved down her frame. He'd gotten her again. It felt good...

No, it didn't. His chest—it hurt. The pain increased. He pressed his hand over his heart and desperately tried to suck in air. It refused to come. Falling to the ground, he jerked violently, kicking and thrashing. He reached for her hand. Mara looked so scared, but he couldn't help her. He couldn't tell her not to worry. He couldn't do anything.

The world went dark.

"What happened? Where are we?"

Mara sat next to him on a mosaic-tiled floor, her skirts bunched up around her shapely legs. Tearing his gaze away from the awe-inspiring sight, he grabbed his chest. The pain was gone. He could breathe easy, unless he looked back at her and forgot to inhale.

"Dougal?" Her Southern accent thickened.

He studied their surroundings. The building didn't look familiar. The wood-paneled walls, the tiled floor, the smell of burning candles... he'd never been there before. The last thing he remembered was walking Mara down the aisle at her sister's wedding.

Wait. Was that... the wedding march?

He motioned for Mara to wait and slipped around a corner. People leaned back in padded pews. A bride glided down the aisle, a lacy white veil covering her face. At the altar waited a young man dressed in a tuxedo, waiting patiently, a goofy grin splitting his face. Dougal blinked. He couldn't believe it.

That was Chase. So the bride had to be Maddie. Even though he couldn't see her face, Maddie walked toward Chase.

Somehow he and Mara must have traveled into the future and arrived at Maddie and Chase's wedding. He eased back to where Mara waited and slid down the wall, sitting beside her. Mara stared into space.

Whispering, carefully quieter than the ceremony, he explained everything. He told of his past in the Irish village. Of the horrible things he had done. Everything of consequence or inconsequence, as the couple standing before the church spoke their vows.

When it was over, Mara knew all there was to know about him. She might regret being pulled into the future, but at that moment, he didn't care. He was the only one she knew, so he had time to work on her. Eventually she would give in to his charms and they would still be wed.

She leaned forward and planted a lingering kiss upon his lips. "I love you."

Dougal clasped her hands in his. It hadn't taken as long as he'd thought. Clearly his charm had survived his adventure intact. He smiled. "Forever and always."

# EPILOGUE

Mara whistled as she vacuumed her own home's carpet. A smile spread across her lips as she thought about her arrival in town. She'd married Dougal two weeks after arriving in Coal Creek. She still couldn't believe that the place which once had held nothing but farms was now a thriving metropolis.

Dougal had gone to work at a local grocery store, and she stayed at home running the house. All was peace and quiet. For a woman who'd traveled from the 1860s to the future, and a man who flew around in beast form when the mood struck him, they seemed like a perfectly normal couple and she couldn't have been happier.

The phone interrupted and she switched off the vacuum to answer. "Hello?"

"Yes, I'm trying to reach Mara Hess."

"Well, you've found her, sort of. I was Mara Hess, but now I'm Mara Lachlan. Can I help you?"

A maniacal snicker poured down the phone line. "Ah, you can help me. You see, I know who you are. And I know where you came from. What I don't know is why you are here?"

"What?" Mara struggled to keep fear from her voice as she massaged her round belly.

"Don't play coy. It doesn't matter, you know. None of it matters. Not Chase's power or Maddie's inheritance, your superhuman abilities, or the little ones on the way. No, none of it matters. All that matters is I know who and what you are, and soon the world will, as well..."

*The End*

# ABOUT THE AUTHOR

**Felicia Rogers,** born and raised in the southern part of the United States, is a Christian wife and mother. She is just your average, ordinary woman, with a side interest—writing.

For eleven years, every waking moment of her life was consumed with changing diapers, wiping noses, and kissing scrapes. But now that her children are growing up and she enjoys a modicum of freedom, in addition to taking care of hearth and home, she writes! She enjoys adding a flavor of realism and humor to her all-too-real romance stories. For what is love without a little laughter!

# ALSO BY FELICIA ROGERS

**Paranormal**
The Key
Mara's Secret
Iceas' Victory
Cian and Arin: Beginning

**Contemporary single titles:**
The Painted Lady
The Holiday Truce
The Perfect Rose
Love Octagon
All I Have
A Month in Cologne

**Meaningful Numbers**
One of Forty

**Wounded Soldiers:**
Diamond Mine
Pearl Valley
Emerald Street

**Historical romance:**
The Ruse
The Rescue

**"Justice" and Miss Quinn Mysteries**
The Case of the Missing Cross
The Case of the Puppet Constable
The Case of the Secret Love
The Case of the Chinese Boxes
The Case of the Hidden Treasure
The Case of the Lost Island

**The Renaissance Heart:**
There Your Heart Will Be Also
By God's Grace
Labor of Love
Beyond a Doubt
Letters in the Grove

**Southern Hearts:**
Millicent
Amelia
Cora

**writing as F.A. Rogers**
**The Board:**
Maralie
Reuben
Vanessa
Simon
Darla
Daniel
Irving
Levi
Francesca
Benjamin
James
The Return to Eden's Hollow

*Where Mara leaves off...*

# Iceas' Victory

## 1

Brendan Donovan pretended to peer inside his open locker. First period had yet to start and the hallway teemed with people. Locker doors opened and closed like rapid-fire gunshots. Feet shuffled, stomped, and skipped. This was high school — senior year. He was almost finished. He couldn't wait. Once he was done with school, he was going to get as far away from Coal Creek as possible. He might travel to the west coast and become a fisherman. He didn't care, just as long as he wasn't *here*.

He peered around the door. Myriad faces passed. It was hard to believe so many varieties existed. Jocks, preps, geeks, Goths, surfers, and the unclassified, all under one roof. By some miracle, the building still stood.

"Hey, dude, what are you staring at?"

The voice called over the racket from far away. A sigh parted his lips. Malcolm was notorious for interrupting a good thinking session.

"Nothing in particular." Brendan grabbed his books and slammed the locker closed. *Take that, noisemakers.*

Malcolm approached through the crowd, but he wasn't alone. John and Matt strolled beside him, occasionally snapping their fingers and winking at a cute girl. Brendan would have rolled his eyes at their antics, but they probably wouldn't notice.

The four of them had been friends since kindergarten. They'd been in Cub Scouts, Boy Scouts, played football, and hung out together since time began. They even lived in the same neighborhood in the sleepy community of Coal Creek, where nothing exciting ever happened. Which was why he wanted to leave. There had to be more to life than *this* place.

Malcolm thumped against the row of lockers. "What are your plans for tonight? The guys and I thought about heading over to the lake. This is like the last weekend of summer and I don't want to waste it."

Brendan shrugged. School had begun only a week ago and he already had a semester-long project looming over his head. If he started now, he might have it done by Christmas. Unfortunately, Malcolm and the others would understand if he skipped the lake for a family event or for a girl, but never for homework.

His friends continued to stare at him. He swallowed. He'd just tell them the truth. If they didn't like it, so be it.

But before he could say a word, Malcolm stood straighter, whistled, and clapped. "Dino-mite!"

John groaned. "Not again."

"What?" Malcolm opened his hands like he was confused.

Matt slapped his forehead. "Isn't it obvious? You've been watching Retro TV again."

"Or TV Land on *Nick at Night*," John added, head bobbing to music only he could hear.

"Yeah, good ole J.J. from *Good Times* is awesome." Malcolm spun on his toe, the way the actor, Jimmie Walker, once had on the show.

Brendan could no longer resist their antics. He raised his hand. "Great, we know he's behaving like an old TV actor, but why?"

"That's why." Malcolm grabbed Brendan's head and angled it to where he'd been staring. "Now do you see? Just look at her." He released Brendan and flowed his hands up and down in the shape of an hourglass.

*No clue.* Brendan cocked his brow and stared at the other two for assistance.

Matt shrugged. "Don't look at me. I don't know what he's talking about."

"Not a what, but a who. John, don't you see her? The voluptuous black-haired beauty? She's standing right down there. Am I going to have to stand next to her and hold my arms out like Vanna White?"

John and Matt shared a quizzical look.

Malcolm's hand flew upward. "You guys are hopeless. Vanna has only been on *Wheel of Fortune* for like ever."

"What is he talking about?" asked John.

Matt shrugged. His classic move. Brendan should record how many times he did that per day, as if he were trying to get into the Guinness book of world records...

Brendan forced down his irritation. "Malcolm, back to the girl. We still don't know who you're talking about."

His hands rose again, mimicking the shape of the girl's frame. "It's that girl right there, with the long black hair, and the umm, and you know, and look at the tight—"

Brendan stared in the direction Malcolm pointed. Heat flushed his cheeks and he fisted his hands at his sides. His heart beat faster and faster. Before he knew what he was doing, he grabbed Malcolm by the collar and shoved him against the lockers. His teeth hurt as he clenched his jaw. "You need to shut up."

Malcolm crossed his hands over his face. "Whoa, man. I didn't mean any offense. The girl is fine. Who is she?"

Brendan couldn't believe he was saying it, but he was. "That's Iceas!"

Malcolm's head shook violently. "What? No way. You're kidding."

Turnabout was fair play. Brendan grasped Malcolm's head and swung his face around. "Look. That is Iceas."

"Wow! What happened to her? She didn't look like that before summer break. She must have been swallowed by a Victoria's Secret model."

John and Matt narrowed their eyes toward the girl's end of the hall. A stream of drool slipped down Malcolm's chin.

Brendan tried to control his temper, he really did. But with a forceful shove, he sent all three of his friends into the row of metal lockers, and the sound echoed along the hall. Was everyone watching? He didn't care. Let them see. No matter if they were friends, they weren't going to ogle Iceas like a piece of meat. She was like a sister to him.

Malcolm broke free and straightened his T-shirt. "Man, I was paying her a compliment."

"Yeah, you should back off and let the man ogle." John's grin spread broadly across his face as he tried to look over Brendan's shoulder — in Iceas' direction.

Brendan's chest rose and fell as his breathing grew heavier and heavier. The hallway blurred. Shoes tapping on the glossy tile floor, fingers drumming on books, someone chewing their nails — the sounds rushed into his ears. Then the room spun. Horrified, he leaned sideways and reached out to steady himself.

"Hey, guys. How have you been? It feels like I haven't seen you in forever."

Just as suddenly as the weird feelings began, they ended. And then she was there. *Iceas.* Malcolm, Matt, and John kept their eyes trained on him and their mouths shut. Which was a good thing. He didn't want to have to hurt them.

Iceas drew her brows downward. "Hey, Brendan, you okay?"

He shook his head, forcing a weak smile to his lips. "Yeah, I'm fine." He paused. "How about you? What have you been up to all summer?"

She lifted a toned and tanned shoulder. "Nothing much. I've been at summer camp helping children, like usual."

Iceas Lachlan, the literal girl next door. She was seventeen and, like him, a senior at Coal Creek High School. Five foot seven, with long black hair and dark lashes covering blue eyes that shone brighter than any sapphire. At the moment, her plump rosy lips moved, but Brendan heard nothing. Her beauty consumed his mind. She might be like a sister to him, but he wasn't blind. She had changed over the summer, and he hadn't noticed, even though she lived next door. Hadn't she just said she'd been at camp most of the time? It didn't matter; he was noticing now. And she was more beautiful than ever.

"That was the bell. I'll see you guys later." Iceas waved as she walked away.

Matt nudged him. "Man, where *were* you? You looked a million miles away. Iceas was talking and you just like zoned out. I think she just gave up and moved on."

"What did she say?" Brendan raked a hand through his hair and wished he could hide in a hole. He'd fussed at his friends for staring at her and then he'd done the exact same thing. Admittedly he thought of her more than any piece of meat; she was more like prime rib, but still.

Malcolm slapped Brendan's back. "I don't know what's gotten into you, bud, but we better get to class before we're late."

Brendan followed his friends to homeroom. *This is going to be an interesting year.*

"I saw you talking to Brendan this morning."

Iceas stopped outside the classroom door and cringed. She hadn't even made it to homeroom and Janice was already on her case.

Plastering a fake smile on her face, Iceas turned on her heel. "Janice, how good to see you. How was summer vacation?"

"It was decent. I spent the whole summer at my dad's beach house."

Janice Russo was five-ten with muscular arms and the facial features of a model. She was also the biggest bully in school and she just happened to have a crush on Brendan. Whether the boy was aware of it or not, Janice and he had a "thing" and no one was allowed to disrupt it.

Iceas feigned interest as Janice prattled on. She'd edged closer to the classroom door, but she'd yet to make it inside. Just a few more steps and she'd be there, safe within the confines.

"Hey, Janice!" Dudley Wainwright, an annoying rich kid who played softball, lifted his hand in greeting.

Janice stopped talking midsentence and abandoned Iceas for Dudley. Iceas wasted no time. She slipped inside the classroom and rushed to her seat, careful to pick a desk surrounded by other people. If Janice wanted to attack her, then she would be forced to do so with witnesses.

Iceas lowered her head to the desk and counted the carvings. Starting at the doorway, moans and groans rent the air and traveled toward her. She lifted her eyes a fraction. Janice walked the aisle flicking people's ears, but then she stopped abruptly, staring. She must have noticed that Iceas was covered on all sides and she couldn't get to her without kicking someone out of their chair.

Iceas again lowered her head to the desk and prayed the teacher wasn't late. *This is going to be an interesting year.*

Thanks for reading! Dingbat Publishing strives to bring you quality entertainment that doesn't take itself too seriously. I mean honestly, with a name like that, our books have to be good or we're going to be laughed at. Or maybe both.

If you enjoyed this book, the best thing you can do is buy a million more copies and give them to all your friends… erm, leave a review on the readers' website of your preference. All authors love feedback and we take reviews from readers like you seriously.

Oh, and c'mon over to our website:

www.DingbatPublishing.ninja

Who knows what other books you'll find there?

Cheers,

Gunnar Grey,
publisher, author, and Chief Dingbat

δ
Dingbat Publishing